Dead Wrong
Written by Stacey Rourke

Octavia Hollows Vol 5

Copyright 2024 Stacey Rourke

Special thanks to:
Melissa Stevens
Melissa Ringsted
Stacy Sanford
Becca Vincenza

All rights reserved. Published by Anchor Group Publishing. No part of this book may be reproduced or transmitted in any form or by any means, electronic or mechanical, including photocopying, recording, or by any information storage and retrieval system, without written permission from the publisher.

Find a full list of Stacey Rourke's books here:
www.staceyrourke.com

This likely won't be the best book I have ever written, but it will be one I am most proud of. I wrote it during one of the hardest times in my life. It was a struggle. But I did it, damn it. I believed in myself, and I accomplished it. That same power is within you. Believe in yourself. Believe in your dreams. And know we can all do hard things we may doubt we're capable of.

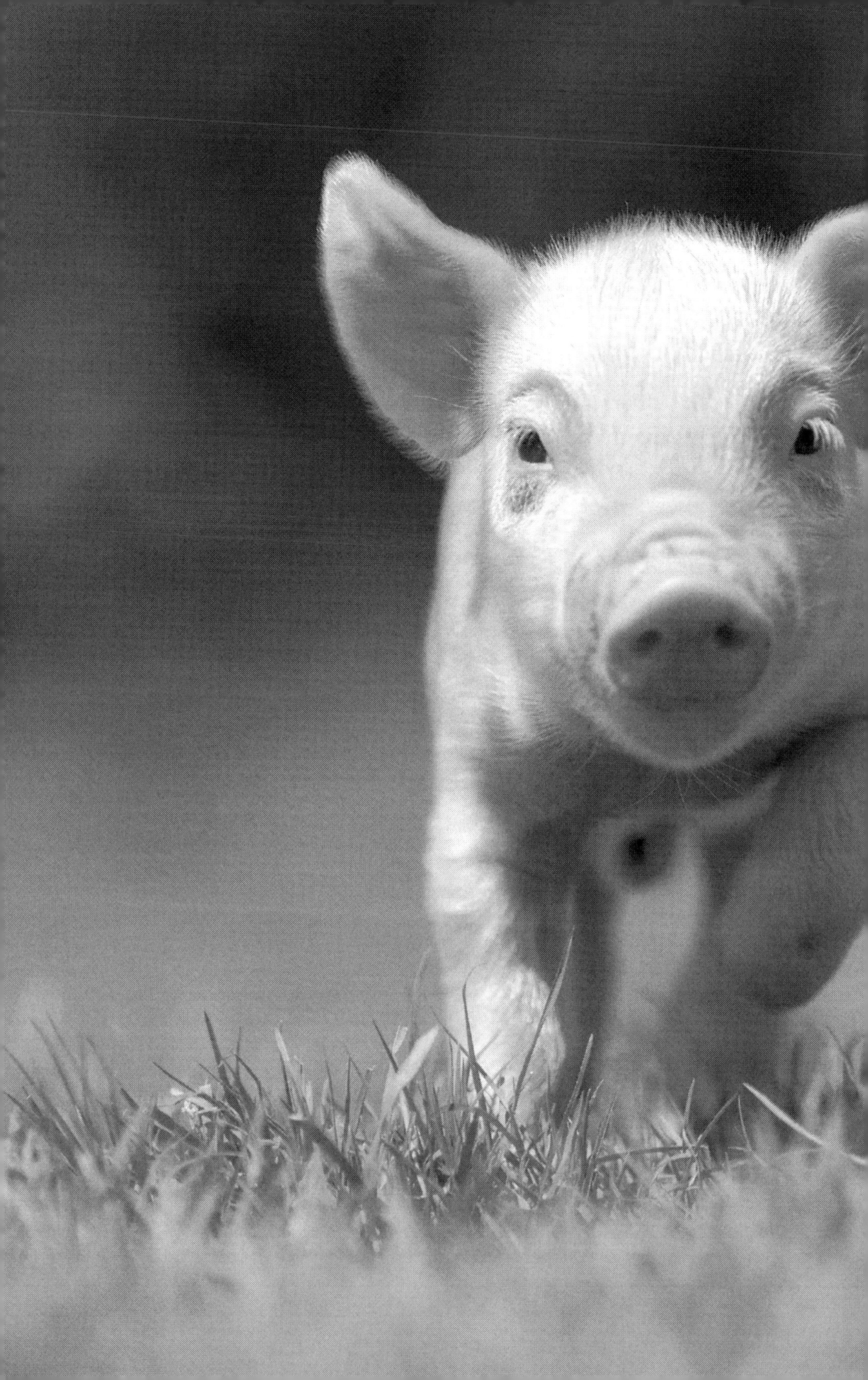

When We Last Saw Octavia Hollows: Bacon

  The piglet laid flat on his back on the bed, sleeping more soundly than he had since being separated from Mama. A knock at the door woke him from his slumber, earning a yawn and a stretch from the pink prince.
  Mama came out of the bathroom dressed in a robe and drying her hair—which perfectly matched his snout—with a towel. She gave her boy a belly scratch on her way to the door. It creaked as it opened for a freckle-faced young man who wheeled in a cart full of delicious smelling food.
  "The meals you requested, ma'am." Dressed in a white jacket with black cuffs, the server offered a warm smile as he pushed the cart inside. "Where would you like it?"
  "By the guest of honor, if you please." Mama jerked her head towards Bacon, earning a happy rump wiggle from him. "You can park it right next to the bed."
  The lad did as requested, then exited the room with a polite bow.
  Mama waited until the door clicked shut before pulling the covers off the platters. The smell of popcorn got the piglet on his hooves, his curly tail wagging in delight. In

addition to that, there was a platter of fresh fruit, one jug of water, a second of almond milk, a giant bowl of mashed potatoes, and… to Bacon's confusion… two rotisserie chickens.

The piglet sniffed at them before giving a perplexed snort.

"Don't worry, bud. Those aren't for you." Shrugging off her robe, Mama revealed she was still dressed in her jeans and t-shirt. She set the fruit, popcorn, potatoes, and milk—poured into a bowl—on the floor. Then, spreading out the towel she had been drying her hair with, Mama dropped both chickens onto it and folded it up like a knapsack. "You fill your belly. I'll be back in a minute."

Needing no further invitation, Bacon dove snout first into his meal. In between munches and slurps, he watched Mama disappear into the wall.

Sitting back on his haunches, his tongue slapped over his lips. A section of the wall of books had opened, exposing stairs that disappeared down into the darkness. The piglet tried to distract himself with another bite of potatoes, but after being without Mama for so long, it hurt his heart for her to be out of sight. One more munch of popcorn and he hopped up to scurry after her.

Down, down, down he went, following the echoes of Mama's footfalls. The ground finally leveled out, making it possible for him to pick up the pace. Ears flapping, he gave his all to catching up. He caught sight of her and was about to call out with a happy little squeal when a sudden movement made him pull up short.

Mama stood in the arched doorway of a dank, musty room. Snatching one of the chickens out of the rolled-up towel, she tossed it inside.

A groan seeped out of the shadows.

Something dragged across the ground.
Bodies appeared, one after the other.
Yet none of them could be confused with humans.
Rotted flesh.
Exposed bone.

A sea of the dead dragged themselves from the blackness, where they tore into the chickens she tossed to them.

Bacon knew Mama. He trusted her. She was his everything. But in that moment… he was scared for her… and of her. Fear getting the best of him, he was backing in the direction he came from when a silver-eyed corpse caught sight of him. A scream tearing from its unhinged jaws, it hurled itself towards the frightened piglet as fast as it could. The others quickly followed, snapping Mama's head in the direction of the disturbance.

One glance at her terrified swine-kick and her eyes bulged. "Oh, shit! Bacon!" Chickens forgotten, she dropped everything and sprinted for her boy. Catching him in a football hold, she ran back towards the stairs that led to her room with her legs pumping for all she was worth. The dead clamored after them, thankfully without the gift of speed in their advanced state of decay. Groans and gurgles chased them up the winding stairs, growing louder when Mama momentarily stumbled. She caught herself with one hand on the stone stairs, emitting a yelp of pain at the nasty scrape she had earned on her bloodied palm.

Catching sight of a ghoul with half its face missing mere inches behind them, Bacon squealed with his whole chest. Mama got her feet under her and made a mad dash toward the light. Exploding back out into the bedroom, her breath came in ragged pants as her fingers fumbled to find the trick book that would close the hidden door. When she finally hit it, it moved at a terrifyingly slow pace, blocking out the horrors chasing them, but not nearly fast enough.

"Come on, come on!" Mama coached, edging away in fear of the worst.

Skeletal fingers scrabbled at the edge of the bookshelf, clawing and scraping to pry it back open. To the piglet's great relief, it clicked firmly into place and locked the dead within the dark corridor.

Setting Bacon on the bed, Mama checked him over in a cursory inspection. "You're okay. My brave boy. I'm so sorry you had to see that, but you're okay now." Relieved that her warrior pig had made it out unscathed once more, Mama gathered him in her arms and peppered the top of his head with kisses. "I'm so sorry, buddy. I've got you now, and I'll never let anything hurt you."

So distracted was she in escaping the army of her creation that Mama had failed to notice the fair-haired detective standing at the bedroom door. How long he had been there, Bacon didn't know. Judging by the slack-jawed way he peered at Mama, it was long enough to be as horrified by the sight as the trembling piglet.

The hush of the moment was broken by the detective's breathless proclamation.

"Octavia … what have you done?"

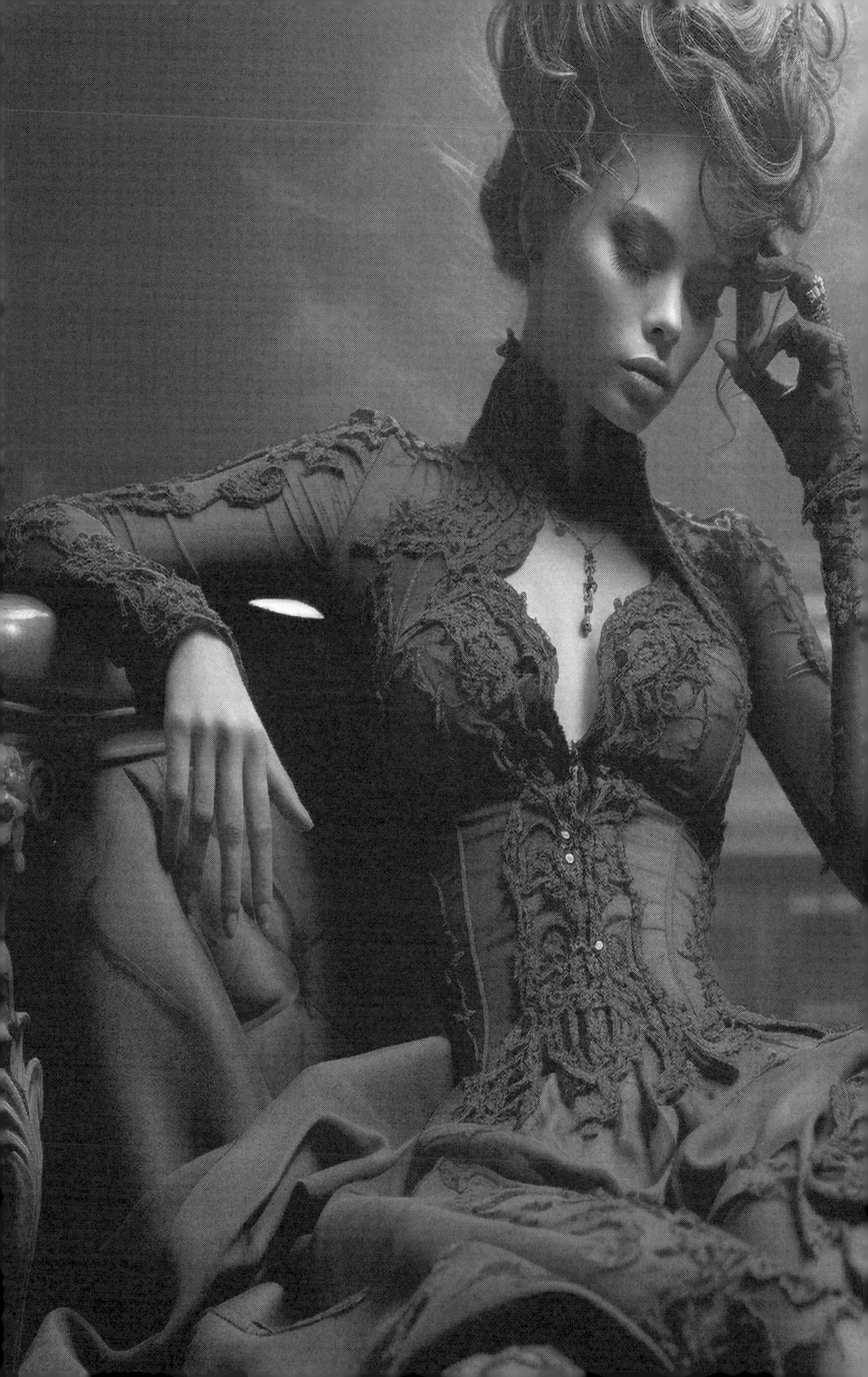

Chapter One
Octavia

My hands shook. The breath lodged in my throat. Still, I battled to keep my voice steady. "You don't understand. Tormund and his hive made me a victim. They kept me trapped in here like a wounded animal. Never again will I allow anyone to make me feel that way, no matter what it takes."

Did it break my heart that Bacon was hiding behind Connoll's leg? Absolutely. Still, I couldn't blame my little porker.

The detective, on the other hand, stared hard at the bookcase and the anguished moans of the dead resonating from behind it. "You can't honestly believe this is the way to ensure that, or is in any way a good idea, do you?" He stabbed one upturned hand in the direction of my hidden horde.

Teeth grinding to the point of pain, I forced the words through jaws clenched tight. "They made me watch you die right in front of me. Do you remember that, or did the blood loss blur the memory? Your fangs were torn out by the root in hopes of driving you mad with hunger. Worst of all, you were manipulated into using your gifts to torture and kill a young woman. You have just as much reason to hate them as I do!"

"I did hate them, Octavia. Past tense. But they're gone. You saw to that yourself." Connoll lowered his voice, his features carved into a mask of compassion that made my chin betray me by quivering.

Dragging my fingers through my hair, I shook my head with frantic intensity. "They're gone, but there's a never-ending supply of other shit out there. Jinns. Wraiths. Serial Killers. Demons. They just keep coming. Never giving me time to breathe or cope with one near death experience before the next one comes crashing into me. It's too much, Connoll! I can't keep doing it!" I didn't realize tears were slipping down my cheeks and dripping to the floor in heavy splats until Connoll closed the distance between us and enveloped me in the comfort of his embrace. Words tumbled from my lips as I soaked the front of his shirt with my pain. "If this is what I have to do to keep the people I care for safe, then this is what I'm going to do. I have to. There's no other way. I've given all I can."

"Shhh, shhh, shhh," the immortal detective murmured against the top of my head. "You said you're doing this to keep those you love safe?"

"Mm-hmm," I managed.

"Just now, it almost cost you Bacon."

My gut twisted at the thought of what could have happened to my adorable pig-tato. "It's no excuse, but he distracted me. My control slipped for a minute and I panicked."

"Are you willing to risk it happening again?" Connoll used the same calm and steady tone I would expect him to adopt if he was talking a jumper off a ledge.

Pulling back, I dried my cheeks with the heels of my hands. "No. You're right. Keeping a flesh-hungry horde of zombies in the basement is not the most practical security system."

Hopping up on the bed, Bacon gave a snort of agreement before plopping his rump down on my pillow.

Connoll gave a nod of confirmation. "Glad we're in agreement. Now how about if you take the needed steps to prevent a zombie uprising?"

Taking a deep breath, I tapped into the energy in my core. Emerald wisps danced down the length of my arms, sparking from my fingertips. "Take Bacon downstairs. I'll let you know when it's safe." Reluctantly, he did as I asked. Before he could reach the hall, I tagged on one more request. "Oh, and Connoll? Could you please close the door behind you?"

Gathering Bacon in his arms, the detective strode out. Hand on the doorknob, he wet his lips and cast a worried glance back over his shoulder. "I know this sounds unlikely, but ... try to be careful."

The door clicked shut behind him and I turned my attention to the task before me. Calling forth my magic, I let it surge and ripple in powerful gusts around me that tossed the strands of my hair around me like wildfire. Armed with the forceful weapon of my own creation, I pulled the faux book that allowed one section of the bookshelf to slide back. Groans and hisses resonated from the darkness. Clumsy corpses fell over each other in their awkward attempts to move out of the way of the receding wall. Only when the partition stilled did they surge forward in a storm cloud of death and chaos.

I drew my hands back by my shoulders and cast everything I had at the incoming horde. A wave of green slammed into them, leveling them in a wave of destruction. As the dust of their remains wafted to the ground, silence fell.

But I wasn't done yet. My winds turned and tossed their crumbled remains back into the darkness of the passage, arranging every particle into a neat and tidy pile. One that could be used again, if the situation demanded it. Only then did I retract my powers.

The heels of my boots scuffed across the polished wood floors as I inched closer to inspect my handiwork. "And no pigs were harmed in this zombie exodus." Pushing the fake Mark Twain book back in, I watched the pile of ash disappear into a blanket of black. "Stay right there, friends. I may need your help again soon."

While I took what Connoll said to heart, I wasn't ready to give up on the security of my army quite yet. There was still the matter of the fairy bitch who was holding everyone I cared for hostage. She would release them, unharmed, or there would be a second coming of my horde… with the sadistic fae as their unlucky target.

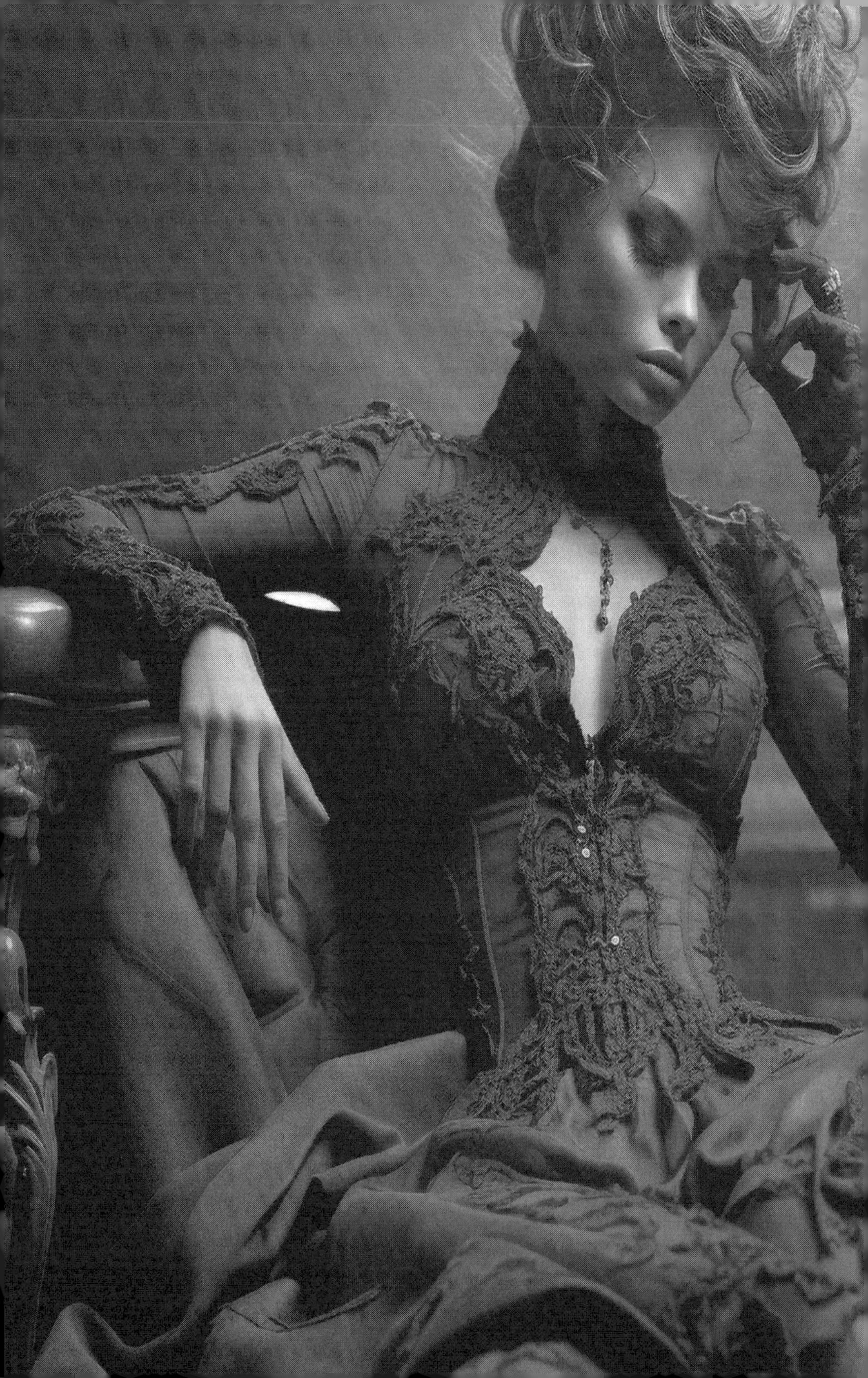

Chapter Two

After a fitful night's sleep as my imagination ran wild with what could have played out if I hadn't saved Bacon from the horde, I woke before sunrise feeling the urge to do something special for my favorite porker. I didn't have Amity's sweet potato pancake recipe Bacon loved so much, nor any talents in the kitchen whatsoever. Even so, for my boy I was willing to give it my best shot. Possible culinary disaster be damned.

Armed with the very first recipe that popped up in a Google search, I hopped on my bike and leaned into the whipping winds as I sped into the heart of Lavender Lotus. Sure, the sun had only seconds ago crested the horizon, casting every shade of orange imaginable across the morning sky. Yet it struck me as odd that I didn't pass a single vehicle along the way. Weirder still, the usually bustling streets of downtown were vacant. Not even one of the rotary club members were out for their morning power walk.

The lights were on in every shop and business, but not a soul was to be seen anywhere around. Parking my Scrambler in an empty parking lot outside the Piggly Wiggly, I pulled off my helmet and shook out my bubblegum hair. A chill of unease skittered down my spine as I watched the automatic doors open and close like hungry jaws, even though no customers stepped over the threshold.

I did my best to physically shake it off, attributing my unease to the early morning hour I rarely saw, and sauntered inside. Jovial music strummed through the sound system, welcoming me the instant I stepped into the brightly lit establishment. Fresh fruit and produce were stacked to my right, the signage announcing a BOGO on avocados. Grabbing a basket, I filled it with the ingredients I hadn't found in the manor's kitchen: sweet potatoes, maple syrup, and brown sugar. Everything else needed for the recipe was available on the shelves in the pantry ... which was surprisingly well-stocked, considered its latest inhabitants were on a strictly blood-based diet.

Armed with my cargo, I edged up to the checkout area hoping at the very least a self-checkout lane would be open. All the lights for the serve yourself options were off, yet sitting at the middle register with their face blocked by a People magazine, I encountered the first person since leaving the manor. Somehow that did nothing to put my mind at ease. With the soles of my boots scuffing over the linoleum floor, I approached the counter.

While my mind was still pondering if I'd somehow landed in the middle of a dystopian nightmare, I offered the salesclerk a smile. "Excuse me, are you open?"

He put the magazine down with a crisp snap and peered up at me with the same half-grin that had graced many Hollywood silver screens. "Not only am I open, I've been waiting for you, Octavia."

Eyes narrowed, I glanced around the store in one direction then the other in search of hidden cameras. What other reason would there be for the insanely hot actor, best known for his portrayal of an infamous Star Wars character, to be behind the counter at my local Piggly Wiggly? I won't say his name, but it rhymes with Shmayden Shristensen.

"Uh … has anyone ever told you that you bear an uncanny resemblance to the guy who played Anakin Skywalker?"

The man's head cocked to the side. "Is that who you see? The chap from the space movies?" He gifted me with the same smirk I'd seen grace countless magazine covers. "Intriguing. What era, pray tell? The sweet, baby-faced Attack of the Clones version? Or later franchise appearances when he's more Daddy Skywalker?"

Feeling heat creep up my neck to the tips of my ears, I awkwardly shifted my weight from one foot to the other. "Any. All. And every version in between. What exactly is happening here? Did I have a stroke? Am I dead? Dreaming? No, this can't be a dream. When that happens, we're both wearing significantly less clothing and the lighting is far more forgiving. Oh, dear God… I said that out loud."

Leaning over the counter, the lookalike took the basket off my arm. Carefully, he scanned and bagged each item. "Relax, Octavia. I'm sure the real Hollywood heartthrob is living a full life somewhere far from here, blissfully unaware that a sweaty-palmed necromancer fantasizes about him."

Yes, I knew I was staring at him in slack-jawed astonishment. But could you blame me? "Who … or what … are you?"

Peering my way from under thick lashes, he caught my gaze and held it in a way that made a flurry of butterflies explode in my stomach. "I… am Death. The being. The personification. The be-all, end-all. I've found that appearing to each individual to whom I need to speak in the form of their celebrity crush prevents them from screaming and running away from me. You see, my true form can be a bit jarring. As you can imagine, that is both a hindrance in the communication process, as well as just being straight-up hurtful for me. That long period of time where there were lots of Elvis sightings after his demise? Yeah, all me. Lots of people were still crushing on The King back then."

"All this," I gestured to the vacant store and town, "is you?"

"Yes, my dear. A conversation between you and I is long overdue." Having bagged the last of my items, Death glanced at the register. "Oh, that will be twelve dollars and forty-three cents, please."

Grabbing my phone from my back pocket, I slid my debit card out of the slot in the back of my case and passed it to him. "I imagine you have a certain amount of animosity towards me, considering what I can do."

"Not in the least. You have a role to play in the grand scheme of things, just as I do." After scanning my card, he handed it back along with my receipt. When I reached out for it, he seized my wrist, his touch instantly morphing my hand to a shriveled claw of bare bone. "But you have disturbed the balance far too many times to be ignored."

Throwing my weight back, I broke free from his hold, my hand thankfully returning to its normal—albeit shaky—form. "If this is about the army of corpses, they're dust now. I saw to that last night."

"Oh, that was just the final nail in the coffin... so to speak. Sorry, I'm a sucker for a good pun." Leaning one hip against the counter, he crossed his arms over his Piggly Wiggly apron. "No, for those keeping score... and I have been... you've been ignoring the delicate balance of things for some time. Your precious pig. The strapping wolf. Your coven. That pack of wolves. Bodies have fallen around you by the dozen and you have brought them back with no consideration to the natural order that must be maintained."

"To be fair, all of those were under some form of supernatural influence, and I made sure I followed the rules so the entire population didn't find out what I can do." Even as I made my heated counterpoint, my voice betrayed me by wavering.

"Silence!" Bellowing that one word, his features shifted. Sharp angled bones protruded from Death's mask of the handsome celebrity. Fiery pits of darkness glowed from his eye sockets for a blink. Quick as they came, the façade of the silver-screen hunk situated itself back into place. "You speak of rules forced on you by the land of the living. Don't be seen. Don't be discovered. Only use your gifts for good." A hint of taunting crept into his tone. Planting his palms on the stilled conveyer belt, he leaned close enough for me to catch a whiff of the scent of earth and foliage that emanated off him. "None of that matters to me. You think I care if people find out what you can do and turn you into their experimental guinea pig? That would be a you problem, little girl. No, my issue is constantly having to counter the scales because of you. What you fail to realize is that some of those you brought back were meant to stay dead. When you didn't return them to that state, I had to snuff out a life when it wasn't their time."

Blinking in horror, the best I could manage was a weak rasp. "What?"

Straightening his spine, Death sauntered through the counter like it was nothing more than a mirage. And maybe it was. By this point I had no idea. "That's right. Your sweet little pig was supposed to be the main course at a family feast. When you kept him around, I plucked another life in his place. Every time you brought back someone whose time was truly up, another soul paid the ultimate price."

My mouth opened and shut, every word in the English language failing me.

Death took advantage of my silence and continued his intimidation by pacing a slow circle around me. With one finger he pushed my hair off my shoulder, letting that lone digit brush across the delicate skin of my neck. "As I said, balance must be maintained."

Tears burned behind my eyes, slipping between my lashes unchecked. "I didn't know. I wouldn't have—"

That smell of moist soil assaulted my senses as he leaned in to murmur against my ear. "Yes, you would have. Because those you know and care for seem far more important in those pivotal moments than those you don't." Swirling away with velvet fluidity, Death threw his arms out to his sides. "Not that it matters now. Those other lives have been taken and can't be restored. They've all met that infinite oblivion."

My feet felt like leaden weights sinking me into the murky depths of despair right next to the display rack of batteries, chewing gum, and breath mints. "Then... what do you want from me?"

He closed the distance between us. Wearing the façade of my favorite silver screen idol, he gathered my face in his hands in a way I had fantasized about countless times before. Though never under such off-putting circumstances. "What I want from you, darling Octavia, is to heed my warning. The yoke of maintaining the balance will no longer rest on me alone. If you continue to abuse that gift of yours, dire consequences will follow. Pain you can't begin to comprehend will befall you, and death will be the only way out."

"Mine?" I squeaked, prepared to lay down my life for those I cared for without an ounce of hesitation.

Death bowed his head, his lips teasingly close to mine. "That would be an easy fix, wouldn't it? Throwing yourself on that proverbial sword. Sadly, I can't allow it. Death will become a weapon you must wield for your own salvation. If... you continue along this path. Or..." The tip of his nose bumped mine before he took a wide step back. A mischievous grin spread across his delectable features. "You can remember to put back the souls you wake, and this little encounter of ours could be our first and last interaction." Death glanced down at his celebrity disguise as if noticing it for the first time. "I mean, I can absolutely understand the appeal of this tall, strapping gentleman. That said, I think a one-time rendezvous would be best under these particular circumstances. Wouldn't you agree?"

Swallowing hard, I managed a nod.

"Good. I'll be seeing you, Octavia. Whether you like it or not." A flirty wink, and he was gone.

The store came alive around me. Shoppers pushing their carts up and down the aisles. Cashiers busily bagging groceries. An announcer reading the daily specials over the PA. Unable to exhale quite yet, I turned in a slow circle all the while battling to comprehend what had transpired.

"Miss? Miss, you forgot your receipt." The soft-spoken cashier behind me waved the arm-length printout to get my attention.

Stumbling to face her, I fought to offer a tight-lipped smile. "Thank you."

"Oh, and don't forget your magazine." The button-nosed brunette returned my smile and passed me the magazine left on the conveyer belt.

I took it without thinking. Glancing down at the cover, the world spun around me in a dizzying blur. The infamous Star Wars star stared up at me from the pages with the blazing pits of oblivion glowing in the depths of his eyes.

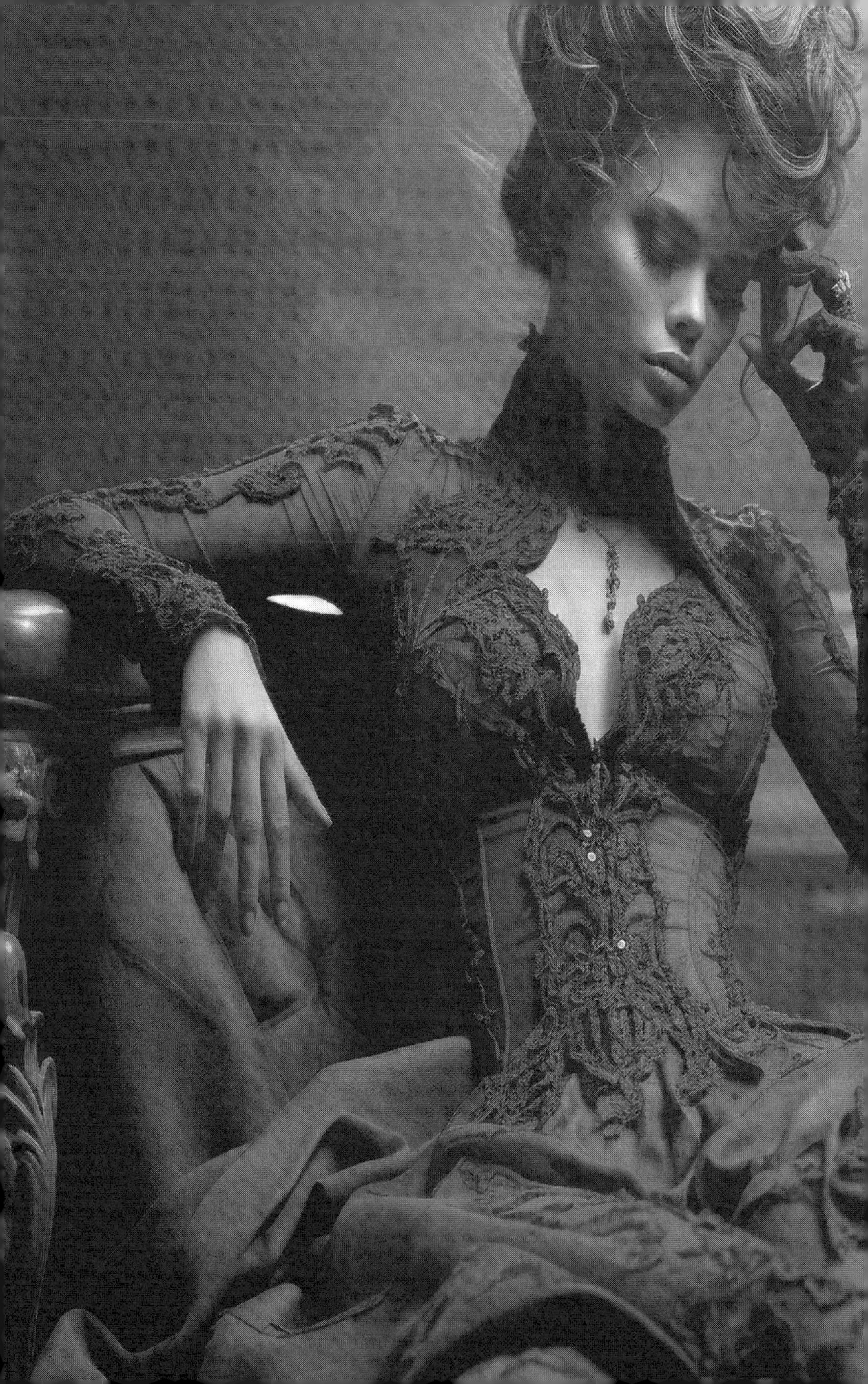

Chapter Three

"Welcome back, Miss Hollows." A tall, gangly man with roughly three strands of white hair on his scalp bent in a formal bow when I returned to the manor. "I am Jareth, the new butler assigned to the manor by Queen Vincenza Larrow and Master Vlad Draculesti after the last person to hold this role was brutally killed by the previous residents."

My eyes narrowed in his direction, sizing this brave fella up. "Yet knowing that, you took the job anyway. Is the money that good, Jareth? Or do you have a death wish?" I placed my purchases in his outstretched hands.

"While the pay is quite substantial, I have been assured you eradicated any threats here and I am perfectly safe. Is this information in any way incorrect?" Jareth's head tilted, not in concern but question.

"No, it's not incorrect," I whispered, not sure if I should be proud of that or not. Saying my method of clearing the house was unorthodox would be an understatement.

"Then, I consider it a blessing to work for such a brave individual. On an unrelated topic, your swine friend is in the kitchen rather aggressively rutting for breakfast." Jareth opened my shopping bags and glanced inside. "Is there anything in here that he would enjoy?"

"I got ingredients to make him sweet potato pancakes. But you don't have to bother with that. I'll make them." I started for the kitchen, only to have Jareth side-step in front of me.

"With all due respect, Miss, I believe your attentions are needed elsewhere. You have guests out on the back patio. Detective Tiresias is out there now entertaining them, and judging by the heated tones that have wafted inside, he could likely use some assistance. If it pleases you, I can have the chef prepare the pancakes for your piglet while you tend to that." Jareth rolled his wrist and gestured to the long hall that led past a fully stocked bar and lounge to the patio out back.

My gaze shifted from the direction of the kitchen, where my adorable little swine-kick awaited, to the patio, where audible shouts could clearly be heard. "Fine, but save me a pancake and take him out on a walk immediately after he eats or you get to clean up his mess. And trust me, his first morning poop is a doozy."

"Yes, ma'am. Shall I report back with color and consistency?" He actually uttered those words with a straight face and complete sincerity.

I, on the other hand, yelped a sharp bark of laughter that I tried—and failed—to stifle behind my fist. "No, that won't be necessary. But thank you." Pivoting towards the patio, I hesitated. "Uh, who exactly is out there?"

Shopping bags looped around his wrists, Jareth tucked both hands behind his back. "I'm afraid questions such as that are of no concern to me. I simply ensure that you have all you need to prepare you for interactions such as this. That being said, you may want to consider a wardrobe change. While your tattered jeans, band tee, and... ahem... frayed flannel have a lumberjack chic charm, you may feel underdressed in the presence of your guests."

My nose crinkled at the insult to my standard wardrobe. "Is the King of England out there?"

"It wasn't my place to inquire as to what realm they may reign over. That said, they do have the air of royalty about them. However, unlike mere mortal royals, these individuals possess an otherworldly beauty that few can attain. As you will soon see." A last bow and Jareth disappeared in the direction of the kitchen.

I watched him vanish into the kitchen in hopes of catching a glimpse of Bacon's curly pink tail wagging. Unfortunately, the door shut without even a momentary swine sighting. Filling my lungs, I glanced down at my clothes and shrugged off the butler's suggestion. I had spent enough time within those walls being forced to play dress-up for the delights of others. Whoever was here could take me as I was or fuck off.

That bravado took me as far as the patio. One step out onto the brick pavers, and I found myself surrounded by the most stunningly beautiful individuals I had ever seen. I was instantly aware of my every flaw just standing near them. Flaxen hair. Features that appeared carved by the gods. Think the elves from the Lord of the Rings movies dressed by Armani or Versace. Figure hugging styles. Elaborate beading. Gold brocade.

Jareth was right.

I should have changed.

I toyed with the idea of shrugging off my flannel and knotting it around my waist to at least accentuate my figure a bit. Unfortunately, I was wearing my Eminem tee with the real Slim Shady flipping the bird times two. That seemed worse instead of better.

I was in the midst of this internal struggle when the gaggle of stunningly gorgeous individuals turned their attentions my way. Instantly, heat burned up my neck to my earlobes.

"I assume this is the pseudo-wizard you spoke of." A platinum-haired gentleman with a jawline that could cut glass sneered in my direction. While his age was undeterminable, his palpable disdain was not.

Thankfully dressed like an actual human in a white t-shirt and jeans, Connoll shoved his hands in his front pockets and swiveled my way. His face was crumpled with pure emotional exhaustion. "That makes it sound like she does tricks for children's birthday parties. As I stated, Father, Octavia is a powerful necromancer. Octavia, this is my father, King Roderick of the Winter Court, my mother, Queen Maraleigh, and their entourage of ass kissers."

A woman with skin as flawless as polished marble batted Connoll's words away with a flick of her delicate wrist. "Connoll, there's no need to be crass. Please, at least pretend we raised you to have some semblance of manners."

I caught a glimpse of rune tattoos poking out from beneath the queen's belled sleeves, while the king had no visible markings on display. Hmmm... it seemed the detective and his sister got their powers from their mother's side. Perhaps Papa resented that and felt the need to flex the authority of his crown?

"My apologies, Mother," Connoll corrected. "Their entourage of royal ass kissers."

Roderick's thin lips pursed in disgust. "I can only assume this complete lack of respect ties back to you allowing yourself to be transformed into a filthy bloodsucker."

A chorus of snickers bubbled up from the crowd of finely dressed onlookers. However, even though Connoll's jaw tensed with annoyance, he kept silent.

That particular talent was not one I possessed. Looping my thumbs in the back pockets of my jeans, I gave an audible huff of humorless laughter. "Allowed himself to be transformed? That's what you think happened? Because who wouldn't want to voluntarily be attacked by a brutal vampire and then left to bleed out and die in front of a friend? Spoiler alert, I was the audience for that little show, and I can promise you that nothing that happened that day was in any way consensual. Your son came to rescue me and paid the ultimate price. Maybe your ass kissers can show you how to pucker up instead of criticizing him."

Roderick snapped upright with haughty indignation, the heels of his loafers clicking together with the motion. "How dare you! I am a king!"

I let one shoulder rise and fall in a casual shrug. "You're not my king. So I don't give two fucks—"

Connoll cut me off by stepping in front of me with one hand outstretched in his father's direction. "While you may not be her king, Miss Hollows does appreciate that we need your help to gain control of Nora."

Roderick turned his head away with a sniff, only to be coached back to civility by Maraleigh's hand tenderly touching her husband's forearm. "Darling, shouldn't we tell them?"

"Silence!" The king's face reddened, morphing his beautiful features into a mask of cruel hatred. "If they want our aid, they will show the respect due to our station! That is my command!"

Connoll bristled, his shoulders creeping towards his ears with contempt barely held in check. In tense motions that made it appear he was wrestling with his own better judgment, the vampire/detective took a knee before his father and bowed his head. "As you wish, Your Highness." Sure, even though the venom he tainted the words with made them sound like a slur full of expletives, he still prostrated himself to honor his father's wishes.

Seeing the king peer down his nose at his son whilst wearing a victorious smirk made me want to roundhouse kick that smug look off his face. My hands were curling into fists at my sides when I noticed all eyes had suddenly turned my way expectantly. "Oh. Are you all waiting for me to kneel? Words cannot express how much that is absolutely not going to happen."

"Roderick, darling, she isn't of our kind," the lovely queen gently interjected. "Perhaps we can offer a bit of clemency to protect the relationships our court has established amongst the humans?"

Roderick stared daggers of disgust my way. His jaw moved as if chewing on her suggestions, before he gave a curt nod. "Very well, but only because I want our son to know how unfounded his claims are and how his actions may have put Nora's life in jeopardy."

Connoll's head snapped up. "What? What does that mean?"

Roderick clasped his hands in front of him, lips screwing to the side. "It means like all vampires, your word is completely unreliable. We went to the address you spoke of. There was no one there. Not a soul. There were traces of fae, therefore we do believe Nora was present on the premises at one point. However, her scent was drowned out by the overwhelming stench of shifters and vampire." Connoll and I exchanged matching looks of confusion as the King of the Winter Court rambled on. "While lupine possess the constant smell of mutt, the Nosferatu scent was an alarming one. Judging by its rather potent smell of copper and dust, I'm guessing it was a rather old one."

Connoll pushed to standing, his brow creased into a deep V. "Octavia wiped out every vampire in the area. I witnessed that firsthand."

The king cast a pointed glance at his son. "Well, not every vampire... unfortunately."

Maraleigh hid a choked sob behind her hand at the blatant insult against her boy. Tears welled in her eyes that she unsuccessfully hid by glancing down at the patio pavers beneath her feet. It seemed King Roderick was abusive to every member of his family. Delightful wasn't a word I would use to describe him. But something else that started with a d...

"Father, I need you to take this seriously. My scent should be faint there now. And even if it was me, I obviously don't carry the smell of the old ones. This could mean that Nora and the others are under the influence of another vampire. I can tell you firsthand how dangerous that could be. Since my change, my powers have intensified in ways I never imagined. Can you even begin to comprehend Nora's powers intensified? That is nothing short of terrifying."

"This matter must be dealt with at once." Roderick glanced toward his minions and circled his finger in the air. Without a word, they all disappeared around the side of the manor in a single-file line.

"What's your plan?" Connoll fell into detective mode like a switch had been flipped. His eyes sparked with the thrill of a new mystery to solve.

Roderick blinked his way without a trace of emotion. "My plan? I have no plan. Why would I put my soldiers at risk over a failure on your part?"

Brows darting to my hairline, my eyes bulged with shock. "Oh, you're the kind of cruel fuck that would really benefit from a boot up the ass."

Connoll held up one hand to silence me... which I openly scoffed at. "Father, we can't just ignore this threat."

"Make no mistake, I'm not," came Roderick's flippant response. "Since you are a vampire, this matter is with your own kind. The issue is yours, not mine."

Connoll's hands balled into fists at his sides, the tendons of his neck bulging. "You can't be serious!" Nostrils flaring, his emotions were barely held in check. "You know what Nora is capable of! If a vampire were to seize control of her power—"

Roderick's features sharpened in inhuman angles, suddenly appearing more monster than man. His ears elongated to points, teeth sharpening to that of a piranha. "Then blame for that will fall on you! You are a vampire! Find whatever foul atrocity has my child and return her to me. For if you fail, I will lay siege on this town. My men will show no mercy. Every man, woman, and child will be slaughtered. Their blood will be on your hands if you dare fail me... again."

With those acting as his parting words, King Roderick turned on his heel and marched off with his queen and court falling into step behind him.

Connoll stood stone still, his nostrils flaring as he watched them disappear around the side of the manor. "Again," he muttered more to himself than me. "As if he ever viewed me as anything other than a failure." A heavy silence fell with him seemingly lost in thought and me unsure of what I could possibly say to make anything better. Yet any words of comfort I may have attempted died on my lips when he glanced my way with a face full of desperation. "And that's why I need your help."

Folding my arms over my chest, I dragged my tongue over my bottom lip. "With all due respect, have you lost your fucking mind? He suggested there may be a new vampire in the mix, and you think I'm going to dive head-first into that sewage swamp? Hell no. You're the only bloodsucker I like, and that's because our relationship was a preexisting condition."

Connoll's shoulders sagged with defeat. "I'm no different than those monsters, Octavia. You've seen what I'm capable of without the benefit of your touch. Imagine the horrific shit Nora could do if her powers were amplified in the same way mine were. Mass genocide. World domination. The fucking purge. Nothing would be out of her reach or unattainable. Worse still, people we both care for were last seen with her. I want to go after them, but I need you by my side. If your touch wears off while I'm there, I'll be nothing more than fuel on the fire."

The idea of coming into contact with any vampire that wasn't him made a fist of panic squeeze tight around my throat. My breath came in rapid, shallow pants. I crossed both my fists over my chest, as if applying pressure could somehow ease that gnawing ache. Survival instinct screamed for me to run. My muscles were set on a hairpin trigger, ready to bolt at a moment's notice. But a vampire… possibly one as cruel and merciless as Tormund… may have taken the people I love. That, I couldn't let stand.

Paisley could be chained to a wall just as I was. Likely triggering horrific memories of the trauma she suffered at the hands of the Equal Opportunity Killer.

Sister Dina might be forced into stifling darkness like she had been in the water tower where she once died.

Reid could be back in the position he was when we first met, reduced to using his talents and abilities to accommodate the whims of another. Robbed of his own free will.

My emotional pain didn't lessen.

Nor did I believe it would anytime soon.

Still, I forced my hands to drop to my sides even though they shook. Swallowing hard, I prayed Connoll didn't see the fear in my eyes, even though I was well aware I wasn't hiding it well.

"We'll find the vampire and get our people out. That's all I can promise. After that, I'll take mine and run as fast and as far away as physically possible. If there's an isolated island in the middle of some never-before explored stretch of ocean, I'm taking everyone I care for there. You can come along or stay here and fight with your father. That's your call. I'm sorry, but that's all I can offer you. Consider that me being incredibly fucking generous."

Sure, I knew my words were coming fast and heated. Even so, that didn't explain Connoll's widening eyes or the anxious way his gaze shifted from side to side. If I didn't know better, I would have thought he was back-pedaling in fear.

"Octavia... what are you doing?"

My chin fell to my chest, searching for what caused his reaction. "What are you...?"

That's as far as I got in that question before I felt the earth buckle beneath my feet. My mouth fell open. Somewhere in the middle of my rant, I had tapped into my energy without meaning to. Braided wisps of black and green energy traveled the length of my arms. They stretched and snaked towards the ground, causing the patio pavers to crack and split in angry fissures. The manor shook on its foundation, chunks of stone and dust breaking free to rain down onto the grass below. I felt the current charging through me but couldn't clamp it down as it crackled, grew, and consumed everything in its path.

All without my consent.

Stumbling back, it took my full concentration to clamp down the flow. I strained against it, sweat soaking my brow and forcing me down on one knee before I could regain control. The earth stilled.

But… how far had my reach stretched?

"Are you okay?" Connoll rasped, breaking the silence.

My bowed head slowly raised. "I… have no idea. That's never happened before. Check the manor and the grounds. I have no way of knowing if I brought anything back."

The detective took a step back, then another. At the third stride, he turned on his heel and sprinted towards the door with his arms and legs pumping for all he was worth. I knew I should follow him. If I had brought something back, he couldn't do a damn thing about it. I hadn't lost control of my powers since I was a teenager, and then the worst thing that happened was inadvertently bringing a chicken tender pulsing to life mid-snack.

This time I could have started a zombie apocalypse… without even trying.

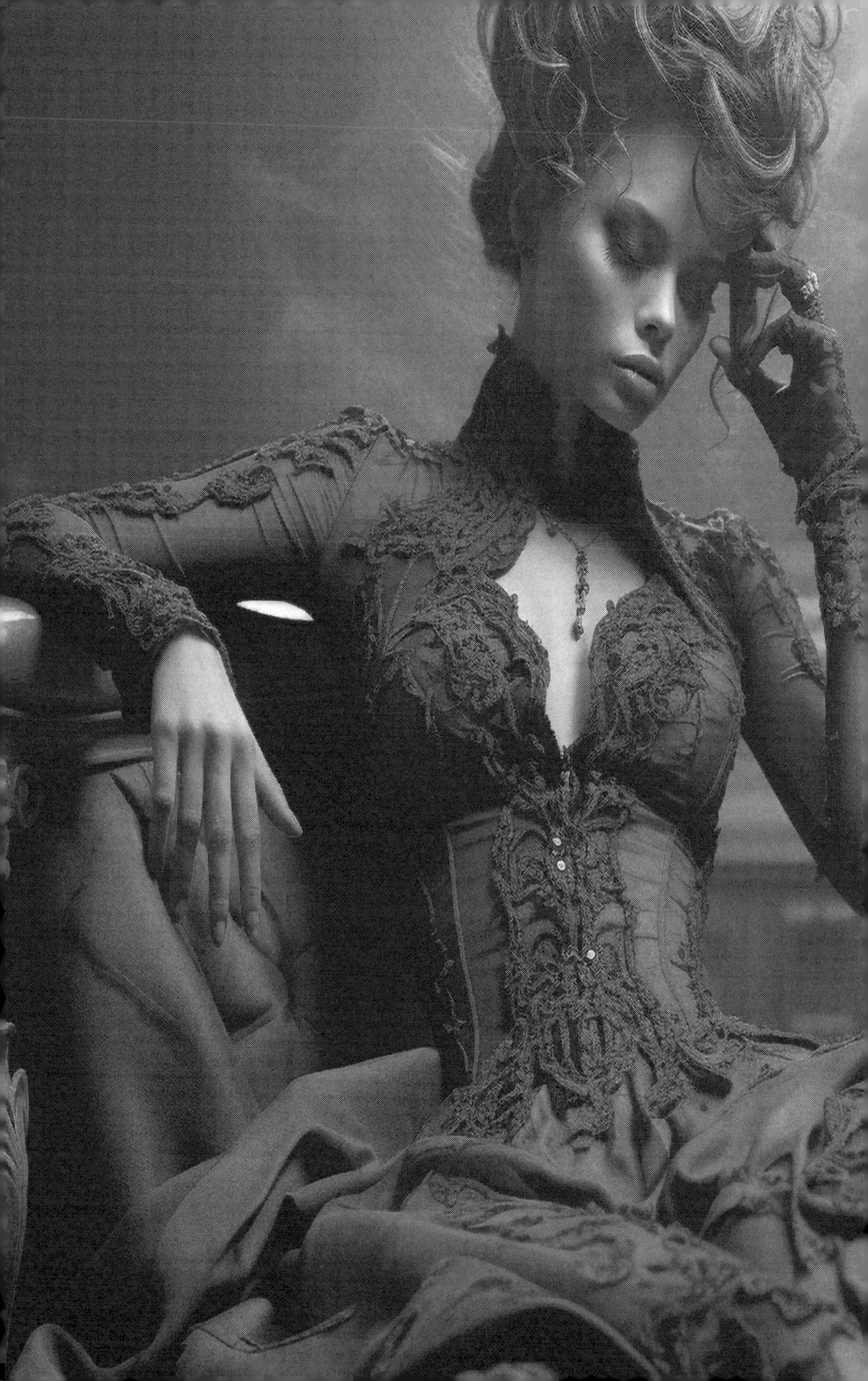

Chapter Four

Connoll searched every inch of the manor grounds and, thankfully, found nothing undead hobbling around anywhere. After the incident with Elizabeth Bridges, mother to the Equal Opportunity Killer, that fact did nothing to put my mind at ease. Accidents could happen. I knew that all too well.

While the detective pushed the issue of finding his sister, I insisted on first taking the time to recite the retraction incantation to draw back any wayward effects of my magic. After which, I wanted nothing more than to lock myself in the manor and do a deep dive into how, or why, I lost control of my powers. To my great regret, time wasn't permitting.

Instead, I forced a warrior's façade… which I absolutely wasn't feeling. Strapping Bacon to my chest, I gunned my Scrambler and followed Connoll's unmarked police car back to Sister Dina's house. Every lash of the wind and each strand of hair that slapped against my neck had me fearing I was losing control of my ability… again.

By the time we pulled to a stop in front of Dina's quaint little house, my legs were shaking from more than the rumble of my motorcycle's engine. The house was dark, all the curtains pulled. Mere hours ago, we'd pulled up to a rager chock full of raunchy debauchery. Now, the house was quiet as a tomb. A chill skittered down my spine when the memory of Amity's lifeless body reminded me of just how true that sentiment was.

"Where do you think they went?" Connoll interjected, startling me out of my reverie.

Unclipping my helmet, I slid it off and shook out my hair. "In my honest opinion?"

"Absolutely."

"My best guess? Whoever abducted the orgy party loaded them onto a moving truck. From there, they took them to a gravel pit where two old school buses were buried deep under mounds of gravel. They made them climb down into them from hatches located on the top of each bus. Inside, wheel-wells were turned into makeshift outhouses while the buses were stocked with flashlights, batteries, peanut butter, jelly, and jugs of water to meet the needs of all those imprisoned until their people—namely the insanely wealthy Red Wolf Pack—meet the demands of the kidnappers."

Connoll blinked my way without a trace of emotion on his features. "Really? That's where your mind went?"

I let one shoulder rise and fall in a nonchalant shrug. "I just watched a documentary about the school bus hijacking of 1976. That's the first thing I thought of."

The detective's brow creased into a deep V. "That is deeply disturbing."

"Spend an hour in my head and you'll never be the same again." I tried to utter the words as an off-the-cuff remark, but even I could hear the traces of sadness that strung each syllable together. Unclipping Bacon, I pulled his leash from my back pocket and secured it into place before lowering him to the ground. I didn't know what was happening at this humble little abode, but I sure as shit didn't want to lose sight of my boy for even an instant.

Wrapping the end of his leash around my hand twice, I squinted in the direction of the cute little cottage. When I first arrived in Lavender Lotus, it was a den of warm welcomes and happy reunions. Since that moment, it had morphed into so much more. Murder scene. Love nest. Boobie trap. Unhinged werewolf rescue. Writhing orgy. Fight club. And now… a haunted grave with a story locked inside, yet to be told.

"Such a sour puss. What's with the long face, sweetheart?" A blonde-haired beauty sauntered around the side of the house with a Betty Boop voice and a Jean Harlow façade. This chick had fully committed to the old Hollywood cosplay. Hair set in pin curls. Eyebrows penciled on. Lips painted a bold red shade. The silver sheath dress she wore clung to every curve. Pert nipples poked out from beneath the silky fabric, making it clear she wore nothing underneath. "Keep scowlin' like that and you'll give yourself wrinkles, doll."

Connoll caught hold of my elbow. Tugging me behind him, he muttered out of the corner of his mouth, "She's a vampire."

The starlet swatted at the air with a flick of her porcelain wrist. "Don't go givin' all my secrets away, sugar! Let a girl have a little fun. The name's Dotty, by the by. And we have a lot to talk about."

The detective took a bold step forward, positioning himself between me and Dotty. "Why don't we discuss this vamp-to-vamp and leave the chick and her pig out of it?"

Dotty pursed her heavily glossed lips and gave a dismissive tilt of her head. "Silly boy, what made you think this had anything to do with you?" She moved in a blur of speed, delivering a flat-palmed push to Connoll's solar plexus that sent him flying backwards, tumbling ass over elbows. By the time he landed with a pained huff in the middle of the driveway, Dotty had planted herself mere inches from me. "Now you, sweet thang, I have lots to talk about with. Namely, the one man I love with my whole heart… Tormund."

I bristled at his name and was forced to clench my fists tight to stop the waves of emerald that threatened to crackle down my arms. "I have some bad news, Blondie."

Her heavily mascaraed eyes narrowed, sharpening her glare with the promise of unhinged violence. "Oh, I'm very well aware that he's dead, and not in the fun way. See, I keep tabs on my boy. I'm never far away from him. Can't bear to be, if I'm bein' honest. It's a flaw I'm workin' on. I wasn't far from that creaky old house you've been holed up in when I felt my boy's light go out."

Pulling on Bacon's leash, I protectively tugged him closer. "How could you feel something like that?"

She raised her hand alongside her head, tapping her long, red-painted nails together in rhythmic clicks. "Tormund was mine. I made him. Since the moment my blood flowed through his body, granting him new life, I have felt his pleasure. His pain. His euphoria. And his agony. Normally, I keep more of a distance. But lately, there was a change in him. Momentary weakenings of our bond. I had to come see what that was all about, didn't I? Couldn't risk losing someone so dear to me. Not long after I arrived in this quaint little burg, I felt him…" a sharp snap of her fingers, "vanish. I got to the last place I had felt him as quickly as I could. And what did I find when I peeked through the windows? A certain pink-haired trollop marching through those dark halls flanked by an army of corpses that tore anything that dared to cross them to shreds. That was you, kiddo, in case you're having trouble keeping up."

My chest rose and fell with panic barely held in check, the pressure of it causing my core to ache. I wasn't worried she was going to kill me. That would be a merciful end. No, I was worried about becoming a plaything to another bloodsucker. I would sooner die and take this blonde bitch with me than to allow that to ever happen again. "So, you came here looking for revenge? Is that what this is?"

Dotty dropped her hand to her side and sashayed a circle around me with her hips swishing from side to side. "I won't lie; I thought about it. I wanted nothin' more than to tear you limb from limb and suck your arteries dry like they're twisty straws. But that seemed too easy." Her coy giggle contradicted the danger looming in the deadly pools of her stare. "Why go for a momentary thrill to assuage what would be my eternal suffering?"

Connoll leapt up, landing in a low crouch with his fangs bared. "Get the fuck away from her!"

Dotty moved in a blink, knocking Connoll's legs out from under him once more before returning to torment me. "Baby vamps can be so self-righteous. But they're all fang and no brain."

Bacon snorted his own agitation at my side, my little warrior pig hopping from one hoof to another in anticipation of a fight. I pulled him tighter beside me, battling to keep control of a spiraling situation. "Not that I'm not enjoying our time together... because you're as delightful as an enema ... but what exactly do you want from me?"

Dotty caught one of her platinum curls and twirled it around her finger. "I didn't know at first. I followed you to this little house hoping to find some way to hurt you the way you hurt me when you tore Tormund away from me."

"I didn't—"

"Semantics!" she barked in a barely human growl. "You were in control of the beasts that ripped him to pieces! I know that now!"

Gritting my teeth to the point of pain, I fought to keep my expression neutral despite the jackhammering of my heart. "How could you possibly know that?"

A vindictive smile curled the corners of her glossy lips. "You wanna play dumb? Okay, let's play. Do you have any idea what kind of wonderful toys I found here? One in particular was all kinds of fascinatin'. She was able to pluck nuggets of information from the heads of everyone here … with the proper motivation, of course."

Icy water ran through my veins. The asshat King of the Winter Court was right. This was a worst-case situation. Nora had fallen under the control of a vampire. "Why do I feel monetary rewards weren't used to ensure her cooperation?"

Dotty clucked the pink point of her tongue against the roof of her mouth. "Fear is much more persuasive and keeps my money in my pocketbook right where I like it. I agreed to keep her alive if she helped me, after adding just enough pain for that threat to really resonate. After that, she was more than willing to tap into the minds of everyone who was here and find the key details I needed. And what did I learn?" Clasping her pearls, she gave a melodramatic gasp. "That you, my pretty little thing, are a necromancer."

"Bold claim. Got any proof to back it up?" My voice betrayed me by wavering.

Dotty pursed her lips, blonde ringlets bouncing off her cheeks as she shook her head. "You're really gonna make me say it? Half the people who were in this house have silver eyes, thanks to you. From what I've learned, that's your calling card. You bring them back, and they have those telltale silver eyes and a pulse to show for it. Practically everyone at this particular party seemed to know about that. Still, they all kept your secret buried deep in their subconscious out of appreciation for you. That really says something."

"And where are all these people now?" There was no trace of Reid, Dina, or any of the others anywhere in sight. I didn't want to think she had drained them all dry, but after all the horrors I had witnessed at the hands of vampires, I couldn't discount the possibility. That said, I didn't hear death chimes. For the moment, I planned to take that as a good sign.

Dotty pressed one finger to her lips and dropped her voice to a husky whisper. "I'll keep that as my little secret for now, darlin'. In time, if ya play nice, I'll return them to you. But first, you have to return something that belongs to me."

Icy fingers of fear clawed down my spine. "You can't mean..."

Hands on her full hips, Dotty's painted lips screwed to the side. "Look at that! I knew you were a smart gal! I'm sure Tormund is a pile of dust now. You, and only you, can change that. Do what you do and return him to me. Once ya do, I'll give back each and every one of these walking blood bags I've collected. I should warn you though, the longer you take, the more likely I am to deliver their lifeless bodies to your doorstep one by one, until I get what's rightfully mine."

Warning sirens blared off the walls of my mind, blurring my vision as tinges of black terror crept in. "What makes you think I'm actually capable of what you're asking? You could end up killing innocent people for nothing."

So distracted was I by the mere idea of resurrecting Tormund, that I completely forgot about the emerald current I had been battling to keep corked. My focus slipped enough to allow green energy to crackle down my arms and dance over my knuckles. Dotty may have looked like a brainless bimbo, but this new development did not escape her notice. (Not that it would take an overly observant person to pick up on the fact that someone nearby had suddenly taken on a radioactive glow.)

However, she was not smart enough to avoid contact. Seizing hold of my wrist, Dotty yanked my hand up and placed it over her heart. My power surged into her like the world's most effective defibrillator. Milky-white skin warmed to a sun-kissed hue. The light of life ignited in the depths of her stare, earning a shocked giggle from the buxom beauty. "Golly! No wonder Tormund was so infatuated with you! My heart... is beating!"

I tore my hand out of her grip, hoping to reduce the amount of time she would get to enjoy my stolen talents. "You really must be Tormund's maker. You share the same lack of personal boundaries."

Dotty stared down at her hands, turning them over in mystified confusion. "It makes my hands sweat. I can feel heat creeping up my neck and to my ears!"

My eyes bulged at the reaction worsening by the second. Sure as shit, the areas she mentioned were beet red and splotchy. "By chance did you have any sort of skin condition in life? Or a hormonal imbalance of some sort?"

Dotty fanned her face with both hands, drops of sweat beading on her upper lip. "My doc said I was starting my change of life early. I had crippling hot flashes right up until I was changed. Goodness, I forgot all about that... until now." Sweat stains soaked the underarm area of her silky gown, destroying her glamorous persona. "I'm burning up! Undo it! I need you to undo it! Take it back at once!"

And just like that, I had the tiniest bit of leverage. "What will I get in return?"

Dotty's lips pursed, her lipstick smudging at the corners with perspiration. "Fine. Have it your way." Raising her hands alongside her head, she snapped her fingers.

I felt him before I saw him. That familiar thrill of potent masculine energy made fingers of longing tiptoe up my thighs. Reid rounded the side of the house, sending my heart into an appreciative flutter beat... that quickly vanished. "What's wrong with him?"

My wolf-man was there in body, that much was obvious. Yet there was a change in him I could see even from a distance. Whatever warm light normally filled his vessel had been replaced by icy nothingness. No kindness. No recognition. No warmth. No personality. Nothing but vacant existence stared back at me from his silver eyes.

He wasn't Reid.

He just... was.

"Reid?" I ventured a step forward, only to be halted by that haunted nothingness peering back at me.

Bacon, on the other hand, wasn't as quick to pick up on body language cues. Tugging at his leash for all he was worth, he caused a rope burn on my palm as he broke free and galloped straight for his wolf-man bestie.

Like he had done a million times before, Bacon waited until he was no more than two strides away and leapt in the air, fully anticipating Reid would catch him. And the shirtless wolf-man did. But not in the loving way my pork-let was used to. Reid's massive hand shot out, catching Bacon by his round little belly and holding him there.

At first, my piglet froze in confusion. When his wolfie bud didn't cradle him in the customary football hold, Bacon thrashed from side to side in a mad struggle for freedom.

Seeing no signs Reid noticed my curly-tailed bud's plight, I inched in close enough to cradle Bacon's rump in one hand and grab beneath his front legs with the other. Oblivious as to what mindset my wolf was in, I dropped my voice to a calming whisper. "Reid, let him go. Please. He just wanted to say hi to his friend. You are that to him. His friend. Please don't betray him by hurting him."

Reid's features didn't change, but thankfully, his hold on my pork belly relaxed, allowing Bacon to scramble into my welcoming embrace.

Cradling him to my chest, I back-pedaled for the sake of my swine-kick. "What the hell did you do to him?" I snapped, attempting to shrink Dotty with my glare.

Still fanning off the effects of my touch, Dotty let one shoulder rise and fall. "I didn't do anything to him. That's all his sister's doing." Platinum curls bobbed as she nodded her head in Connoll's direction. He had fought his way back to his feet, but wisely opted to maintain his distance. "I'll give you your wolf's body back; that's the fun part, anyway. But if ya want his mind, along with your other friends, you're going to have to bring Tormund back to me… alive and well." Clapping one hand on Reid's shoulder, the curvaceous bombshell shoved him in my direction.

"And if I don't?" Ever the rebel, challenge curled my upper lip into a snarl.

"Then your sexy wolf-man will be the first to die. I'll see to that myself. The rest will swiftly follow. They'll pile up on the doorstep of your manor like a morbid delivery service. In the end you'll be broken, with all those you love ripped away. But it doesn't have to come to that. Give me back my love, and we can avoid this getting any messier. Deny me," she gave a dismissive lift of one slender shoulder, "and I'll paint this whole town with their blood. The choice is yours."

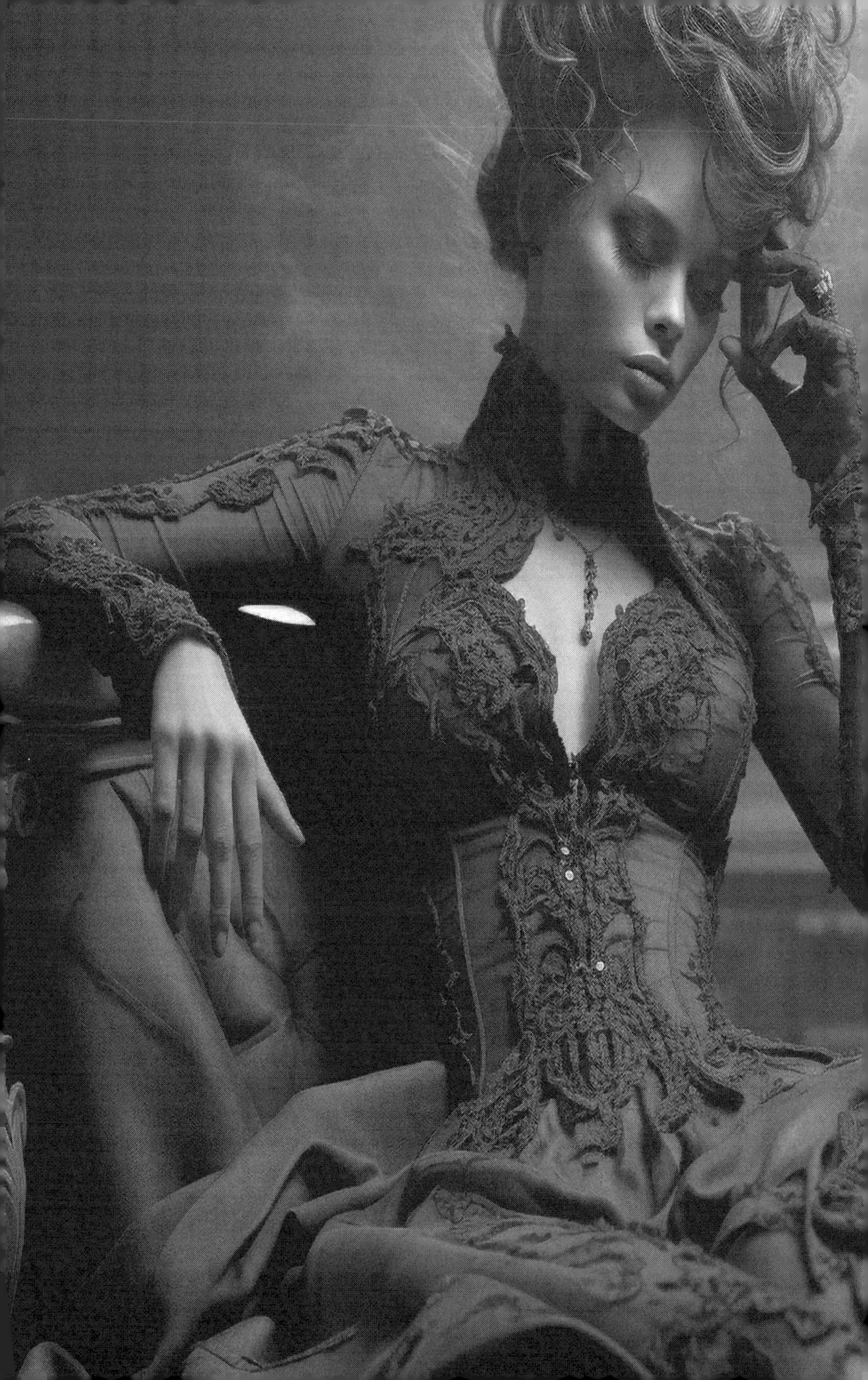

Chapter Five

Back at the manor, Connoll sat in front of Reid in one of the many empty rooms with one hand clasped on his shoulder. Icy blue eyes narrowed, the oracle peered deep into my wolf-man's vacant stare and tried to break through whatever walls had been erected in his mind to trap him inside. Each minute that ticked by felt like an eternity. Even Bacon had abandoned hope and curled up on the black velvet chaise in the corner for a nap.

I couldn't begin to relax. Not with another bloodsucker prowling the streets of Lavender Lotus, making insane demands. Bring back Tormund? No fucking way. As I paced from one floral wallpapered wall to another, I wrung my hands and said a silent prayer Connoll would get through to Reid.

If he could tell us where the others were being held...
If he could confirm they were safe...
Once again, my life was reduced to questions of if.
A heavy sigh from Connoll made me pull up short.
Spinning on him, I saw how his shoulders sagged and knew he wasn't armed with good news. "How bad is it?"
One corner of the detective's mouth tugged back in a sardonic half-smile. "For him? It's not bad at all. What Nora

managed to do in his mind is truly incredible. He's physically sitting here with us now, but in his mind, he's living a blissful secondary reality. Best I can tell? My sister is holding his mind there, while his body is here in the form of a mindless henchman."

"You can't break through what she's done?" The toes of my right foot tapped in agitation.

Connoll's jaw tensed, his attention fixated on Reid. "She's woven such an intricate web in his mind, I'm afraid to try. Pull at the wrong thread, and I could unravel his very essence. This big, strapping beast of a man could be reduced to having the mental capacities of an infant. I don't trust myself to even attempt it."

As we talked, Reid sat on the edge of his chair. Back straight. Gaze fixed at the opposite wall. Hands resting on his knees. None of this registered with him. Did he sleep? Eat? Use the restroom? How deep did Nora's influence run?

Knowing Connoll likely couldn't answer but that time would, I opted for the next question swirling through my mind. "But the faux reality he's trapped in, he's happy there?"

Connoll swiveled in his chair. While the smile he gave me was meant to be reassuring, I couldn't help but notice the hints of sorrow that clouded his eyes. "Wherever he is, he's content."

Unable to speak around the lump of emotion lodged in my throat, I managed a nod. I wrapped my arms around myself tight, as if I could squeeze hard enough to stop my anxious heart from hammering out of my chest. "If we can't get through to him, we have no other way to find the others and get them away from that vampire bitch. That means I have to sweep together the pile of ash that remains of

Tormund and," a chill shuddered through me, "try to resurrect him."

A pit formed in my stomach, causing bile to scorch up the back of my throat. I barely escaped Tormund the first time. There was no telling if I could manage it a second time.

Connoll's chair squeaked as he rose to his feet and closed the distance between us. "We only have about ten minutes until my heart stops beating again."

My brow furrowed at the odd timing of his comment, but I nodded just the same. "Yeah, I'll top you off before I go use a broom and dustpan to assemble a serial killer."

A lock of flaxen hair fell across his forehead as the detective shook his head. "That's not what I meant. When the change happens, if I can control it long enough, I could put him under and keep him under. I can't do what Nora did to Reid. How to even attempt something like that boggles my mind. But I might be able to keep him out long enough to dig through his memories and learn all we can about this Dotty chick. The more we know about her, the better our chances are to bring her down."

My stare strayed to Reid, mind silently pleading for him to look at me with the tenderness I had taken for granted just a short time ago. Instead, he peered back at me with the detached aloofness of a stranger.

"Do you think you can maintain your control long enough to manage that?" I asked, doing my best to pretend that seeing Reid like this wasn't shattering my heart. Even I knew it was far from a Golden Globes-worthy performance.

"If you stay close in case anything happens, I can try." His own apprehension made the words come short and clipped. "I'm not making any promises. I don't trust that side of myself. Still, I owe you this. We can't unleash Tormund on the world a second time. If we can get information out of him, we could bring this all to an end before my father decides to escalate this situation to a ridiculous degree. I hate to say this, Octavia, but, unfortunately, this might be our only chance."

"And if you lose control, leaving me to face two deranged vampires?" Even as I posed the question, I nervously chewed my lower lip.

That look of sadness clouded his features once more, only to be chased away by steadfast resolve. "Then I suggest you have your swords primed and ready. Do not hesitate to take us both down if you have to."

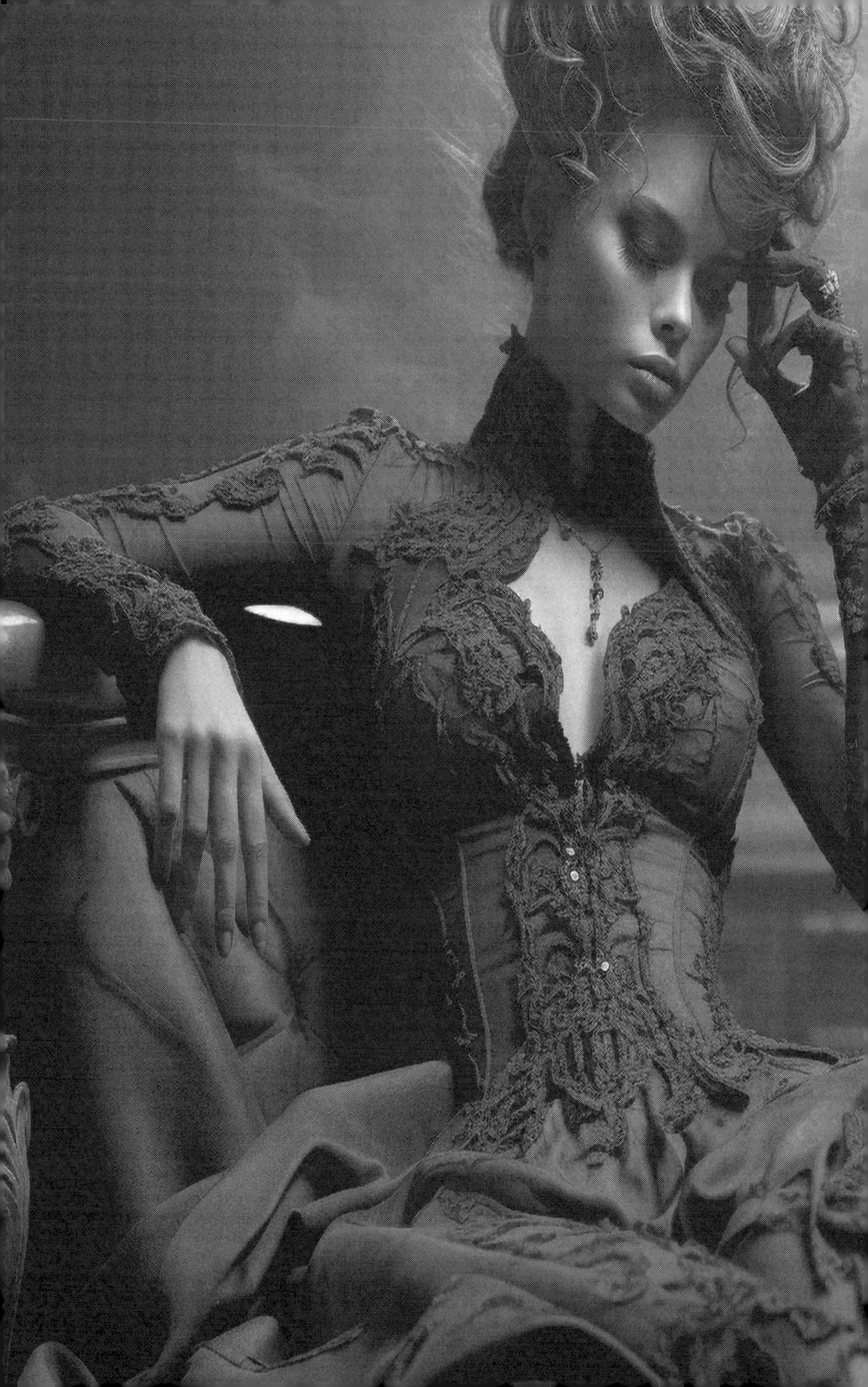

Chapter Six

"I know this was my idea, but I'm not sure I can go through with it." Down in the dungeon of the manor, Connoll stared down at the pile of dust that was all that remained of his sire.

Tormund's screams still echoed off the walls of my mind, and the image of him being ripped apart by my army of the dead burned behind my eyes. "Now is the time to decide, before I even attempt to wake him up. Because, in case you missed the memo, that's at the very bottom of the list of things I have any desire to do. This was your idea. If you have doubts of any kind, we can march back upstairs and scrap this whole plan. Hell, you can go back to riffling through Reid's mind for answers if need be."

Standing statue-still by my elbow, Reid didn't acknowledge his name had been spoken. Instead, he stared straight ahead, showing just as much emotion as the stone wall before him.

Connoll rubbed one hand over the back of his neck. "That's useless. But it doesn't make what I'm about to attempt any easier. You remember what happened to that caterer when I didn't have the benefit of your touch keeping my humanity in check? What I did was monstrous. Unspeakable. It turns my stomach to even think about. I couldn't live with myself if I hurt you or anyone else like that. Even now, I can feel your influence wearing off. My thirst is building. I'm not going to lie, Octavia. It wouldn't take much for me to lose control."

Raising my hand alongside my head, I snapped my fingers, creating an emerald spark that crackled from my digits. "I'll be ready in case you start to slip."

A jerk of his head and the detective dropped fang. "When my strength is at its fullest, it won't be hard for me to overpower you. I could have my fangs plunged deep into your throat before you lay one sparking finger on me."

Despite the dungeon only being lit by the flashlights on our phones, I caught Connoll's stare and held it firm. "I refuse to believe that sharing a bloodline with him means you have to be the same sort of monster. The situation with the caterer happened right after you woke, when you had no idea what ravenous bloodlust was all about. You fed into your darkest desires; I'm not arguing that. Even so, that one moment doesn't define you. This is your chance to prove that to yourself. That you can be better, and do better, by controlling your own impulses. Then maybe you won't have to rely on me quite so much."

Far from convinced, Connoll pressed his lips into a stern line and shook his head. "I just don't know if I can trust myself. How is unleashing me any different than unleashing him?" He jabbed his thumb in the direction of the dust pile. "Or your army of corpses, for that matter?"

I shined my light at the detective's face. His complexion had paled, his features sharpening. The change was coming quicker than Connoll realized. That fact sparked an idea that bordered on insane... yet I was going to throw myself into it just the same. Thankfully, I left Bacon upstairs napping. If things got ugly… and it was likely they would… my boy didn't need to be anywhere near the shitshow likely to follow.

Realizing this was a disaster idea, I basically doused the space with gasoline and tossed a match. "Dotty controlled Reid so easily in this state. How do you think she did it?"

Connoll's top lip twitched into a hint of a snarl. "Are you even listening to me? I know you're upset about your boyfriend, but if you could focus, please."

"This is completely pertinent, I swear." Brushing a lock of cotton candy-hued hair behind my ear, I narrowed my eyes in my wolf-man's direction. "Maybe it's a simple command. Reid, seize him."

Connoll gave a humorless huff of laughter. "Cute. We don't have time for this. Could we—" His words morphed into a grunt as Reid seized him from behind in a tight bear hug. "What the hell? Let go of me!"

Even as he thrashed, Reid held firm.

"Don't let him go under any circumstances," I commanded, fighting to keep my features impassive despite my shaking hands.

"Octavia! Call him off!" The detective's voice changed, deepening with threat and danger as he bared his fangs. "Get this mangy mutt off of me!"

As Connoll's change overtook him, his strength grew. To keep his hold, Reid called on his inner wolf. Ears elongating to points, a canine snout stretched from his face.

Vampire and wolf-man wrestled against one another, with Reid maintaining his hold solely because Connoll hadn't drank blood as of late.

As Connoll battled for his freedom, I launched into step two of my poorly thought-out plan. "You're agitated, and for good reason."

Connoll's features contorted with rage. "Of course I'm agitated! You sicced your dog on me!"

Instead of matching the venom of his tone, I kept my voice smooth and steady. "If you can gain control of yourself here and calm the fuck down, I think it's safe to say you could work your mojo on your resurrected sire without going on a spree. Wouldn't you agree?"

Nose scrunched and jaws clenched, Connoll threw his weight to one side and then the other. Still, Reid's hold didn't budge. "Tell him to let me go, or I'll rip his head off and hand it to you!"

I clasped my hands behind my back, trying to hide how they trembled. "If that's your attempt to convince me you're in control, it sucks. Maybe less saliva foaming at the corners of your mouth would help? Or, ya know, stop threatening to kill your friends."

"You haven't begun to see threatening." The detective bent forward, causing the wolfman to move with him.

A low rumble quaked from Reid's chest. Fur sprouted from his knuckles as he held firm with the ferocity of a dog with a bone… pun intended. Things were escalating from dangerous to deadly fast.

While every instinct screamed for me to run like hell, I made myself edge closer to the enraged vampire. As I neared, I allowed emerald wisps to ripple down the length of my arms. "I can touch you, Detective Tiresias, and restore you to what you were. All you have to do is ask. But resurrecting Tormund and suppressing him was your idea, and you can't do that without your heightened vampiric abilities. I believe in you, Connoll. I truly do. That said, this won't work if you can't trust yourself. Right here and now, you need to prove to yourself that no matter how bad shit gets, you've got this."

I paused for a beat, letting my words sink in. To my great relief, Connoll stilled. While the tendons of his neck still bulged and his hands remained curled into tight fists, he stopped resisting. Dropping his arms to his sides, he slowly straightened his posture. The hatred that had morphed his features was replaced by icy resolve. Looking me dead in the eye, he opened his mouth enough for me to see him retract his fangs.

He fought an epic war to earn back his control, but damn it, he did it. "There are a lot of lives at stake," he grumbled, his voice a gruff whisper. "More than anything, I want to rip your boyfriend's head from his shoulders and punt it across the room. If I can suppress that desire, I can keep control long enough to do what needs to be done with Tormund."

"And if you can't?" Rolling my fingers, I watched wisps of green dance from one digit to another.

One corner of the detective's mouth tugged back in a smirk that brought him back from monster to man. "Stay close and stay charged… just in case."

Swallowing hard, I prayed I wasn't making a mistake and uttered the words that could seal our fate. "Reid, let him go."

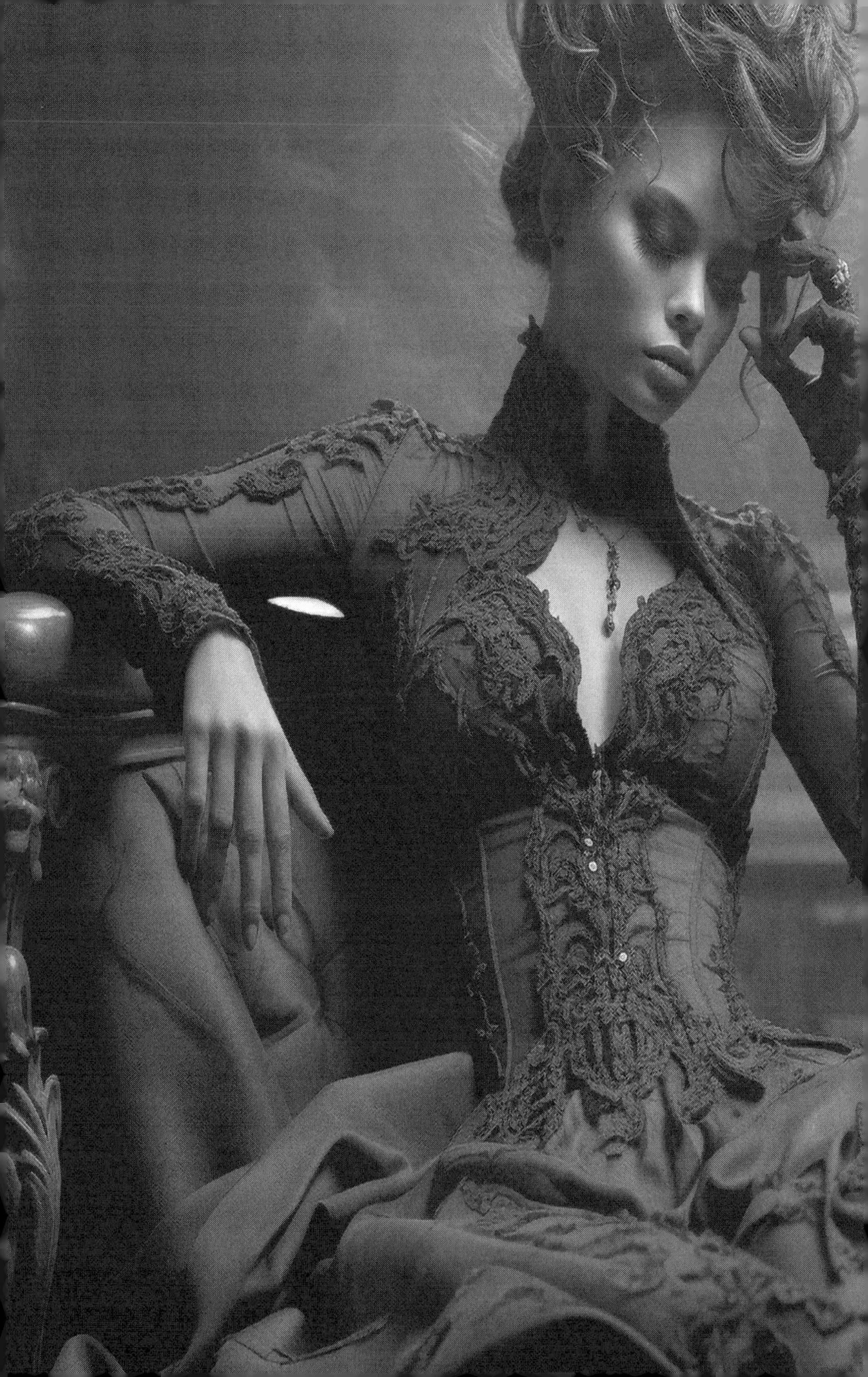

Chapter Seven

I wouldn't let myself think about what I was doing. I couldn't. A moment of introspection would have made my task impossible. Instead, I let the waves of emerald roll while I held my breath and prayed this wasn't an enormous mistake. Puffing my cheeks, I exhaled through pursed lips and stretched my trembling hand over the pile of ash that had once been Tormund.

As it began to take on a human shape, I mentally coached myself. This time I'm not alone. This time there are people in my corner, namely a badass wolf and a mind-controlling vampire. This time... will be different.

Only time would tell if I was kidding myself.

I tried to keep my gaze down, battling not to watch my former captor take shape. Morbid curiosity won out over blind terror. My stare flicked up... and my heart forgot how to beat.

As his silhouette took shape, I was transported back to the night I spent trapped in a bed by his side. Hours stretched by with him forcing me to pour my power into him against my will. So lost was I in that nightmarish memory that I let out a yelp when Tormund's eyes snapped open.

It shouldn't have happened yet.

Spots of his flesh were still ashen and crumbling.

Yet somehow... the monster awoke. Hands curling into claws, he sucked in a deep, ragged breath. His exhale morphed into a scream of anguish that echoed off the stone walls surrounding us. Souls come back often in the same emotional state they were in when they died, and—thanks to me—Tormund died being ripped apart by my zombie army. I didn't harbor even one ounce of guilt that he was haunted by his final moments. He earned that trauma.

Still, seeing him reanimated caused my throat to constrict in an unforgiving vice grip of fear. Squatting beside the vamp, I fell back on my ass and scrambled backwards in an awkward crab crawl. Had I stayed still, I might have been better off. My movement turned Tormund's attention my way. Head lifting from the ground, his silver eyes tracked my motion.

Seeing recognition register in the depths of his mercurial stare, my mouth fell open in a scream that died on my lips. I inserted as much distance between us as possible until my back smacked into the stone wall behind me, effectively trapping me on the opposite side of the dungeon from the exit.

Rolling to his side, Tormund pushed to standing on legs that wobbled beneath him. Fragments of dust fell from his frame, leaving a divot in his exposed shoulder. He dragged one foot towards me, then another. Fingers, black with decay, stretched for me.

His gray lips parted to form one single word. "Mine. Miiiiiiiiiiine."

I couldn't move.

Couldn't blink.

Frozen in terror, I shrunk down, praying the earth would open up and swallow me whole. Tormund filled my vision, blocking out the rest of the world.

"You... are... miiiine!"

Tears were blurring my vision when Tormund froze. His body went rigid an instant before he collapsed to the floor like a felled tree.

Connoll stood behind him, one hand outstretched at shoulder level with his lips moving in an incessant chant. "Sleep. Sleep deep. Sleep. Sleep deep."

Face down on the dusty floor, Tormund's muffled snores wafted up from his resting spot.

The detective shifted his weight, contemplating stepping closer only to reconsider. "Are you okay?"

Pulling my knees in tight, I hugged them to my chest. "Not in any way, shape, or form."

Face vacant of emotion, Reid strode straight forward and offered me a hand up. I moved without thinking, latching onto him and launching myself into his arms. Clinging to him, I prayed for a returned embrace that didn't come. Reid dropped his arms to his side, giving me nothing but ice.

For a moment...

Then, one hand slid around my waist and came to rest on the small of my back. Hot breath tickled over the crook of my neck. "Octavia, Octavia, Octavia... was my warning in some way unclear?"

It wasn't Reid's husky voice purring against my ear, but a pure velvet cadence I'd heard only once before.

Shoving away from him, I backpedaled and peered into the beguiling face of Death. Sure, he wore the façade of my panty-wetting celebrity crush, but his eyes were pits of darkness that threatened with the ominous secrets of the great beyond. Connoll. Reid. Tormund. The manor. It all vanished around me, thrusting me into an inky void that stretched as far as the eye could see.

Pink hair brushed across my shoulder blades as my head jerked in one direction then the other. "Where are we? What happened?"

Death plunged his hands into the pockets of his designer slacks and offered me a crooked smile. "Consider me a selfish man who wanted you all to myself. To accomplish that, I created a little oasis just for us. Did I miss the mark? Perhaps something a bit more appealing?" A roll of his fingers and a luxurious hotel suite materialized around us. Its floor-to-ceiling windows offered a stunning view of what I guessed to be the New York City skyline.

Yet the beauty didn't end there. Cream colored walls warmed the space. The bathroom door was open, revealing a free-standing bathtub filled with steaming water and tempting bubbles. Back in the expansive bedroom, a beige upholstered headboard accentuated what I assumed would be impressively high thread count bedding. What even was a good number? Ten? One Hundred? A thousand? Six million? I had no clue.

Settling into this new scene with ease, Death sauntered to the walnut bar in the corner and poured himself two fingers of Scotch. Rolling the sleeves of his cobalt dress shirt further up his muscled forearms, he raised his glass in my direction. "Join me for one?"

There are all sorts of sayings about Death. Flirt with Death. Dance with Death. However none of them warned about drinking with Death. That made it safe, right? Or so I convinced myself as I closed the distance between us and accepted the offered glass.

Before it touched my lips, I had enough sense to hesitate. "It's not poisoned, is it?"

Death threw his head back in a genuine chuckle. "Why would I ever commit such a heinous act? Would heaven strike down the Gryphons who protect their gates?"

"Is that rhetorical? Because I have no idea."

Death's amused smile lingered at the corners of his delectable lips. "No, Miss Hollows, fate has much bigger plans for you than to meet your end by a toxin."

"Mhm," I muttered for lack of a better response and drained my glass in one gulp. As it burned down my gullet, I pressed the back of my hand to my lips. "Okay, I'm good and lubricated. Go ahead with your threats."

Death gave a playful wiggle of his eyebrows. "So eager. Darling, at least allow me a bit of time for foreplay before we get to the naughty fun."

Maybe it was the fact that he wore the face of my celebrity crush, or the velvety seduction of his tone. Either way, warmth crept up my inner thighs as I watched him pour himself a second drink.

"What exactly do you have in mind?" I battled to keep the longing out of my voice, with little success.

Don't judge me.

There's a reason there's a saying about flirting with Death.

He's hot as fuck.

Not that I had any intention of betraying Reid, but no harm came from looking. Right?

Death bought the glass to his lips, his eyes lingering on mine. "What are you offering?"

Mouth dry. Palms sweaty. I shifted my weight from one foot to the other and silently wished he would look anywhere but at me. "A drinking partner for another round, if you're pouring."

His fingers brushed mine as he took my glass and topped me off. Handing it back to me, Death clinked his glass with mine. "Despite what you believe, I'm not a threat to you, Octavia. The balance of nature is. Yet you continue to push the threshold in a way that could have detrimental consequences you can't possibly comprehend."

Another gulp of the amber liquor burned down my throat. "I brought Tormund back out of necessity to save lives. The second we get the information we need out of him, I'll put him back where I got him without hesitation or regret."

"One returned, while so many others still walk the earth." Death swirled his glass, letting the liquid splash up the sides. "I come only with a disclaimer, dear one. Ignore the balance, and there will be a price to pay."

"Tormund is a monster. I wouldn't risk a splinter over a vile turd like him," I seethed. "I need time to get information out of him, then I will happily return him to a pile of ash. I give you my word."

Death pursed his lips and blinked my way for a bit as if contemplating if I was telling the truth. After a beat, he wagged a finger my way. "You know the thing about merely existing that few beings ever truly comprehend, is that mortals can do... anything they want." Moving close with feline fluidity, he used the knuckle of his forefinger to tip my face up to his. Hot breath tingled over my cheeks as his lower lip brushed mine in an intimate caress. "Any desire... or naughty little inkling... could be acted on if one was so inclined."

I hated how my body responded to him. How every nerve ending was set ablaze at the thought of him closing the bothersome chasm of space separating us. Words left my lips in a throaty whisper. "Doesn't acting on those primal impulses reduce us to animals?"

His hands snaked around my waist, lingering at my hips in tempting suggestion. "Oh, but we are animals. Willing to hunt, kill, feast, and fuck to our heart's desire."

Hearing Death himself utter the f-word unlocked a new kink within me I doubted any others shared. Mouth suddenly arid dry, I tried—and failed—to tear my attention away from the sexy curve of his lips. "Then why doesn't the world just give in and erupt into carnal chaos?"

Dipping his head, his warm breath teased over the delicate skin of my neck as he whispered against my ear. "Because, my beautiful marvel, every action has consequences. And that is what you have yet to realize. You've lived with the belief that what you can do is unflappable, without any kind of limits. If you keep this up, you will lose the ability to grant life. Remember, beautiful one, no one can have victorious climax after climax without the occasional moment of impotent letdown by fate and circumstance."

"This may have inadvertently become the filthiest conversation I have ever had, and I'm completely here for it." Even as I uttered the words, I became painfully aware that I still lingered at a body-skimming proximity to him. However, I had yet to find the motivation to correct that matter.

Raising one hand, he stroked his fingers through my hair from scalp to end... giving a little tug that caused heat to throb in my core. "Oh, the fun we could have together... and I have no doubt we will. But not quite yet. To fully embrace what you are, you must be humbled by your own limitations. When that happens," Death took a step back, retracting the tantalizing warmth of his touch, "your power will reach unfathomable new heights that I ... for one ... am practically panting to behold. For now, your destiny has yet to play out. You decide what actions, and consequences, will follow. The future is yours, Octavia Hollows. Where will you let it take you?" As he spoke the words, his form shifted to that of Reid.

My Reid.

With the warm light of love behind his eyes and that easy smile that made me feel I was home. I didn't hesitate, but launched myself into his arms. Squeezing him tight, I breathed in his scent and tried to convince myself this was real. That everything that came before it was just a horrible nightmare. That's when I noticed the markings of reality. The room dimmed to the oppressive darkness of the manor's dungeon. No big surprise there. What crushed my heart was the realization that Reid wasn't hugging me in return. His arms hung at his sides, his posture rigid.

I wasn't the only one who noticed.

"Octavia?" Connoll softly interjected, his tone one of sincere empathy.

It was all too much.

Too raw.

Shoving away from Reid as if contact with him scalded me, I pushed away and stumbled back a few steps. It wasn't enough. A galaxy of distance would still have been too near to this anguish.

"I need a minute," I muttered to no one in particular before bolting from the catacombs beneath the manor. The soles of my boots hit the ground in time with the hammering of my heart, resonating off the stone walls as if taunting me with what was and may never be again. I took the winding stairs two at a time. Bolting down the hall, I sprinted for the front door, all the while feeling the walls closing in around me.

My lungs hurt.

Every breath I sucked in gnawed at the gaping hole that felt like had been punched through my soul. Wrapping my arms around my middle I hugged me tight, as if that pose was somehow holding me together. Bursting outside, I sucked in one ragged breath and then another in my stagger down the porch steps. The instant grass crunched under my boots, my legs failed me. Knees buckling, I crumbled to the ground. Shoulders shaking with gut wrenching sobs, I soaked the earth with my tears. An animalistic wail tore from my lungs, brought on by all I'd endured, with no sign of an end in sight.

Everyone I'd lost.

Every sacrifice I made.

Everything I cared for that had been ripped away.

The saying goes that life never gives us more than we can handle. Yet I felt my limit had been reached eons ago. There had to be a threshold of how much a human could withstand, and I'd surely hit mine.

Comfort came in the form of a cool snout nudging my elbow. Bacon edged in close, concern creasing his sweet little face.

The butler stood at the open door, watching the scene unfold at a respectable distance. "He was pawing at the door, trying to get to you, Madame. I hope this is okay?"

I gave a curt nod, which he returned before shutting the door behind him to grant us some privacy. Alone with my boy, I pulled him into my lap and dotted a kiss to the top of his head. "Remember when it was just us against the world, buddy? A different town every night with no one to worry about but each other? Sure, monsters were always trying to kill us, but we avoided emotional trauma ... for the most part."

Bacon gave a soft snort and snuggled deeper into my embrace.

"Octavia?" Connoll tentatively broke the hush from the front door. "I have Tormund in one of the bedrooms, locked in a resting state. I can begin to read him whenever you're ready."

Filling my lungs to capacity, I exhaled through pursed lips. Tucking Bacon under my arm, I pushed off the ground and wiped the tears from my cheeks with the back of my hand. "Ready has nothing to do with it. Survival demands we push on."

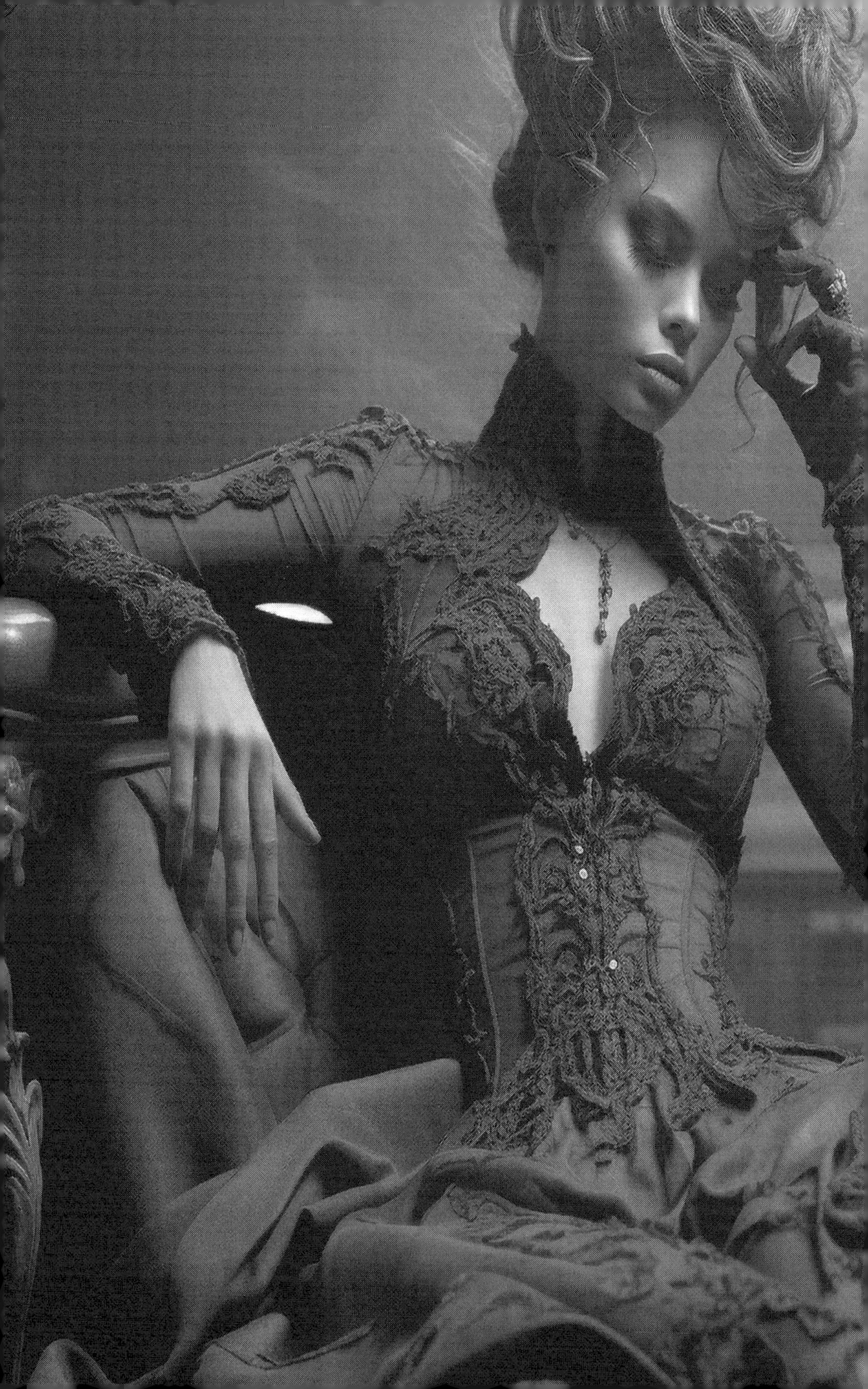

Chapter Eight

Connoll

Octavia was in a bad place. That much was obvious. For the most part, she seemed her usual strong and sassy self. Unfortunately, snaked between those moments—when she thought no one was looking—she would shrink in on herself. Her shoulders would hunch and her arms wrapped around her torso in a tight self-hug. Reid walking around like a human puppet was a big part of her trauma, but her anguish didn't end there. I bore my share of guilt for her pain. Tormund had subjected her to torture I couldn't begin to fathom, and I convinced her to bring him back. I was well aware of the asshole move that was.

Still, my reasons were valid and necessary. Lavender Lotus wouldn't withstand the fury of wrath my father would unleash if Nora wasn't returned to him. The Winter Court had arranged my position with the Lavender Lotus police department in a way that would benefit the city while lining my father's already overflowing pockets. With time, I had come to appreciate my work, the town, and the people here. Call me crazy, but I had no desire to see them all annihilated.

To prevent the very worst from happening, I needed to get inside Tormund's head and learn as much about this

Dotty person as I could. In theory, it sounded simple: tap into his thoughts and learn her weaknesses. Piece of cake. If the cake was a powerful vampire who would likely kill us all if I couldn't keep him unconscious, that is.

Reid, the stoic minion, was the one who carried the limp shell of my sire up to one of the empty bedrooms. Now, with my audience of three watching, I fought an internal battle between life… and death. I had a crucial job to do. Yet, my focus was stolen by the pulses of the living resonating around me and awaking a ravenous bloodlust. My fangs ached, threatening my gumline. Octavia could douse the blaze of my longing with a touch of her hand, but without my heightened vamp abilities, we couldn't get the background on Dotty we needed. Maybe the necromancer would reward me for a job well done by letting me eat Tormund.

One could only hope. She hated the guy. So, it was a possibility. A slim one, but still. All I had to do was ignore my overwhelming desire to rip anyone's throat out. I could do that.

Probably.

Possibly.

Okay, it was a slim chance, but stranger shit happened for us daily.

Hands shaking with the urge to grab Tormund by the shoulders and sink my teeth in his neck, I took my position at the head of his bed and scanned the room. Octavia was seated on the floor in the corner of the suite closest to the bathroom, chewing on her lower lip while cuddling Bacon in her lap. Reid stood by the footboard with his arms folded over his massive chest. He had been prepped with instructions to hold Tormund still if he started to wake up, or pull me off him if I lost control and dove for his throat. Bases were covered. I couldn't stall anymore.

After exchanging nods with Octavia, I turned my attention to the challenge at hand. Dropping my chin to my chest, I closed my eyes and placed my hands on Tormund's shoulders. In an instant, I was launched into his past.

Growing up in the nineteen-thirties, Tormund's life was one of extravagant splendor. Beautiful homes. Grand parties. Boarding schools abroad. Travel to exotic locations. His every whim was answered with any luxury money could buy… except for the time and attention of his parents. Nothing mattered more to Leopold and Valencia Gracy than their elite roles in high society. Not even their own child. Tormund's care was handed over to nannies and tutors while they sauntered to this gala or that dinner. The young gentleman hid his loneliness behind polite smiles, all the while trying to excel at everything he did in hopes of making them proud and capturing even a moment of their attention. His mother would breeze past him without so much as a glance, while his dad would ruffle his hair, pat him on the back, and tell him to keep up the good work.

For years, those were the moments Tormund lived for. Until sorrow descended. Leopold Gracy perished in a boating accident off the coast of Greece. Now in his late teens, Tormund received no comfort from his mother. No, Valencia sunk her claws into the first wealthy bachelor that came along and let him whisk her away to a new life without offering so much as a backwards glance at her one and only child.

The reason behind her actions soon revealed itself. The Gracy family was utterly broke. The lavish lifestyle they enjoyed landed Tormund in a mountain of debt he held no hope of digging himself out of. His home, the cars, and any possessions that held any value were seized by the bank. Tormund was left penniless and alone, forced to work in a match factory just to scrape by. Twelve-hour days laboring away there allowed him to make enough to pay for a room in a boarding house where he collapsed in exhaustion each night. The one day a week he got off, he spent capturing joy in the only way he could to reminisce on the life he'd been forced to leave behind. He meticulously dressed in the one nice suit he managed to keep, swept his hair back in a gentleman's fashion, and ventured to the local opera house.

    He couldn't afford a ticket inside. That luxury was now well above his station. Instead, he sat on a park bench right outside and listened to the muffled vocals wafting out in a bittersweet reminder of days gone by. Days that faded a little more every day like a photograph yellowing with age as its crisp colors blurred. During intermission and after the final curtain call, he would hold his head high and venture into the lobby. He wanted to brush elbows with those inside, purely for nostalgic purposes, without risking calling attention to himself. If the ushers noticed him, Tormund would likely be kicked out. To avoid that, he hung back by the wall and simply listened.

    To the clink of champagne flutes.

    The symphony of laughter.

    Discussions of extravagant lives.

    Genuine merriment.

    It was hard to say what he found more compelling: the sounds of the opera itself or listening in on fragments of the lives of those attending it. Weeks went by with him repeating this pattern without being noticed or caught... until he caught the eye of a stunning blonde standing across the crowded lobby. Dressed in a red velvet dress that hugged her curves, a white mink stole was draped around her delicate shoulders.

Dotty.

A vision worthy of the silver screen, she made Tormund's pulse lurch with a glance. He instinctively took a step in her direction, only to have the harsh reality of his station halt him where he stood. He no longer had anything to offer a woman as fetching as she. Her beauty far surpassed the cot and creaky chair he had to offer back at the boarding house. Yet again, life was denying him any chance at happiness. A lump of equal parts rage and sadness formed in his throat. Fearing it would tear from his lungs in an enraged howl, he pushed his way through the crowd and escaped outside. Bursting out the door, he bolted across the street before folding in half with his hands on his knees. Breathing in the crisp night air, he battled to quiet the screaming in his mind. An endeavor that proved pointless as soon as she spoke.

"You ran out of there so fast, I half wondered if you were a pickpocket." The curvaceous beauty stood before him with one hip cocked in a seductive pose.

Tormund's mouth opened and shut, words of any kind failing him in the presence of such a striking beauty.

Dotty gave a flirty giggle at the visible effect she had on him, her breasts bouncing with the motion. She appeared girlish and playful... to Tormund. He was too bewitched to see the calculating look swirling behind her eyes. Her stare swept over him, taking in every detail and missing nothing. Of course Tormund missed that, seeing as how his attention ventured into the depths of her cleavage and got lost there.

Dotty took full advantage of his distraction by sauntering closer, her hips swaying in a seductive swish. "But then I got a good look at ya. Ya fit the part of a gentleman, for sure.

The posture. The haughty lift of your chin. Even that fancy way you flip your hair. You've known the finer things in life, that's for sure."

A carnation pink blush filled Tormund's cheeks, his chest puffing with the feeling he was being seen for the man he wished he still was. "That I have, Miss...?"

"Dotty," she filled in for him. "But if I had to guess – and I think I do, because you're not offerin' it up on your own – I think those days have passed you by."

Features falling, Tormund stumbled back a step like she'd punched him in the gut. "I beg your pardon?"

"There's nothing to be ashamed of." Dotty let one exposed shoulder rise and fall in a nonchalant shrug. "We don't all get the same opportunities in life, and sometimes fate can be a real bitch. Judging by the black grime under your fingernails, you've been doing time in the factories." Leaning in, she took a whiff of him and gave a knowing nod. "You carry the scent of stale air and week-old bread. I recognize that from the unfortunate nights I've been forced to spend in boarding houses myself. You, my beautiful boy, have fallen on hard times. Haven't you?"

Her faux sincerity and concern were enough to cause tears to well behind the naive twenty-year-old's eyes. Sniffing them back, he forced a tight smile to hide his show of emotion. "Times have been hard, for certain. Still, I remain a gentleman at heart and will work my way back to being a man of station worthy of a woman such as yourself."

Dotty placed one palm softly on Tormund's cheek. "A woman confident in herself doesn't need a man to provide her with a life she can lavish in. She needs a partner she can build a beautiful future with." Her blonde curls bopped as she tilted her head to consider him. "I see something in you, handsome. A sadness mixed with the desire to succeed. It makes me think you and I could accomplish anything we set our hearts to together. The world could be ours. Would you like that?"

"Y-yes," he stammered, unsure how the conversation had taken such a glorious turn.

"Good." Dotty dropped fang, earning a shocked gasp from her prey. "Then let's begin."

Tormund was given no chance to run before Dotty lunged for his throat.

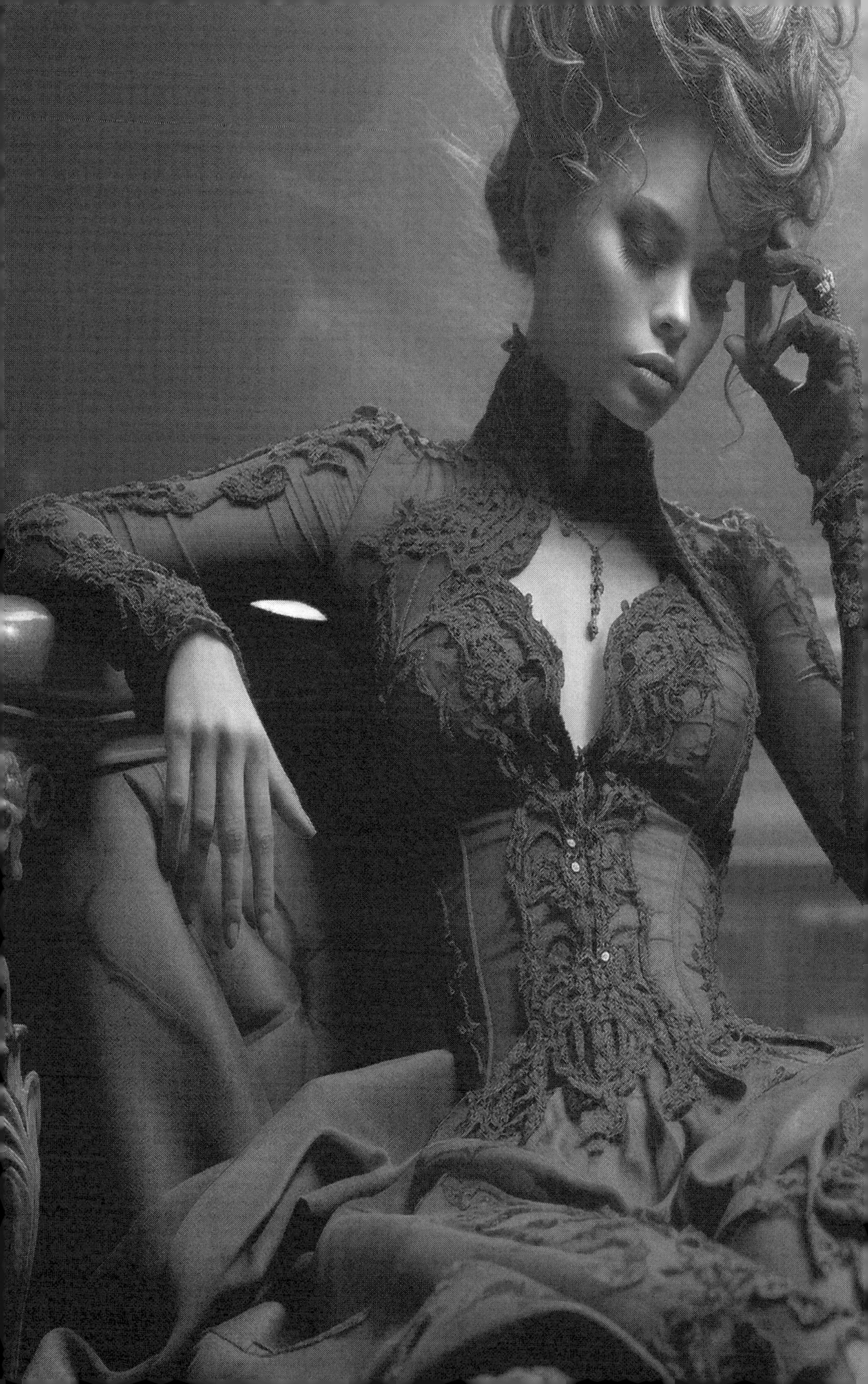

Chapter Nine

My skin sizzled with emotions barely held in check. Seeing Tormund lying there, his chest rising and falling with each breath, ground salt into the open wound of my emotional trauma. I had watched truly amazing people have their lives cut short in merciless ways. Meanwhile, this piece of shit got another chance to torment the world by simply existing.

Seated on the floor with my legs stretched in front of me and Bacon nestled in my lap, I anxiously shook one foot in agitation. The intensity of my vibrating eventually caused Bacon to climb off me with a huff and go find somewhere else to lay down that didn't feel like it was hopped up on Acme earthquake pills.

His departure did nothing to help my mood. Sure, I was a scrappy chick, but I never considered myself openly violent. Until now. To the right of me was an antique rolltop desk and chair. With every ounce of my being, I wanted to heel-stomp one of the legs off the wooden chair and stab it into Tormund's chest. He wasn't immortal anymore. A stake to the heart wasn't necessary. Even so, the idea of splintered wood shredding his pulsating ventricles gave me a dark thrill I probably shouldn't have admitted even to myself. Not only did I want to end him, I wanted to do it in the most agonizing way imaginable.

Grinding that chair leg in deep.

Gouging through tendons.

Life pouring out of him in torrents.

So lost was I in my own dark reverie, my vision tunneled to all around me... until I felt something cold and wet bump my forearm. Brow furrowed, I blinked back to the here and now to find myself face-to-furry face with a massive black wolf. In full canine form, Reid whimpered and nudged my arm a second time. Not following what he was motioning to, I glanced down... and gasped. I turned my hands over, my jaw hanging slack. Every vein was visible beneath my skin, surging with a pulsating green glow. The effect made me look like a patchwork quilt coming apart at the seams. Panic tightened my chest. My breath came in frantic pants as I felt the control over my abilities slipping. One of my arms was knocked skyward by a big furry head. He wasn't looking for scratches. The intelligent, empathetic look in his silver eyes read far deeper. It was him. Truly him.

"Reid?" His name left my lips in a shaky breath.

Ears perked, he licked my cheek with a messy slurp that earned an unexpected chuckle.

I was wiping away his slobber when I noticed the green veins fading back to a normal hue. He got me out of my own way... for the moment, at least.

Hands on both sides of his face, I ruffled his thick coat. "Look at that. Nora couldn't get to Bacon when she took down the rest of you, and she can't influence your mind when you're in wolf form. Lucky for us, her mind melding has limitations."

Reid whimpered and backed away, his stare shifting from me to the door and back again.

"Trust me, I'd love to leave, too. But we can't leave Connoll alone with Count Douche Canoe over there." I jerked my chin in the direction of the detective and the unconscious man he was mind probing.

(Which sounds a lot dirtier than it was.)

Reid-wolf did not agree with my stance on this matter. Flipping his massive head, he barked his annoyance.

Snapped out of a seemingly hypnotized state, Connoll pulled his hand away from Tormund's forehead. "What did you do? Why is he a wolf?"

I opened my mouth to argue, only to clamp it shut with an indignant snort. "Listen, man — a lot of my friends are wolves and I have shockingly little to do with that metamorphosis."

Our furry friend was far from amused by our banter. Hackles raised, Reid barked, his jaws snapping in urgency.

"Dude, if you have to go outside, just say so. No need to wake the comatose serial killer." Even as his ruckus continued, I cast a questioning look at Connoll. "Wait, is that a possibility? How deep is he under?"

Fangs fully extended, Connoll's attention was locked on where my pulse throbbed in my throat. "What? Sorry." Snapping himself out of it with a visible shake, he forced his gaze up to my eyes. "Oh, nothing to worry about there. He won't wake until I want him to. This house could burn down around him and he'd sleep right through it."

Tired of being ignored, Reid swiped one giant paw at me with enough force to knock me sideways. Confident he got my attention, he darted to the window and jumped up with his front feet on its ledge. Massive frame filling the glass, he unleashed a flurry of pissed off woofs.

Something in his behavior curled Connoll's top lip into a menacing snarl. The vampire-detective moved in a blur of speed. Instantly, I bristled in fear that he would launch into an attack with Reid as his target. It wasn't that I didn't trust him. But I had watched him drain a caterer dry just days ago, therefore my apprehension seemed justified. I was on my feet in an instant. Though what I planned to do if a vampire and a wolf actually got into a scuffle remained a mystery even to me.

Thankfully, I didn't have to risk life or limb throwing myself between them. Side by side, they peered into the woods that surrounded the manor with growls rumbling from both their chests. Which, as omens go, seemed like a pretty ominous one. Reid pushed away from the ledge first and trotted to the door where he paced and whimpered for me to open it.

Brow furrowed in confusion, I looked to Connoll for some sort of explanation. Face locked in an expressionless mask that was impossible to read, he spoke in a tone that left no room for arguments or discussion. "Take Reid. Scan the woods surrounding the manor. Now. If at any time you can suddenly see your own breath… run like hell."

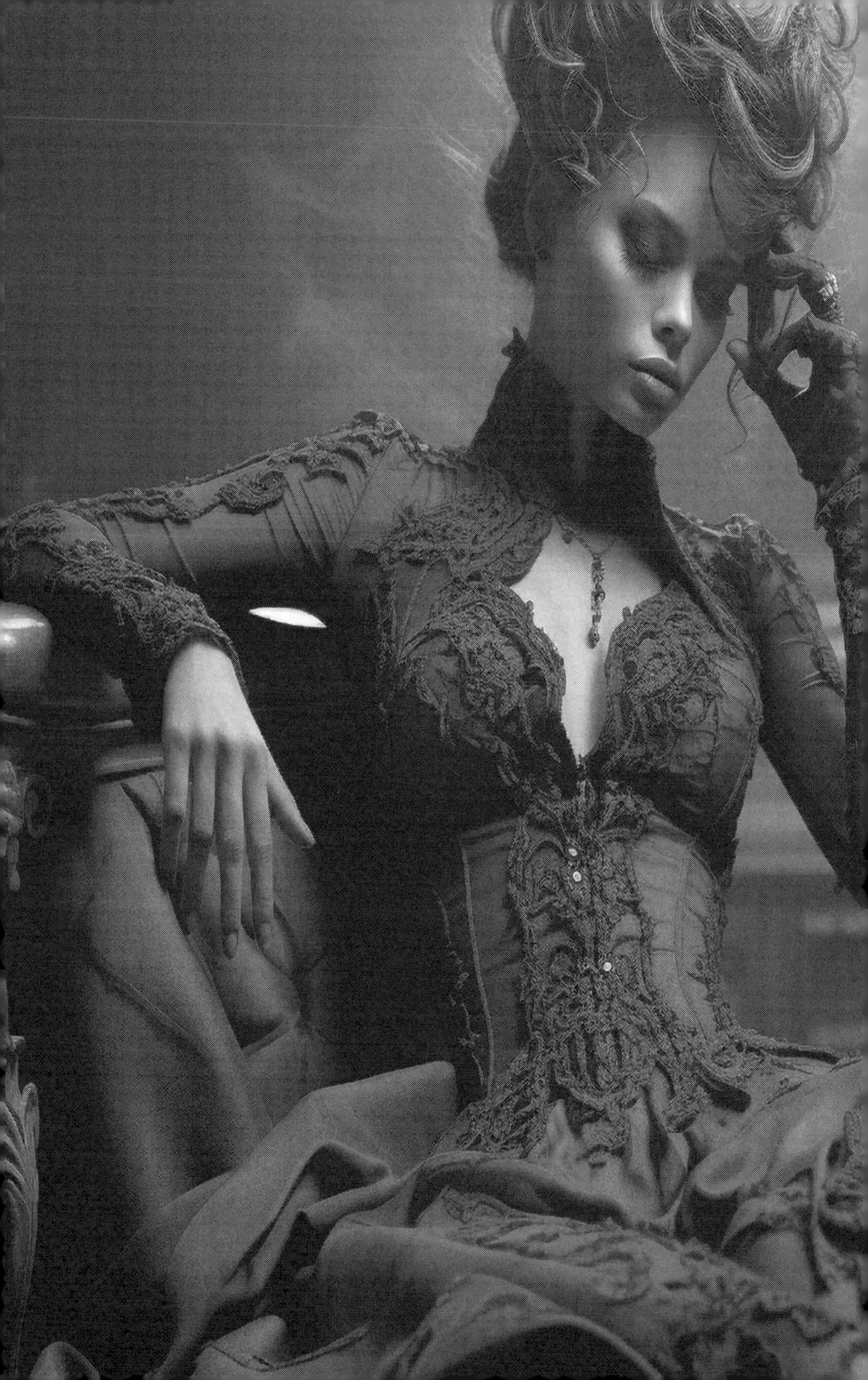

Chapter Ten

Connoll

I couldn't say for certain that my father's influence was at work. It was the time of year when the leaves normally turned brown and frost nipped at the air. Still, I detected a stillness resonating from the woods that put me on edge. The King of the Winter Court said he wanted immediate action, and patience wasn't a virtue of his. Planting fae soldiers in anticipation of a strike was completely in character for him. Be that as it may, for the moment I had to fully trust Octavia and her wolfman to uncover if my father had planted any traps in the trees.

Because I had work to do. We needed to know how to bring Dotty down, and my last trip into Tormund's mind got us no closer to answers. If I was right, and a threat was in fact surrounding us, there wasn't a moment to lose.

Putting my trust in Octavia, I approached the head of the bed and placed two fingers against Tormund's temple. Closing my eyes, I let myself be drawn back into his past.

Waking up as a vampire wasn't as much of a shock to the system for Tormund as it was for the others. (Namely the oracle-turned-gifted vamp who was watching these second-hand memories.) Tormund's situation was far different. He'd had his life of luxury stripped away. Safety, security, and family were torn from him, leaving him scared, vulnerable, and alone. But when his eyes snapped open and he felt the power surging through his veins, Tormund... grinned. The sensory assault of sounds, smells, and sights was a lot to take in. Still, his awakening proved to be a moment of power in a time where he felt impotent in the world. Instead of shying away from it, he embraced the new strength surging through his veins.

Dotty brought him a homeless woman and allowed him to sate his ravenous hunger. That seemed to be the beginning of something truly miraculous. Tormund felt strong and unstoppable... until reality set in that he could still be a disappointment to his maker. Dotty had expensive tastes, which he couldn't begin to provide for, thanks to the financial problems his family had dumped on him. Her appetites were extravagant. The finest clothes. The fanciest cars. Suites that would make anyone on a budget faint. Tormund felt he couldn't compete. Yet somehow, Dotty seemed to have limitless means for them to enjoy every aspect of grand splendor.

For a time, the pair lived their afterlives to the fullest. Fine hotels. Extravagant clothes. Engaging theater and, Tormund's favorite, operas. Each night ended with them finding a couple they could play with in any debaucherous way they liked. Drinks and dining inevitably led to a bloodbath of lust and violent hunger. They wouldn't kill their playthings. That would be too risky. Instead, they stopped short of killing them, then supplied them with enough of their blood to heal them. To ensure the couples wouldn't speak out against them, they robbed them and then positioned their bodies splayed out in public spaces in a way that would mortify them upon waking. Nothing like inadvertently waking up in a dog-collared pegging scene to send both parties scurrying inside as quickly as possible to never speak of it again. For Tormund and Dotty, it was all an orgasmic blur of gore and animalistic desire... until a pivotal moment put a halt to their bloody spree.

Tormund came back to the hotel with his arms flung over the slender shoulders of two sequin-clad follies girls. The two fresh-faced beauties had eyes only for their dark-haired gentleman suitor and giggled up at his handsome face at every word he said.

Yet darkness clouded his features the instant he saw Dotty standing outside the hotel with their bags packed. Her usual sultry smile was replaced by a somber pout. The instant she spotted Tormund, she let out a pained sob and elbowed the showgirls aside to throw herself into his open arms.

His snacks all but forgotten, Tormund enveloped Dotty in his embrace. "My dearest, who has caused you pain? I'll tear their head off with my bare hands."

"Not a who, but a what, sugar. We spent all our dough and we can't stay here no more. What are we gonna do?" She gave a little hiccup-whimper for added effect.

Tormund cradled her face between his palms, yet failed to realize she hadn't mustered even one fake tear. To his credit, he went into full hero mode for his damsel in distress. "I'm stronger than I've ever been because of you. We will figure this out one way or another... together," he vowed.

Tipping her chin, she dotted a kiss to the heel of his hand. "I have one way, doll... if you're up for it. Do ya trust me?"

"Yes, of course, my daring." Peppering her face with kisses, he was completely oblivious to the sparkle-clad girls growing bored and sauntering away. "Simply tell me what you need, and I'm committed to it."

Any trace of sorrow vanished from Dotty's features, replaced by a conniving smirk. "I was hopin' you'd say that."

Time skipped forward through Tormund's memories, finally settling outside a three-story brownstone. On the sidewalk by the stoop, the one-time gentleman of station cast a nervous glance at the building as if it was a viper coiled to strike. "Dotty, my darling, this is insane. There are easier methods to acquire the funds we need. With our strength and speed alone, we could have a bank vault emptied before anyone sounded the alarm."

Dotty's flashy clothes had been replaced by a demure button-up blouse and an ankle-length skirt, then topped off with a tweed coat. Her blonde hair had been straightened into a sleek bob which was accentuated by a stylish cap angled on the side of her head. "We'd be caught in no time. I ain't risking it. The people inside this house are nasty fellas. We're about to give them exactly what they deserve."

Seeing an elderly couple sauntering down the sidewalk arm in arm, Tormund hooked his hand around Dotty's waist and led her closer to the front door. His voice dropped to a whisper meant for her alone. "What these men want is despicable. Why would you voluntarily subject yourself to that?"

Dotty's head tilted as she clucked her tongue against the roof of her mouth. "I'm not subjectin' myself to nothin', doll. You're gonna swoop in and save me as soon as you hear me signal. These rich guys have more money than brains. I've met their kinds before. They think they can do whatever they want with no consequences. We're gonna teach them otherwise. What they want to do to me in there? We're gonna make sure they can't do it to any little filly ever again."

Lips pinched in a thin line, Tormund shook his head. "Signal early, and know if any of them so much as harm one hair on your head, I'll break their spines and drain them dry."

"That's what I'm countin' on, dollface," Dotty purred and gifted him a saucy wink.

Tormund hated this with every fiber of his being. Unfortunately, he was unable to do anything but watch as Dotty entered the brownstone. Rising up on tiptoe, he craned his neck to peer inside. He counted six men waiting for her in the sitting room. One had enormous ears and a bulbous nose. Another held a cigar between his thick lips. The third was overweight and sweating profusely. Next to him was a bald man wringing his hands in giddy delight. The last two Tormund could see hung back in the shadows, making it impossible for him to notice any distinguishable features.

He didn't need to see every detail of them to know they had a sinister agenda. "Dotty!" he called after her before the house swallowed her whole.

She glanced back over her shoulder, seemingly unruffled by whatever atrocities were about to play out. "Everything okay, doll?"

Tormund took a step closer, his hand out-stretched with a deep desire to seize her by the wrist and drag her as far from this ordeal as possible. "Don't do this. It's not worth it. We'll find money another way. We can bunk in a boarding house and wash dishes at an eatery until our luck changes. As long as you're by my side, that's all I need." He offered her his hand, palm up. "Come away with me, I beg of you. I would rather sleep under a bridge than for you to accompany these men."

Something in Dotty's expression hardened. Nostrils flaring with aggravation, she tightened the belt of her coat. "We could do that, but why would we? These are men who entertain the world's elite through violent means and vile manipulation. That's what they plan to subject me to. But I can trust that you won't allow that to happen."

Stepping up the front stoop, Tormund edged up beside her to whisper against her ear. "They are dog shit on the bottom of our shoes. Of that, we agree. That still doesn't explain why you should step foot into this house."

Dotty's mask of civility slipped just enough to let the dangerous gleam of her rage flash through. For an instant her playful dialect dropped, revealing a cadence of stone-cold resolve. "The plans are already in place, Tormund. We have discussed them to a bothersome degree. No sentiment you can utter can or will change my mind. Therefore it is in your best interest to drop it. Do not question me again. Have I made myself clear?"

Never before had she spoken to him in such a harsh manner. His mouth was still hanging agape as she fixed her demure visage back into place. "Now, if you'll excuse me, dollface, it's rude to keep these fellas waitin'."

With that, Dotty stepped over the threshold, earning a chorus of catcalls and whistles of appreciation from the men clustered inside.

Chewing on the inside of his cheek, his fangs threatened against his gumline. Tormund was well aware Dotty was stronger than all the men in there combined. Still, he couldn't help but worry that something would go wrong and Dotty would lose her upper hand.

Tormund had super vamp hearing but tried not to listen. If there were grunts or groans of pleasure, he was quite certain he would slaughter them all.

He had a heightened sense of smell, but refused himself even a whiff of the air out of fear the musky scent of sex would awaken the beast within and he would lose all control.

Tormund occupied himself as best he could, pacing the sidewalk in front of the brownstone, studying everything except the doorway he wanted to bust through. The one wilted pink rose in an otherwise healthy plant in the neighbor's flowerbed. An old woman sitting on a bench, tossing breadcrumbs to pigeons as the twilight hour was blanketed by night. A long, lanky dog being walked by a man whose mustache twirled up at the corners. None of it distracted from the storm clouds of dangers churning in his mind, warning that something horrendous was coming.

As if thinking the worst manifested it, a bloodcurdling scream shattered the hush of the otherwise quiet night. The soles of his shoes skidded over the brick pavers as he spun on his heel and bolted inside. Fangs snapping from his gumline, his nose crinkled into a snarl in preparation for the battle to come.

Throwing open the door, Tormund pulled up short. The scene was horrific, yet he couldn't wrap his mind around what he was seeing. Blood had sprayed up the walls. A slick gore sloshed underfoot. Bodies writhed and moaned on the floor, praying for death. Dotty stood in the middle of it all, looking every bit the innocent flower she'd presented herself as when she first stepped inside.

"They got fresh," she explained with a shrug, licking off the blood that dripped from her fingers.

Limbs had been ripped from torsos.

Torn out jugulars glugged and gurgled with crimson gore.

The stench of death filled the air, causing his stomach to knot. Dead man's blood; a fatal cocktail to vampire kind.

A heavy silence fell like the hammer of judgement on a final verdict.

Dotty had killed them all.

Not one man was left standing. Knowing what they paid to do to her, Tormund couldn't feel the least bit sorry for them. What he did feel was a rising sense of unease. Dotty didn't seem the least bit bothered as she grabbed a still twitching severed arm off the floor and sucked the exposed veins dry like they were the straw in a juice box. Blood slathered her face and painted the front of her dress as she drank deep. Casting the severed appendage aside, she tried to force her features back into a victim's mask ... an impossible task when you've slaughtered a room full of men without batting an eye.

Still, Dotty attempted to play on his sympathies. "I know I was supposed to scream for ya, doll, but things got out of hand quick."

Tormund took an involuntary step back, repulsed by the scene as much as by the stench of dead-man's blood. Sure, they'd had feeding frenzies on humans before, but they never killed. Until now. "We were supposed to do this together," he managed, battling to keep his panicked tone at a shaky neutral.

Blood-dripping fangs on full display, Dotty tilted her head and attempted a mask of innocence that fell far short of her goal. "I always need you, lambchop! Things just... got a little out of control."

Tormund blinked once and then again, trying to shake off the image of her sucking on that severed arm. "What… happened?"

Dotty tried to clean her blood-smeared face with the back of her sleeve. "They were boorish, doll. Simply barbarians. I had to defend myself, didn't I?"

She claimed to be the victim.

However, Tormund heard their screams, not hers.

"What happened?" he gasped, wrestling to make heads or tails of this.

Dotty let her arms drop to her sides, her voice taking on a whiny tone. "I protected myself. Protected us. Ya can't fault me that, can ya?" Her trembling chin played on his emotions, prompting him to open his arms and envelop her in an embrace. She ran to him without hesitation, faking a choked sob as she buried her face in his shoulder.

Even as Tormund held his maker tight, doubt clawed at his heart. He had trusted Dotty with his entire existence since the second he met her. Now, for the very first time, he feared her … and what she was capable of.

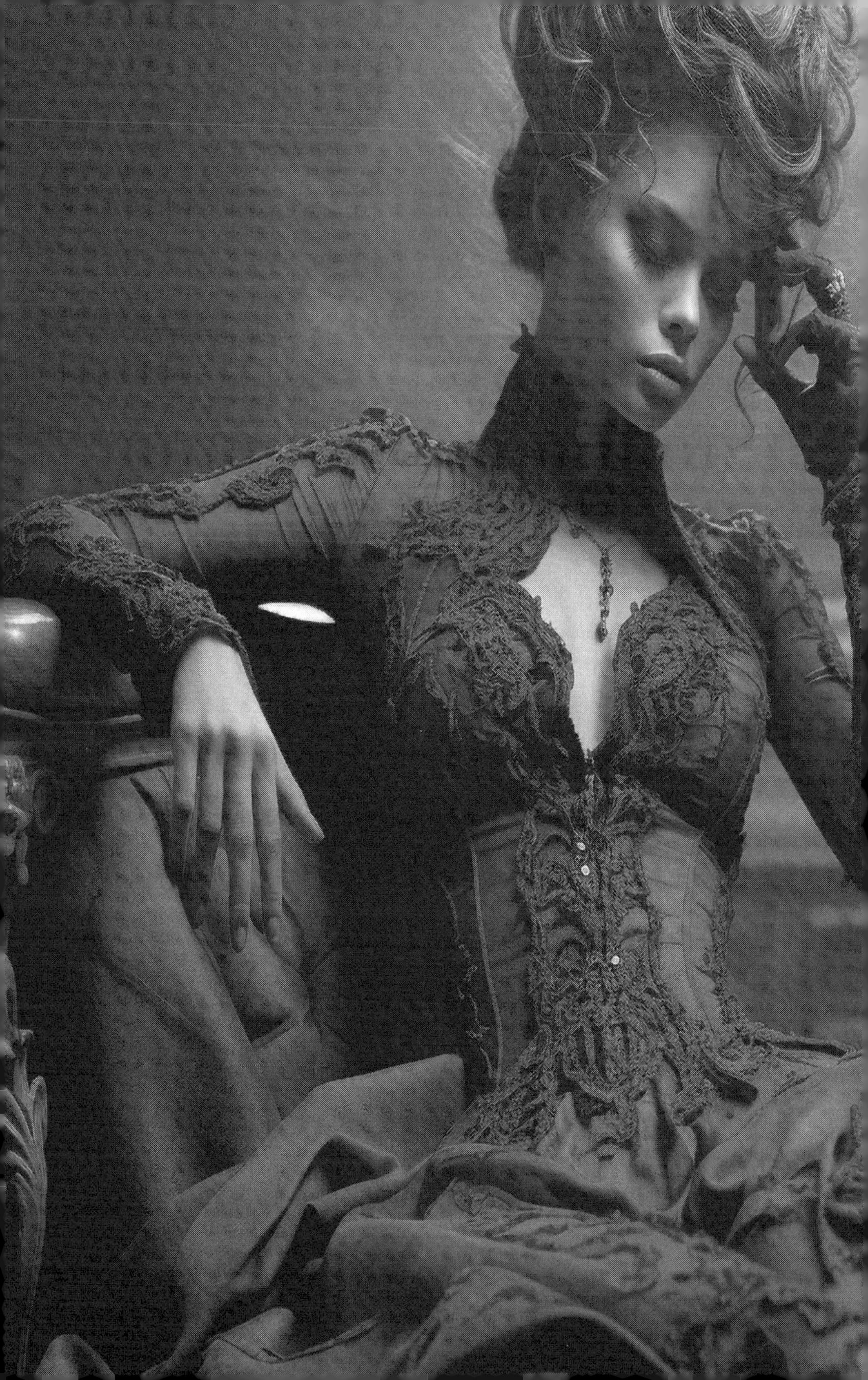

Chapter Eleven
Octavia

"Run if you see your breath? What does that even mean?" Rubbing my hands up and down my flannel-clad arms, I tried to fight off the chill of the dropping temperatures. "It's Alabama in the late Fall. Jack Frost isn't nipping at our noses, but he is taking a few solid snaps in our direction."

I got exactly no response.

Apparently, Bacon picked up on the same vibe I got from Reid that he was himself in his canine form. Reid-wolf was crouched down in a playful pounce pose with his furry tail wagging behind him. Bacon did his best to imitate the pose with his curly little tailed bottom merrily wiggling his happiness at the return of his beloved friend. Both gave false starts in the other's direction before launching into a game of chase with Bacon in the lead and Reid in hot pursuit. They ran a lap around me, Bacon squealing a jovial chorus all the while.

I wanted to revel in this moment of normalcy. But when I exhaled, I noticed my breath suddenly left my lips in a white cloud. A chill skittered down my spine that had nothing whatsoever to do with the plunging temperature. "Uh... guys, I don't want to ruin your sweet reunion, but... has anyone noticed the sudden cold front moving in?"

Reid paused mid-playful swipe in Bacon's direction. Posture suddenly at attention, his ears perked. Muzzle twitching, a deep growl rumbled from his chest.

Protective pig-mama that I am, I patted my leg with one hand. "Bacon, come here, bud."

Instead of trotting over like the good little pork chop he is, Bacon let out a stunned snort followed by a flurry of frantic squeals.

Head whipping his way, I let a string of expletives fly. The earth appeared to be eating my piglet. He sank into the frost covered soil up to his belly. Flailing and writhing, he tried to break free with no success. Without hesitation, I dove for him, ready to dig him out if I could. Just as I was hooking my hands under his front legs to stop him from sinking deeper, an ear-piercing yelp rang out.

Pulling up short, I blinked as if I could deny what I saw.

Nope, I wasn't hallucinating.

We hadn't ventured deep into the woods around the manor, yet we were surrounded by enough trees for it to be foreboding when they turned against us.

A weird sentence, I know. Trust me when I say it's far more disturbing when it actually happens. Tree roots slithered out of the ground, snaking their way around Reid's legs and pinning him where he stood. Jaws snapping, he threw his weight against the force holding him. Unfortunately he didn't have any more luck than Bacon did.

With my boys incapacitated, my muscles were tensed on a hairpin trigger for the attack I knew was coming. Keeping my hold on Bacon, I jerked my head in one direction, then another in my search for an enemy who had yet to reveal themselves. Reid was snarling. Bacon was snorting. I didn't have the heart to tell them I had the unmistakable feeling this whole situation was about to go from bad to worse.

Turns out that premonition was spot on.

The first lash struck my cheek with a freeze that settled deep into my jawbone. Clapping my palm over the pain, I spun in search of the bitch who hit me. Nothing but frostbitten trees and my panicked friends loomed before me.

"Did you guys see—Fuck!" My question morphed into a pained exclamation when that same bone-chilling freeze snapped against my lower back. Spine wrenching at an angle that made muscles I didn't know I had ache, I forced out a frosty breath from burning lungs. "Wh-wh-what is this thing?" I managed through chattering teeth, the cold ravaging me and chilling straight to my bones.

Bacon read my mood like the compassionate little cutlet he was. His snorts quieted, coming in an ominous chorus of huffs at the viable threat before us. Reid added to the soundtrack with a low growl escaping his quaking jowls.

Not knowing what we were up against, I called forth my emerald energy. It crackled down my arms, casting a jade glow over the sepia tones of the forest.

I thought I was ready.

Prepared for anything to come.

Turns out I didn't have a damned clue.

A strong gust of frigid air blew past my cheeks, its bite burning my skin on contact. A second attack breezed across the back of my neck. The arctic shock of it extinguished my green flames and blued my lips on contact. Fingers and toes numb, my limbs froze to leaden weights I had to struggle to move. The only thing that kept me going was the inferno burning within. The one hellbent on preventing me from ever being a victim again.

"Show yourself!" I screamed at the trees, my voice broken by my violently chattering teeth.

"Gladly," a husky voice whispered in my ear before knocking me to my knees with yet another icy blast.

Frost inched up my fingers, causing bone-rattling chills to quake through me. Craning my neck to see who or what hit me from behind, puffs of white air left my lips and haloed around my face.

They formed from the winds.

Pale beings, whose genders were undistinguishable. All had sharp features, snowy white skin, and pointed ears that peeked out from beneath icicle-blue hair. Each wore the same navy blue with silver trim tunic, which would have looked like pajamas on anyone else, but they somehow made it look regal.

"We speak on behalf of Roderick the Just, King of the Winter Court," they recited in one unified voice.

Battling past the chills coursing through me, I forced myself back to my feet. "Y-y-you'll find m-m-my commu-u-unication sk-sk-skills are-"

"Silence!" One of the Pissy Jack-Frost look-alikes lifted one hand to quiet me. An act that would have enraged me further if I wasn't in the process of losing the feeling to my appendages. "Prince Connoll knows very well what his father, the king, is capable of. You and your animal sidekicks are another matter. A bloodsucker can't be counted on to think of the greater good when their kind are nothing more than beings of death and destruction."

"Y-y-yet you're the one freezing my t-t-tits off," I managed, hugging my arms tight to my chest in hopes of trapping in even a touch more body heat.

If they picked up on any trace of my sarcasm, they didn't let on before launching into verse two of their eerie chorus.

"We will surround you before you know we're there. We will destroy you without lifting a finger. We are nature. Disasters you can't begin to fathom will slaughter all you hold dear if you fail to honor His Highness's orders! You have been warned."

With those acting as their final words, the frost beings dissipated into a snow flurry and rode an evening gust off into the horizon. As quickly as our attack came on, the violent invasion of the foliage retracted. Our trio was set free, left to blink our confusion at the suddenly still forest.

Free from the dirt, a trembling Bacon dashed over to me and threw himself into my arms.

Reid snapped and snarled at the disappearing fae. Still, he didn't charge after them. Which I saw as proof he was as traumatized as the rest of us. After giving a snort of appreciation that he had successfully chased them off, the wolf took his place by my side. His titanium-hued eyes blinked up at me expectantly.

Shaking my head, I uttered the painful truth as I saw it. "It occurs to me now that we are truly and utterly fucked."

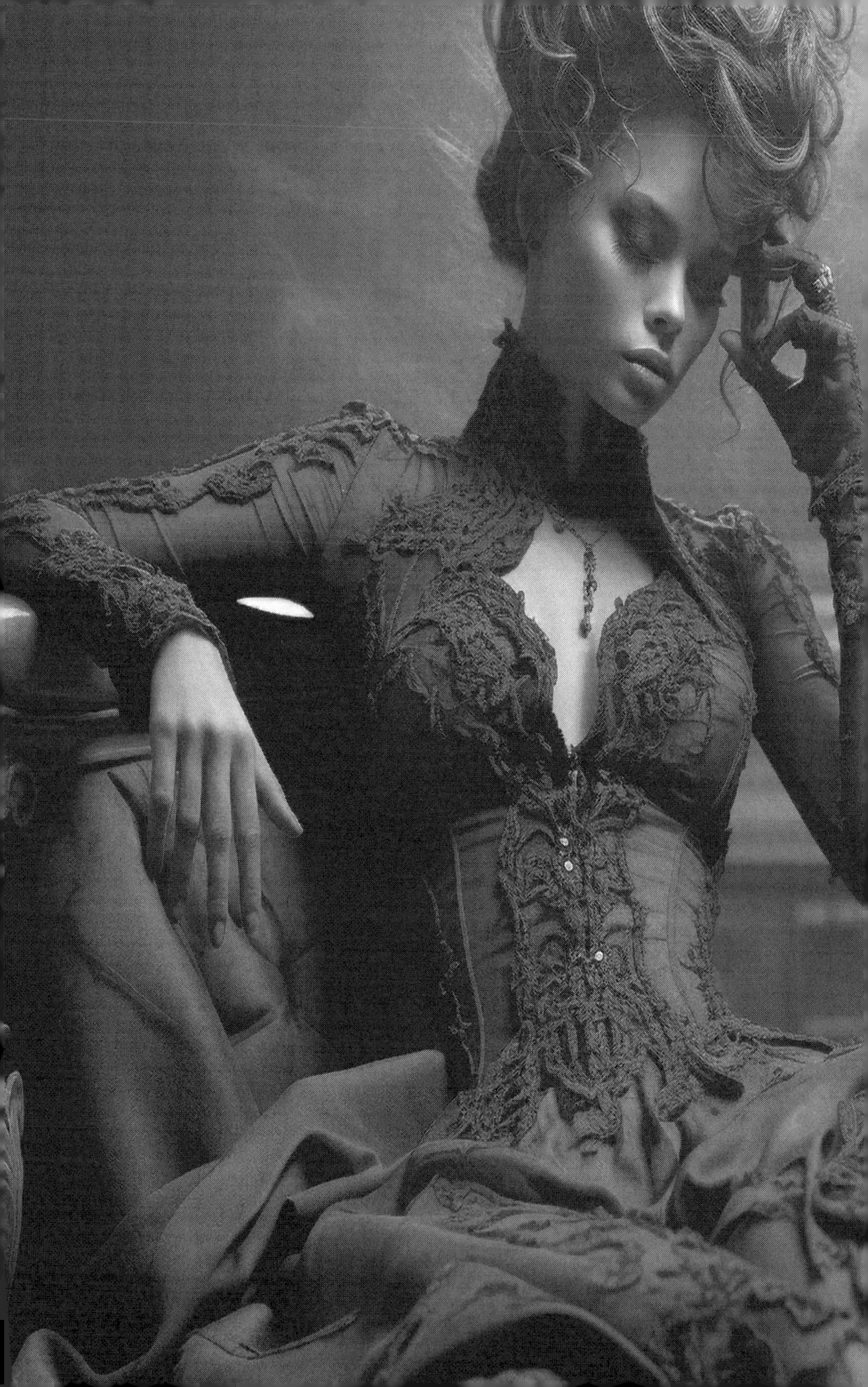

Chapter Twelve
Octavia

"It seems something like 'oh, by the way, my people can turn into fucking shrubberies' would have come up in conversation!" I paced from one side of the bedroom to the other, blatantly ignoring Connoll's exasperated facial expression.

Standing at the head of the bed by the unconscious vampire, the tattooed detective fought back a grimace. "My father held me down so the other men in my family could scar every visible part of my skin. What part of that made my people seem like a caring lot by any stretch of the imagination?"

I threw my hands skyward only to let them fall to my sides with a slap. "I don't know! You're a decent fucking human being so I figured your kind would be, too."

Tips of his fingers hovering at Tormund's temples, Connoll offered me a tight smirk. "We master in mind control and manipulation. I'm the exception to the rule that fae are not to be trusted."

"But you're a good guy!" I countered, pointing a finger of accusation his way. "I figured others like you would be, too!"

Reid and Bacon shifted on their feet by the door, both ready to have my back by whatever means necessary. The wolf and the pig, unlike in all ways except for being ride-or-die by my side.

Connoll glanced down at Tormund and spoke through tightly clenched teeth. "We aren't good people, Octavia. Never forget that."

My throat constricted at the visible pain contorting his features. "You are a good man, no matter what anyone else might think. That's why you're digging around in that crusty twat's head for answers. We need to find Nora, Dina, and the others, and you are doing your damnedest to make that happen. I just ask that you, maybe, do it a little quicker. Preferably before the trees attack again, because that shit was terrifying."

The detective finally pulled himself away from his vampiric specimen. Rounding the side of the bed, he planted himself in front of me. "You want my advice? Leave the property as quick as you can and don't look back. Scour Lavender Lotus until you find the others. Hell, send up flares when you do. Maybe my father will burst in and handle this matter for us. Whatever it takes to appease him. Meanwhile, I'll stay here and work on our back-up plan. One way or another, we need to deliver Nora to him… or he will reduce this town to ash."

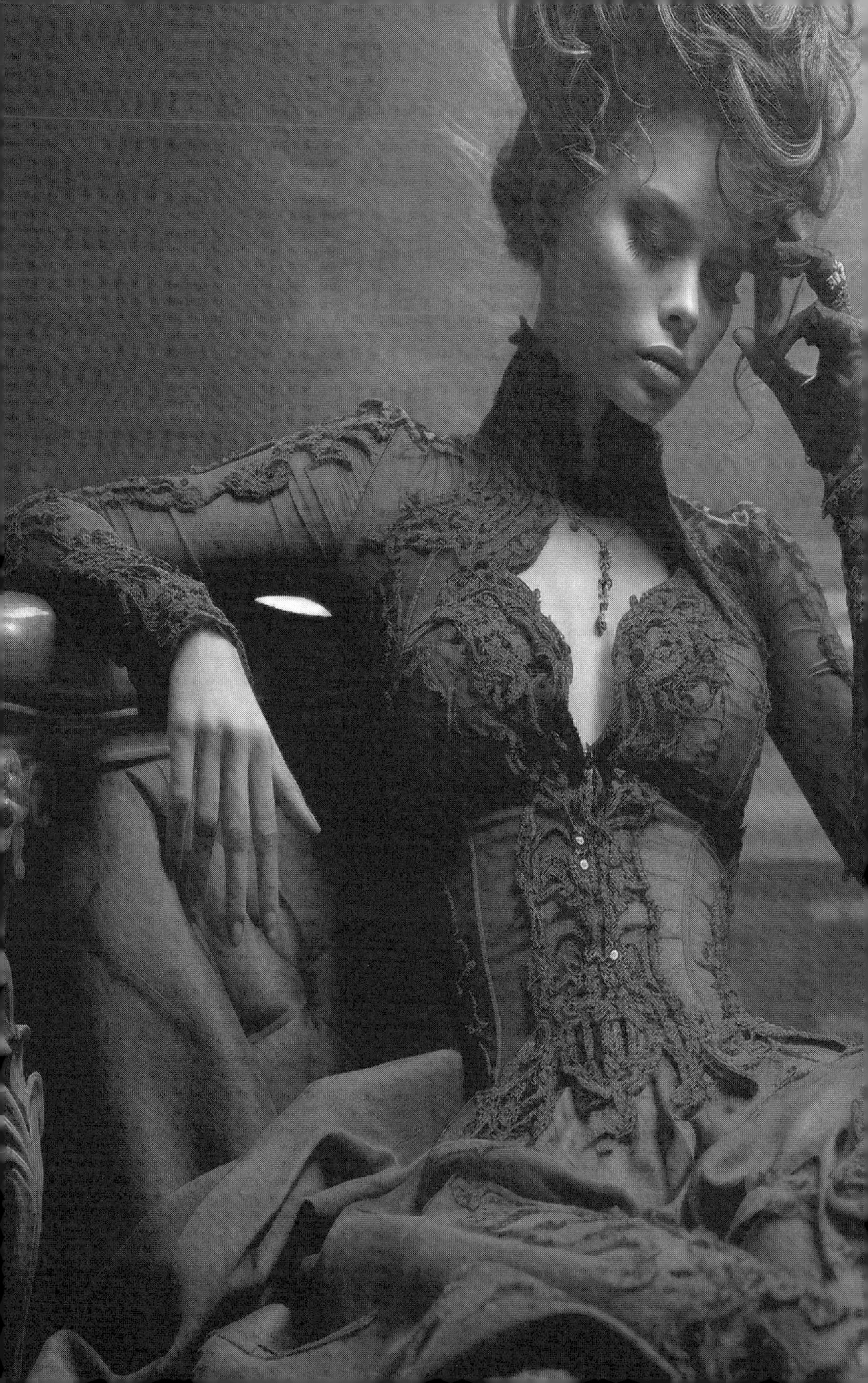

Chapter Thirteen
Connoll

My father was escalating things faster than I anticipated. I was right to send Octavia away, if for no other reason than to allow myself time to concentrate as I ventured deeper into Tormund's mind. Judging by the nauseating massacre I'd witnessed the last time, whatever came next wouldn't be pleasant. But it might deliver answers.

Swallowing my own desires at the memory of carnage dripping from Dotty's chin after she drank her fill, I placed two fingers to Tormund's temple and let him take me where he would.

Tormund hoped Dotty's one-time massacre would be her last. A thrill to quelch her dark thirst, perhaps. To the young vamp's great regret, the virginal victim scam quickly became her favorite. Finding the wealthiest men in a town, she would offer them the opportunity to do anything they wanted to her under the pretenses that she was a young, impoverished beauty with no other choice. Then, the moment the door clicked shut, she would kill them one by one without mercy or regret. After yet another bloodbath,

Tormund promised himself he would talk to her and convince her she was drawing unnecessary attention to them, even if it meant enduring her wrath.

No longer did he wait outside. He couldn't bear the screams or witness the horrific tableau of her handiwork. Instead he waited at posh resorts, which they could now afford thanks to the money she pilfered from her prey. Each time, she came home fully satisfied with a belly full of blood. Seated in a chair by the bed, he patiently waited for her to shower off the blood that covered her in a grisly slick before dressing in a silky negligee that hugged her curves in all the right ways.

When she sashayed towards him with the fluidity of a contented cat, he rose and presented her with a glass of sparkling champagne he had poured and waiting for her. "Darling, you've run this scam time and again. You've punished these filthy men—who well deserve your wrath, might I add. Need I point out we are now comfortable in our finances, thanks to you?" He waited for her to bring the champagne flute to her luscious lips before climbing onto the pillow soft mattress and curling one arm behind his head. His button-down shirt was open to his navel, the shirt sleeves rolled up his forearms. While he still wore his trousers, his feet were bare. "However, if we keep up with spectacles like this, we will draw unnecessary attention to ourselves. We can stop this charade. Travel up the Greek Isle and bathe under the moonlight on a private gondola. What say you, my love? Will you escape with me before the disappearances of the men you have feasted on are traced back to us? We may be immortal, but we are not without our weaknesses. Run away with me and let us leave this blood-splattered land behind."

Dotty hitched up her skirt to climb on top of him. Straddling his hips, she ground sweet temptation against his swelling enthusiasm. "We'll travel the world a hundred times over. Just you and me, the way it's always meant to be." Taking his hand in both of hers, she placed one to the curve of her breast and sucked the fingers of the other. "But there is one more job we need to handle first. One last trick that promises to pay triple what any of the others have. We can't pass that up, now can we, doll? We do that, and then we can move on and go anywhere we want in the world." Her hips moved in a hypnotic rhythm, clouding his rational thoughts with passion. "Can we make that deal, baby? Just one more trick. Then," she sucked his finger from base to tip, letting her tongue swirl around its length, "I'll do absolutely anything you want to do, for as long as you want."

Tormund let out a moan of appreciation, his thumb caressing her perking nipple. "When you put it that way... Whatever you need, it's yours. You need only speak the words."

Shifting her weight onto her knees, Dotty lifted her hips and reached between them. Unzipping his pants, she took him in both hands. "In that case, I want you to be all mine, Tormund. Forever... and ever... and ever."

Eyes rolling back, Tormund gave himself over to the growing crescendo of his desire. "Yes... my love. Oh... yes. Anything you want. Anything at all."

Tormund stood in the drizzling rain holding an umbrella over Dotty's head to protect her perfect pin curls from frizzing or flattening. Dressed in a black suit topped off with a slate gray peacoat, he made himself appear human by adjusting the collar further up his neck to fight off the chill mortals would have been suffering with. "You're saying the Johns on this trick are interested in me?"

Dotty swatted at the air between them. "Please, don't bore me by being narrow-minded. You're better than that, doll face."

Tormund rolled his eyes. Letting one hand snake around Dotty's narrow waist, he pulled her closer. "You, more than anyone, have seen firsthand that I have no problem quenching my desires with persons of any gender. This isn't about that."

Pressing one hand to his chest, Dotty leaned in and purred her words against his lips. "Then what's the problem? Ya go in, get your rocks off, kill 'em if ya want, and bring back the money."

His mouth opened and shut, brow creasing into a deep V of confusion. "I'm not saying I'm opposed to it, but this has always been your con. Why the switch?"

Something flashed behind her eyes Tormund couldn't quite name or place. Vindication? Delight? Whatever it was disappeared before he could put a name to it. Dotty drummed her fingers once and again before answering. "I need you to understand why I do what I do. Once you do, we will be closer than any two souls have ever been. Nothing and no one will ever stand in our way. Then, we'll take this final payday and go wherever we wish. What do you say, doll?"

A cluster of men strode past, casting lingering glances in Tormund's direction. Measuring him. Undressing him. Violating him. All with nothing more than a glance. Others who could have been easily victimized would have felt unease. But Tormund had power beyond most men's comprehension on his side. Feeling his fangs threaten, he fought back a snarl. He believed himself untouchable, and that was his downfall. Maybe, without it, he would have caught a whiff of the looming threat in their pheromones. Perhaps he would have heard the crackle of danger sizzling through the air in the buzz of their anxious chatter. Unfortunately, those things faded into the background thanks to predatory instincts that convinced him he was the most dangerous creature to walk these streets.

He would soon find that wasn't the case.

Peering into Dotty's angelic face, the raven-haired vampire dotted a kiss to the tip of her upturned nose. "I will do this for you, my pet. Then, we'll be done with this scam once and for all."

Tormund's memories became clouded and staticky the second he stepped inside the brick manor uptown. A professional would say extreme trauma was to blame for that. As it was, the story played out in flashes of scattered images and feelings. The faces of the men in the room blurred the second the door clicked shut behind him. Tormund couldn't have picked them out of a line-up if he had to, but their ill intent pulsated through the air like a live charge.

Their hostile energy should have been the first red flag.

The set-up of the room the second.

None of the men were dressed for a night of passion. No. Still wearing button-down shirts and slacks, all had donned leather butcher aprons and rubber gloves that stretched up to their elbows. A gurney had been placed in the center of the room with leather wrist and ankle restraints. Beside it was a stainless-steel cart holding an assortment of tools whose purpose could be for healing or hurting… depending on whose hands wielded them. And these men did not give the appearance of helpful healers.

Sure, Tormund was undead.

But he wasn't an idiot.

Turning on his heel, he was bolting for the door when a burning sensation clamped on to his wrist. A yelp tore from his throat, his skin blistering on contact with the silver cuff forced onto his flesh. The young vampire was still reeling from the surprising pain when he was hit from behind and knocked to his knees.

"She was right. The silver worked!" one amongst them crowed, grabbing Tormund's free arm with more force than necessary and wrenching it behind his back to clap on the second cuff.

A titter of ominous laughter filled the room.

Two men grabbed him under the arms, chuckling as they forced him onto the gurney. "The blonde said as long as we don't cut off his head, drive silver through his heart, or feed him dead man's blood, he can't be killed."

The lot of them surrounded him, securing the leather restraints over his cuffs, wrapping his ankles in silver chains, and ripping open his shirt in the first of many ways they would expose his vulnerabilities. Tormund thrashed and screamed for all he was worth in his battle for freedom. To his great regret, the silver held firm and his cries fell on deaf ears.

With no further pomp or circumstance, the unthinkable began.

How long it went on, Tormund couldn't say.

His consciousness spared him by letting him sink into dark oblivion time and again when the pain became too much.

The men fed their psychotic delights by carving, burning, stabbing, and ripping into him in unfathomable ways. They fish-hooked the corners of his mouth, splitting his cheeks into a ghoulish grin. A scalpel sliced through his flesh from throat to navel, allowing his muscles and ribs to be cracked open with bare hands when gloves became too slick with blood. They cut into his testicles. Stuck straight pins into his eyes. Any tender or delicate piece of him was tortured and maimed in unspeakable ways. Even though Tormund pleaded for them to kill him and end his torment, they never crossed any of those pivotal lines that would grant him the sweet release of death.

It was in the midst of his fifth or sixth blackout—he had fast lost count—that an explosion rang out, shaking the floor beneath them. A fresh wave of screams rang out. This time, not from Tormund. Which was good, considering he had long since shrieked his throat raw. As his world swam in and out of focus, he felt sticky warmth splattered over him. It was accompanied by a gruesome soundtrack of slurps, gurgles, and crunches that painted the picture of a god-awful massacre playing out. Then again, that could have been Tormund's mind disassociating with what he was being put through. That seemed a likely scenario until something crashed into the side of the gurney and Tormund spilled to the floor.

Forcing his puffy, red-rimmed eyes open, he watched a severed head roll across the floor and settle slightly askew beside him. A beat later Dotty crouched beside him, using a key she miraculously pulled from her bodice to unlock the handcuffs.

"I've got you; lean on me," she murmured, catching him in her arms as she released his restraints. Dotty held his slack frame in her arms, her angelic features growing cross that his vampiric attributes weren't stitching his wounds back together as quickly as they should have. "Do you understand now, doll? Monstrous creatures like them deserve every bit of pain I've delivered to them. They need to be wiped off the face of the earth. You and I have the ability to make that happen. I know this was a painful lesson, but I did this for you. For us."

Tormund slapped one palm onto the floor and used every ounce of strength he had left to push away from her. "You... did this to me. You set this up, told them our weaknesses, and how to restrain me."

"To make a point," she countered, her nostrils flaring. "Nothin' more!"

Tormund held up one hand to halt her. "Stay the fuck away from me. I mean it. I never, ever would have done something like this to you. Because I loved you. But you killed that, just like these men would have killed me, given more time."

"Don't be crazy, handsome. I was right outside the door if things got too carried away-"

He tried to get his feet under him, only to crash back down on one knee. "You listening while they tortured me is proof of your love? No. I mean it, Dotty. Stay the fuck away from me. I reject you as my maker and swear on the blood of Vlad that I will grant you the final death myself if I ever see your hellish face again!"

Tormund's rib cage gaped open, forcing him to physically hold his innards in with one arm as he made his final stand against his maker.

That last vision proved to be too much for Connoll to endure. Spinning away from Tormund's sleeping form, he dry-heaved in violent wretches.

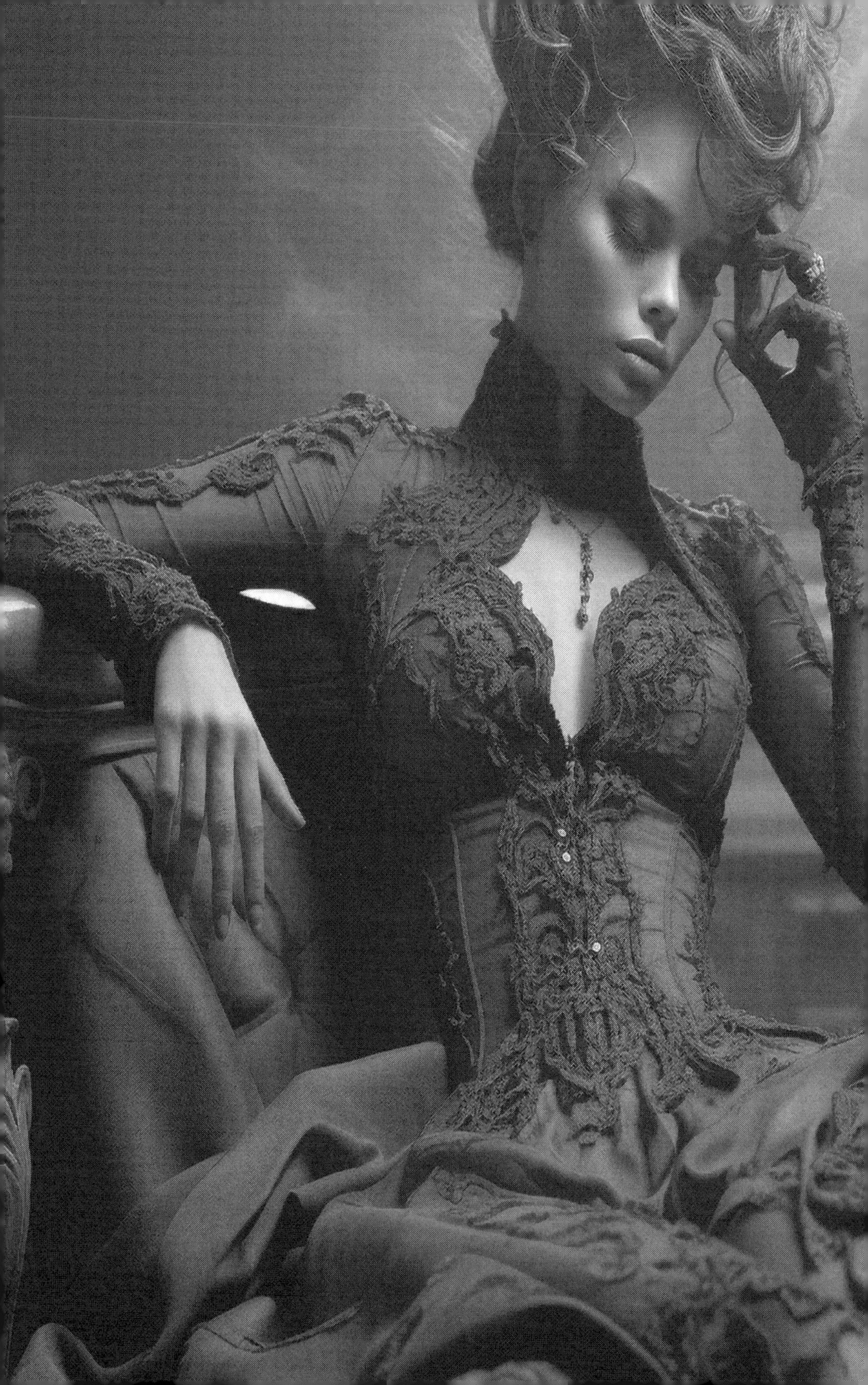

Chapter Fourteen
Octavia

With Bacon strapped to my chest, I supported his weight with both hands to prevent him from knocking the air from my lungs as I ran to keep up with Reid. Still in wolf form, he darted through the trees at a speed I couldn't even hope to match. Not that I blamed him for running like his tail was on fire. We had no way to know if the fae soldiers were still around. That said, if the foliage was going to suddenly turn on us at any moment, we were right to get away from it as fast as possible. Black dots were dancing before my eyes as a painful reminder that I needed to do more cardio when I saw the enormous black wolf suddenly dart to the right and disappear around a towering oak tree. I trailed after him, his lead time seconds, at best. Rounding the bend, I pulled up short. He was gone. Not a trace of him to be found. Not a tuft of fur or giant paw print remained. One second running at full speed, the next seemingly blinked out of existence. And he didn't go alone. Bacon no longer occupied the infant carrier I wore.

Mouth falling open in confusion, I spun in search of answers. Instead of clarity, I found the world had fallen silent around me. No birds trilled. Not one cricket chirped. Maybe it was that chilling hush, or the skitter it caused to prickle down my spine, but I felt Death's presence before I saw him. Thick fog bellowed in around the base of the trees, clouding the leaf covered earth in a heavy, opaque blanket.

My celebrity crush sauntered out from behind an ash tree looking as handsome as ever. Hands in his pockets, he gave me a sexy smolder that would have made my panties melt away into a pool of nothingness... if I wasn't well aware he was the gatekeeper of oblivion.

"Octavia, Octavia." He clucked his tongue against the roof of his mouth. "You're just not quick on picking up hints, are you? Was our last conversation so easily forgotten?"

Despite the ragged breaths causing my chest to rise and fall, I battled to keep my face a mask of indifference. "Oh, I remember every ominous word crystal clear. But here's the problem: people I care about are in danger. I'll sacrifice whatever I have to in order to protect them. Something I'm sure you can't begin to understand, with your chosen vocation."

His gait was as smooth as a waltz, the look in his cobalt eyes one of pure seduction. "Thinking I chose any of this shows how little you understand. Actions have consequences, Octavia. That's what I've been struggling to make you understand from the moment I first beheld that wonderous pink hair... and fantastic ass of yours." He murmured that last part against my ear as he skirted around behind me with the fluidity of a circling shark.

"Is there a lesson in this or are we falling in love?" I kept my tone sharp, hoping it would hide the quiver in my voice at having him so close to me. "Because I'm kind of in a rush."

With one finger, he brushed my back. A straight line right across both shoulder blades. His touch electrified me in a way that made my breath catch. "That's why I'm here. You're on the wrong path, my beauty."

Needing the spell of his nearness broken, I took a couple steps away to insert some much-needed distance between us. "Why? Because I'm going to tip the scales of balance and lose my abilities? What makes you think that's not exactly what I want? I've been a fucking freak my entire life. Did you ever think I would jump at the chance to be ordinary?"

Sauntering closer, he caught one strand of my hair and twirled it around his index finger before giving a firm but gentle tug. "You would never truly desire a mundane existence. You can fool others into believing that, but not me." Death dipped his face to mine, the warmth of his breath tickling over my lips and tempting me to close the lingering distance between us. "Because you and I are two halves of the same coin. Beings with godlike powers few know of and fewer still could even begin to comprehend. I understand you, and the hypnotizing power you feel at how easily you can do the impossible. Life gifted with a touch. Souls shuffled with a simple incantation. We aren't like mere mortals, and neither of us would want to be, if we're being honest with ourselves."

I couldn't help but fixate on the inviting curve of his lips. "So, if you think you know me so well, why bother to pop in and warn me at all? You know damn well I'm not going to listen."

To my great regret, this time it was him who pulled away. "Oh, I'm not warning you. I am completely invested in seeing how this whole dramatic tale plays out. I come only with a gentle reminder of those blasted scales of balance. Your control is slipping, causing your abilities to become unhinged and unreliable. Which—while incredibly fascinating to watch unfold—will be made infinitely worse if you stay on this particular course."

"That sounds like a warning." Wetting my suddenly dry lips, I hitched one brow. "Is that concern I'm picking up on? Are you worried about me?"

"Miss Hollows, are you flirting with me?"

"Maybe a little."

Raising his hand alongside my face, he gently brushed the backs of his slender fingers from my temple to my jaw. "Oh, the things we could do together. Kingdoms crumbling. Cities rising from the ash. Waves crashing. Volcanoes belching their fury to the skies. Granted, it would be completely apocalyptic. But damn, would it be fun…" Shoulders sagging, he sighed. "Sadly, for today, I will merely offer counsel and not intervene. Stay on this course if you will. Hell, as a token of good faith, I'll even help you escape the fae."

Time and space blurred around me, a sound like an industrial fan whirring in my ears. Reality steadied, but my gaze was still locked on him and his beautifully carved features. One corner of his mouth tugging back in a knowing grin, he jerked his head in the direction of the building beside us. "I believe this is the establishment you're looking for."

Suddenly understanding the phrase flirting with death to a painful degree, it took every ounce of my strength to drag my stare off him and shift focus. When I did, my nose crinkled. "I promise you, the Bowl-A-Rama has never, and will never, be what I'm looking for. Maybe it was a childhood growing up in foster care, but a place that forces you to wear borrowed shoes while loud noises crash all around sets my teeth on edge."

I glanced back, my eyes hungry to devour another glimpse of him. To my great regret, he was gone. The spell of his presence was broken when a certain black wolf came galloping straight for me and Bacon suddenly weighted down my shoulders, sending a twinge into my lower back as he reappeared in his carrier. While I was still blinking hard and trying to make sense of what just happened, Reid-wolf skidded to a stop. The way he shook his head from side to side, ears flapping, made it clear he was just as perplexed by the change of landscape as I was. Even so, it was disconcerting for all parties involved.

Reid snapped me from my reverie with a huffed snort and a plaintive bark.

All I could offer was a confused shrug. "If I had an explanation, I would give one. Rumor has it this is the place we're looking for. Whatever that means."

Reid's ears perked and his head jerked in the direction of the cement block building. In typical canine fashion, he didn't begin to explain his motives before galloping around the side of the bowling alley. With a sigh, I supported Bacon's rump with one hand and jogged after my wolf.

I rounded the side of the building to find Reid bounding up the metal fire escape stairs heading to the roof.

For a beat, I watched him and considered my options. "Death warned about my path. Which could have meant marching in the front door, or trusting those rusted-out stairs. I didn't think to ask for clarification. But here goes nothing. If these things rot out from beneath us, I'll do my best not to land on you," I whispered against the velvety ear of my little swine-kick.

Bacon kicked his dainty hooves in appreciation of that idea.

Swallowing hard, I gripped the rails and meandered up a set of stairs that creaked their protest. In no way did I trust them not to crumble to dust beneath me. I didn't exhale in relief until I reached the roof in one piece. Thanking Hecate, Budda, Lilith, Gaia, and any other higher beings listening, I planted my hands on my knees and peered up from under my lashes in search of my canine sentry. I found him pacing by a skylight, his hackles raised and muzzle twitching in a growl.

"Yeah, I have that same reaction to this particular sport," I muttered under my breath before ambling over to see what prompted such a reaction. His fur brushed the back of my hand as I peered over the edge down into the bowling alley below.

At a glance, everything looked normal. Seemingly happy people knocked down pins and shared smiles. But something wasn't right. The vibe of the place felt… forced. Brow furrowed, I crouched down to get a better look. Sister Dina and Paisley were in lane three. Dina had just finished her turn and was walking back after a spare with her right hand—from which she'd just released the ball—trembling. The blood dripping from the tips of her fingers proved to be the reason why. And she wasn't the only one. All the bowlers were blemished with battle scars from what must have been hours and hours of playing.

Bloodshot eyes with bags of exhaustion under them.

Fingers, wrists, and knuckles bruised and bloody from constant play.

Backs hunched from walking the floor over and over.

They all wore forced smiles even as tears zigzagged down their cheeks.

It didn't take long for the cause to reveal herself.

Reid saw her before I did; a low growl rumbled from his throat.

Dotty strode though the alley, trailed by a disheveled Nora.

"The wolf was mine! You knew that!" the fairy princess steamed, her hands curled into fists at her sides.

Dressed in an ivory slip dress with a white mink stole, Dotty flipped one edge of it over her narrow shoulder and resumed her sashay. "I ain't havin' this conversation again. I had my reasons."

In a rather ballsy move, Nora caught hold of Dotty's slender arm and spun her around. "No, I don't understand. Why don't you explain to me why you handed over the very guy I came to this miniscule speck of a town for in the first place!"

Dropping fang, Dotty looked from Nora's hand to her face until the fae had sense enough to let go. "It was an act of good will to inspire the necromancer to give back what's mine. Her favorite boy toy, for mine."

"He wasn't yours to give!" Nora sputtered. "I already lost him once, and I had no intention of doing it again!"

Dotty stepped threateningly close. "He wasn't yours, either. You made him your marionette puppet, just like the rest of these meat sacks. He didn't choose to be with you. But what he wanted never mattered to ya, did it?"

Nora jerked back as if the vampire slapped her. Her mouth opened and shut like a screen door on a windy day. "I... love him."

Dotty's nose crinkled in disgust. "Ya never bothered to ask if he felt the same, or if you're the one he would choose. Why? Because you're a selfish little twat. You desire him. What about the rest of these people?" She threw her arms— clad to the elbow with silk gloves—out wide. "This was all your doing. You were manipulating their minds long before I ever came along. If this was about him, why bother with the others?"

Nora peered around at the fake smiles of her victims, her shoulders sinking with defeat. "I... just wanted a family of my own. People to surround myself with."

Dotty's hand shot out, catching Nora by the hair and wrenching her head back at a sharp angle. "The notion of family is a lie." Throwing all boundaries of normal social conduct aside, she dragged her tongue over the panicked fae's jugular. "The only real connection is blood. Churning, pumping blood. That's what binds us. That's who we are. And there's no escaping it. Take you, for example, little princess. What do you think your father would do if I drained you dry and tossed the husk of your corpse at his feet?"

I had to give Nora credit: fires of challenge blazed behind her eyes. "He would use every resource he had to hunt you to the ends of the earth until your head was on a spike for his entire kingdom to see."

Satisfied with that answer, Dotty released Nora with more force than necessary. The princess stumbled to regain her footing. "My point exactly. That's the true bond." The vampress moved in a blur of speed, seizing hold of a random bowler by the throat. "You claim this herd is your new family. Do you even know this one's name?"

Her chosen victim had sandy hair with a spray of freckles across his cheeks. His face was morphing from red to purple as Dotty applied pressure to his trachea.

"I'll be damned," I murmured, stunned by the genuine look of panic that blanched Nora's lovely features. "She had her own private fight club in Dina's backyard, but when someone else pulls the strings, she gets fidgety."

Lips pressed in a thin line, Nora frantically shook her head. "I don't. I'm sorry. I call him Carl, but that was only after I started coming up with names alphabetically after Allen and Becky. Regardless, you've made your point. Please, just let him go."

Platinum curls bobbed as Dotty tilted her head, her calculating eyes narrowing in genuine confusion. "These people were toys to you. Are you telling me you've sincerely come to care for them?"

Nora's stare lobbed from Carl to Dotty and back again.

Prompting her to respond, the flaxen-haired vampire squeezed Carl's throat hard enough to make his eyes bulge from their sockets.

"Yes!" Nora erupted. "Yes, I care for him. I care for all of them. Please, I'll do whatever you ask. Just don't hurt any of them."

Dotty kept her hand raised, but she released Carl, allowing him to fall to the floor in a heap. "Good girl. That's what I wanted to hear. Now, if ya want to keep the rest of your pets alive, you will continue to control their minds and keep them your brainless puppets. Otherwise, I'll kill them all one by one in front of you. Understood?"

Nora started toward Carl, likely wanting to gather him in her arms and protect him. Yet something in Dotty's venomous glare rooted her where she stood. Even from the roof, I heard how her voice betrayed her by wavering. "I'll behave. I promise. Just... don't hurt them."

Dotty lifted one penciled-on eyebrow in victory. Striding past Carl, she patted the fairy princess on the top of her head. "That's a good gal. Have your minions sleep wherever they fall. All of them are lookin' a bit haggard, not to mention being incredibly ripe. We'll handle that second part tomorrow. Now, I'm going to find me someone to eat who doesn't smell like gym socks and ball sweat."

With that she sauntered off, her hips swaying with each step.

Nora glared after her for a beat. Then, she lifted her chin and closed her eyes. Arms held akimbo at her sides, she cast her intention out through the alley. That simple act was all it took. All the sad, exhausted bowlers rose up and assumed battle-ready poses. An army willing to fight for her every whim was instantly formed, absent of bothersome thoughts of self-preservation. The similarity to my own army of corpses was not lost on me, and a hot rush of guilt burned up my neck to my ears.

Nora could have attempted to overthrow Dotty right then and there. And maybe she would have, had Carl not gasped in his desperate attempts to catch his breath and launched into a hellacious coughing fit brought on by Dotty's attack.

Even from above, I could see how Nora softened when she peered down at him. He was exhausted. They all were. Granting them the mercy of rest, Nora shut her eyes once more and let them all sink to the floor. Eyes shut. Bodies fell slack. Some drooled. Others snored. Paisley and Dina managed to cling to each other in comfort even as the twilight hour claimed them. Showing compassion I didn't anticipate, Nora eased Carl onto his back and held his head in her lap until his breathing regulated.

Tears slipped from her lashes, raining down on his sleeping face. "I'm sorry to all of you. I wanted my freedom. To finally have a life and friends of my own. Now, my own selfish desires could be what gets us all killed. I will do whatever it takes to prevent that, I promise you. I'll die before I let her hurt you, and I will find a way to set us all free."

Filling my lungs, I took a step back from the skylight. "We need to get back to the manor. That little fairy just became our ally on the inside, and she doesn't even realize it."

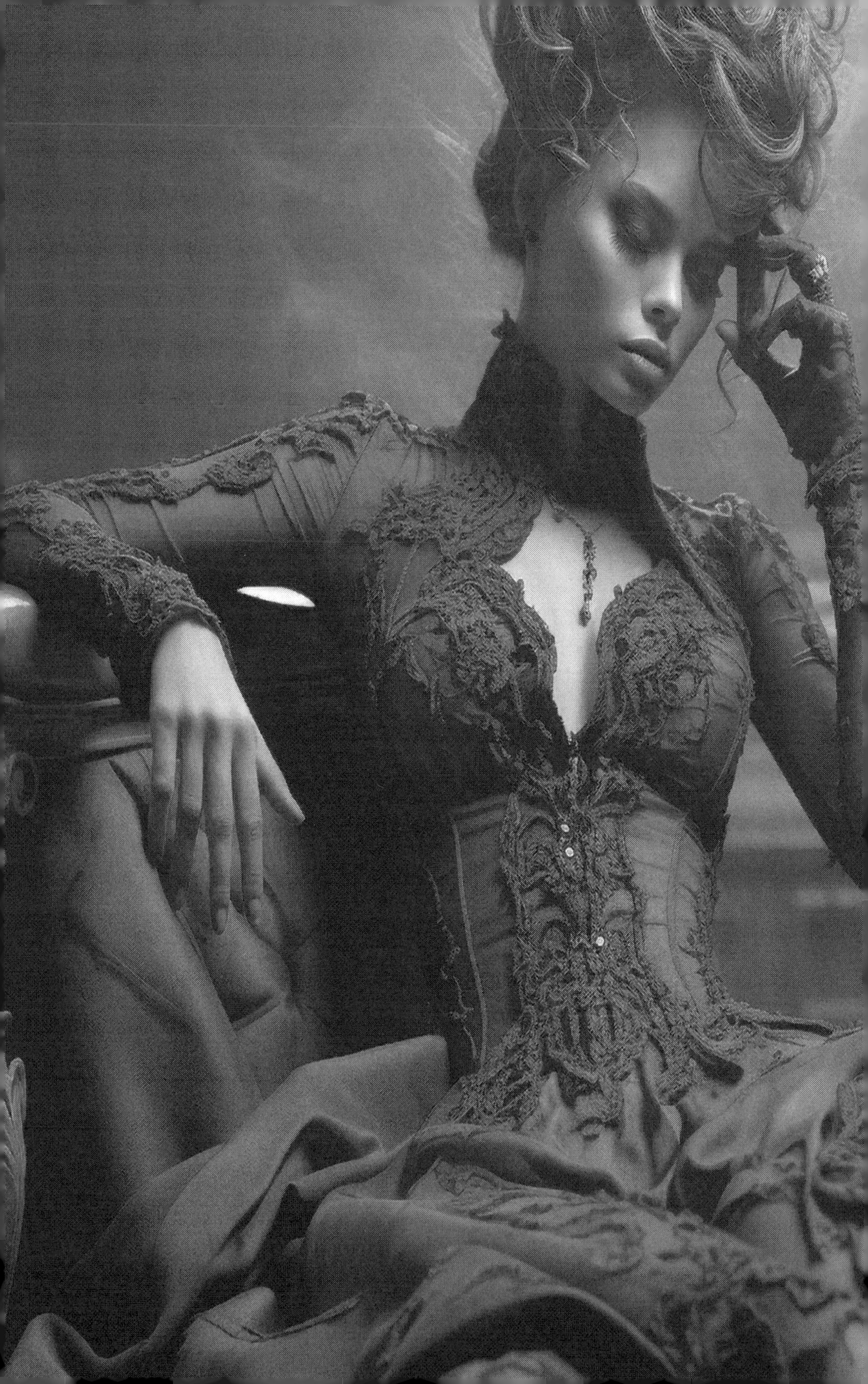

Chapter Fifteen
Connoll

"We ran into your father's goons on the way back." As Octavia filled me in, she unfastened Bacon and lowered him to the ground. Hooves scampering over the floor, he bolted out of the room and towards the kitchen in search of snacks. "I made a compelling case and they let us pass."

I didn't want to ask, but felt I had to. "What was that?"

Octavia shrugged off her black leather jacket and dropped it on the foot of the bed beside Tormund's unconscious form. "Exact words? I said we're on the same side, dickface. Then I blasted him with an emerald jolt which I absolutely did not intend to do, but it proved to be an effective strategy. The combination did the trick, and they let us by."

Leave it to that pink-haired beauty to earn a huff of laughter from me despite the mountains of horrendous shit I had trudged through in Tormund's mind. "You seriously called him dickface?"

"Followed by a little shock therapy, yes."

My sweat-dampened hair slapped against my forehead as I shook my head. "Those who have resided in the fae courts their entire lives only understand painfully literal speech. Truth be told, he was probably more stunned trying to decipher why you thought his face looked like a phallic symbol than the jolt you gave him."

Octavia leaned one hip against her black wolf's side and nonchalantly scratched behind his ears. "Not the first guy I left confused and trembling. Won't be the last. So..." She nodded towards the sleeping vampire. "What have you dug out of his head? Anything useful?"

I chewed on the inside of my cheek, instantly regretting it when a protruding fang stabbed into the tender tissue of my mouth. But my hesitance was for good reason. What I had learned so far painted a picture of pity owed to the same man who had killed me and held Octavia hostage. That information would not be well received by Octavia. Seeing as her abilities had been on the fritz lately, I decided to avoid electrocution by playing my cards close to my chest. "No, nothing yet."

Lifting one brow, her lips screwed to the side. "How about mediocre? Or at least slightly less dire? Anything along those lines?"

I forced a tight smile I hoped she wouldn't see right through. "Don't ask questions you don't want the answer to."

Slapping both hands to the front of her legs, Octavia pushed off the unwavering side of her canine sentry, who looked anything but menacing with his tongue hanging out the side of his mouth. "I hate to sound like a broken record, but answers are key if we want to avoid a full-fledged war with your people. Because Dotty does not have your sister's best interests at heart, and your dad fully intends to blame us for that. If the circumstances were right, I fully believe we could sway Nora to our side. But she won't take the risk unless she's sure shit will turn in her favor. To make all the pieces of that particular chess game come together, we need some inside information from the psychopath's mind." She jabbed her thumb in Tormund's direction. "I'm going to let you get back to that while I go hunt for something to feed Reid that won't make him feel like a dog."

Reid-wolf gave a whiny bark in response to being called out in such a bold way.

Octavia rolled her eyes. "Really? You want to be sassy? I'll absolutely serve you kibble."

His woolly head shook with a snort of disgust.

Pushing my sleeves up my forearms, I tried to mentally prepare myself for yet another walk through the twisted vampire's mind. "Wolf-boy seems more like himself and less like a puppet. How did you make that happen?"

Octavia glanced down at her wolf with a face full of adoration. "Turns out Nora's abilities don't work on swine or canine. Didn't intend for that to rhyme, but I'm okay with this being poetic justice. Her powers don't work on animals, which is why she wouldn't allow him to go full wolf. The second he did, he was free. That said, from what I can gather, he's afraid to risk shifting back out and going full mindless marionette again."

Reid barked his agreement.

Lifting one shoulder in a shrug, Octavia rambled on. "So, for the time being, he plays the part of Lassie in this melodrama. At least until we can find a way to stop Dotty… and Nora… and your father… and his army… and Death, who is sexy in a really confusing way—"

My brow furrowed. "What was that last part?"

She swatted my question away with a flick of her wrist. "Never mind. Least of our worries right now. I have a wolf to feed, and you have the emotional turmoil of a psycho to wade through. I'll leave you to it." A whistle for Reid to follow and she strode out, all pink hair and sass.

Watching her leave, I deflated. Not because I was still harboring a crush on her. Those days had long passed. Turns out, after being murdered for a gal, any romantic inklings you may have been clinging to tended to die as the pulse faded. Plus, there was a certain voodoo practitioner I was still hoping to make a play for once I was convinced I could, in fact, be alone with a non-rotting person for a long period of time without eating them. Tormund definitely did not count. The man smelled as bad as he looked.

No, these melancholy feelings were because I knew my break was over and it was time to dive back into the shit show of Tormund's afterlife. Taking my place back at the head of the bed, I stretched my neck in one direction and then the other. When that did nothing to relax me, I opted for two fingers of Scotch from the bedside table. I let it burn its way down my gullet as an injection of liquid courage. After saying a silent prayer this would be the last time I would have to step over the threshold into his violent existence, I placed two fingers to his temple and let myself be transported into the unknown.

However much time had passed since the horrific torture Tormund suffered in the townhouse, he somehow managed to look even worse for wear than right after the attack. From the looks of things he clearly hadn't bathed, or so much as fallen in a river, since that day. The filthy button-down shirt he wore was open and ripped to tatters. His feet were bare, sliced up, and oozing black vampiric blood. His formerly well-coifed hair was matted with dust, grime, spiders, and anything else he picked up while spending the days sleeping in light-tight graveyard mausoleums. Dried rats' blood was crusted on his face, with drips dotting his torso where they fell when he fed. It was a horrific existence. Yet, he still preferred it to spending another minute in Dotty's presence. He said goodbye to her that day, and he meant it. If he had to see her face again in this eternity or the next it would be too soon.

Each new day, as the sun rose, he tried to find the strength to step into it and let himself fry. He stood under its rays until his skin cracked and smoldered. Gritting his teeth, he withstood the pain as long as he could until it became so intense he couldn't bear it a moment longer. Cursing his own weakness, he dove for cover wherever he could find it. Huddled in the shadows, he would openly weep and berate himself for being such a coward. Slinking back to the stone confines of the cemetery with his skin smoldering, he would seal himself away, all the while vowing to himself that next time he would follow through. Next time, he would finally be free from the horrid curse of his existence.

"Follow the smell. He's over here," a muffled voice barely broke through Tormund's slumber.

Hours passed.

The sun had set.

Even so, a heavy cloak of exhaustion had settled over Tormund and refused to budge.

The deep, throaty voice that filled the crypt echoed off the stone walls in a deep boom. "Rau was right; this guy's a mess. One look at him and the NPI bill will be set back decades."

Arms hooked under Tormund's pits, the man dragged him out of the corner where he was huddled. Giving no more response than a weak groan of protest, his chin fell to his chest.

"Woo-ee! He smells like a pig in shit!" another voice with a thick southern drawl cut in. "Nice to meet you, son. Sorry it's under these circumstances. Believe it or not, we're here to help. Vampire society wants to be a part of civil society. To make that happen, our maker is rounding up wayward souls like you to bring into the fold."

"In other words," a female voice interjected, "today is your lucky day."

Head lolling to the side, Tormund tried to pry his eyes open only to find they were crusted and blistered from his last outing in the sun. "Same maker?" he rasped, his voice gruff from lack of use. "Are you triplets?"

The female gave a sharp bark of laughter. "Triplets. I like that. Three beings as different as we can possibly be, but... sure, let's go with triplets. Whatever you want to call us, we're here to bring you in."

The deep voice rumbled close to Tormund's ear, proving he was the one currently propping him up. "We're going to show you that what you've been enduring isn't vampire life. Not really. You found yourself in a bad way because of bad people. Our kind are cultured, respectful, and eager to break into mainstream society. If you'll let us, we want to take you somewhere where you can be safe... without having to feed off vermin anymore."

Roused by his raw determination, Tormund tried to plant his feet and struggled against them—a pathetic attempt, considering his depleted strength. "I won't kill people! I refuse to!"

"Good." The baritone's relief was audible. "Then you're just the type of man we're looking for."

Had he even an ounce of strength left in him, Tormund likely would have fought back. After all he'd endured, trusting strangers seemed the farthest thing from plausible.

Fortunately, something within him detected that he was, indeed, safe with these newcomers. Or else he'd given up and just didn't give a damn what happened to him. Either way, his mind faded to black, coherency returning in blurred glimpses.

Carried into a grand estate.

Gently laid on a bed.

Filth-covered clothes cut off.

Every inch of him delicately washed with a basin of warm, sudsy water.

His hair gently combed.

Tormund swam in and out of consciousness while nimble fingers buttoned clean pajamas on him.

When Tormund's lashes fluttered open what could have been hours, days, or weeks later, he felt stronger than he had since he was brutalized.

"Look who's waking up." The voice that spoke could only be described as that of a kindly old grandmother.

Tormund's hair fell across his forehead as he turned his attention towards whoever was speaking. She had a round, kind face with rosy apple cheeks and her gray hair was twisted into a bun at the nape of her neck. The knitting needles she held clicked with a rhythmic beat as she worked on what was either a narrow blanket or a really wide scarf. An I.V. tube was connected to one of her arms, pumping fresh blood from her to him.

"You're... f-feeding me?" he stammered, his voice gruff from not using it in weeks.

Finishing one row, the woman started on the next. "That I am. And may I say your color has taken on a vast improvement! You looked like a sickly Victorian child when I came in here. Now, you've upgraded to a milky white. For anyone with a pulse, that wouldn't be a compliment. In your case, it definitely is."

Tormund tried to sit up, but only made it as far as propping up onto one elbow. "Aren't you worried I'll hurt you?"

Blood-donor Granny stopped knitting and blinked his way with genuine surprise. "Not in the slightest, young man."

"Why? Did they drug you or influence your mind in some way?"

"Goodness, no!" Folding her knitting in her lap, she laid her hands on top of it. "First and foremost, you might be getting stronger, however in your current state, I'm still fairly certain you'd crumble like a piece of paper under a strong breeze." Tormund opened his mouth to argue, only to have the sassy grandma hush him with one raised finger. "I am not done speaking, young man. My second reason being if you were feeling froggy and decided to hop, he would see to it you didn't get far." With a dip of her head, she nodded toward the mountainous individual standing stone-still in front of the six panel bedroom door.

Tormund followed her stare to the enormous Black man who folded his arms over the expanse of his chest and glared down his nose at him. "I wouldn't advise that." Tormund instantly recognized his booming voice as one of those who dragged him out of the crypt. "Not if we want to keep things friendly here."

Still traumatized by his assault, when the giant of a man approached the side of his bed, Tormund couldn't suppress the urge to drop fang and snarl. "Is that what this is supposed to be? Friendly?"

The hulk of a man didn't break his stride. "It could be, if you allow it to be that way. Believe it or not, son, we want to help you."

With a soft smile playing across her thin lips, Donor Granny went back to her knitting.

Tormund's top lip twitched to show a flash of fang. "Don't call me son."

His visitor's broad features softened with compassion. "You'll soon learn you don't have to be on guard here. This hive is open and welcoming to all who toe the line of adapting to a mainstreaming lifestyle. That means not killing or hurting anyone, and only feeding off willing donors. Think you can do that?"

A jerk of his head and Tormund retracted his fangs. "I don't know... What was your name? I didn't catch it in the midst of me swimming in and out of consciousness."

That earned a brilliant smile from the building-sized man. "I liked being one of the triplets. It made me feel adorable."

Granny glanced up in confusion. "Triplets? What did I miss?"

"That's what he called me and my recovery team when we brought him in. He'd been holed up in a crypt living off rats' blood." The lone triplet caught hold of one end of her knitting and gave it a cursory inspection. "This looks great, by the way."

"Thank you, dear." She grinned. "And rats' blood, you say? That's what started the plague, you know. I am no vampire, but I certainly wouldn't be feeding off vermin if I was."

"What is this? What the hell is happening here?" Tormund's agitated shouts interrupted their playful banter.

Granny raised her brows in silent judgement and went back to her knitting.

The triplet, however, spoke to him in the calm tone one would use to soothe a toddler's temper tantrum. "This is a safe space, Tormund. Nothing more. Respect the boundaries given, and you can stay as long as you'd like. Go on a frenzy or violent tirade of any kind, and you'll be booted out. Think you can manage that?"

Brow creased in a deep V, Tormund shifted his gaze from Granny to the triplet and back again. "I'm willing to try. But at the first sign any of you are doing anything untoward, I'll leave. Try and stop me and I'll burn this place to the ground. Of that, you have my word."

"I assure you that won't be necessary." The triplet graced him with a jovial grin.

For the first time since being betrayed by Dotty, Tormund let a bit of the tension leave his shoulders. What the future would hold, he didn't know. Yet, for the moment at least, he felt safe. Cared for. While his attention remained on high alert, he allowed himself to enjoy this momentary reprieve from his nightmarish existence ... knowing full well it wouldn't last forever.

To his shock and pleasure, it did carry on long enough for Tormund to not only adjust to hive living, but to thrive in it. The triplets left to return to their maker and continue building the foundation for the Nosferatu Presumption of Innocence bill, which they hoped would one day allow vampires to have the same rights as mortals. With them gone, Tormund was left with roughly two dozen vampires occupying the estate who shared the same spirit of caring and mutual support. They taught him how to feed without killing, including techniques to reduce the pain felt by their well-cared for donors. Hive members educated him on the importance of a caring relationship built on trust between vampires and the mortals who willingly allowed themselves to be drank from.

Most importantly, they showed him what it felt like to have a family. His mother and father provided for him without granting him the attention he craved. The hive changed all that. They would dress in their best and attend the theater together, once again returning Tormund to his beloved operas. When daybreak approached, they would gather together in the parlor in front of a crackling fire to wind down over shared stories of the lives they had before, and adventures they'd embarked on since their afterlife began.

Tormund listened with a smile on his face, keeping his stories of murder, pain, and torture quiet. Pushing all that agony to the back of his mind, he healed his soul by listening intently to their tales. As the others spoke, he saw the scenes playing behind his eyes so vividly, he could have sworn he was right there with them. Running with lions in Africa. Trekking through the rainforest. Taking center stage in a Broadway musical. Morning after morning of listening to their stories before his rest, Tormund found himself filled with fresh hope that his death wasn't the end. Not by a long shot. There was still much he could do that would allow him to escape the mindset that he was a monster. With his hive by his side, he could rejoin society with others like him.

He had found happiness.

Family.

One not of blood, but choice.

Somehow that made it even more special.

A treasured artifact he was determined to protect … which would be a necessity sooner than he realized.

Unbeknownst to Tormund, darkness was closing in fast. It surrounded his merry scene, determined to taint it with vile intent. As Tormund and his hive put out the morning's fire and prepared to take to their caskets to rest, a ripple of fabric appeared outside the parlor window. Dotty stood in the yard in a dressing gown as if attempting to insert herself into the cozy scene. Hurt and anger morphed her features into a mask of hate. Her boy had not only dared to leave her, but he'd had the audacity to achieve some element of bliss without her.

For that, she would make him pay, in the most horrific way possible...

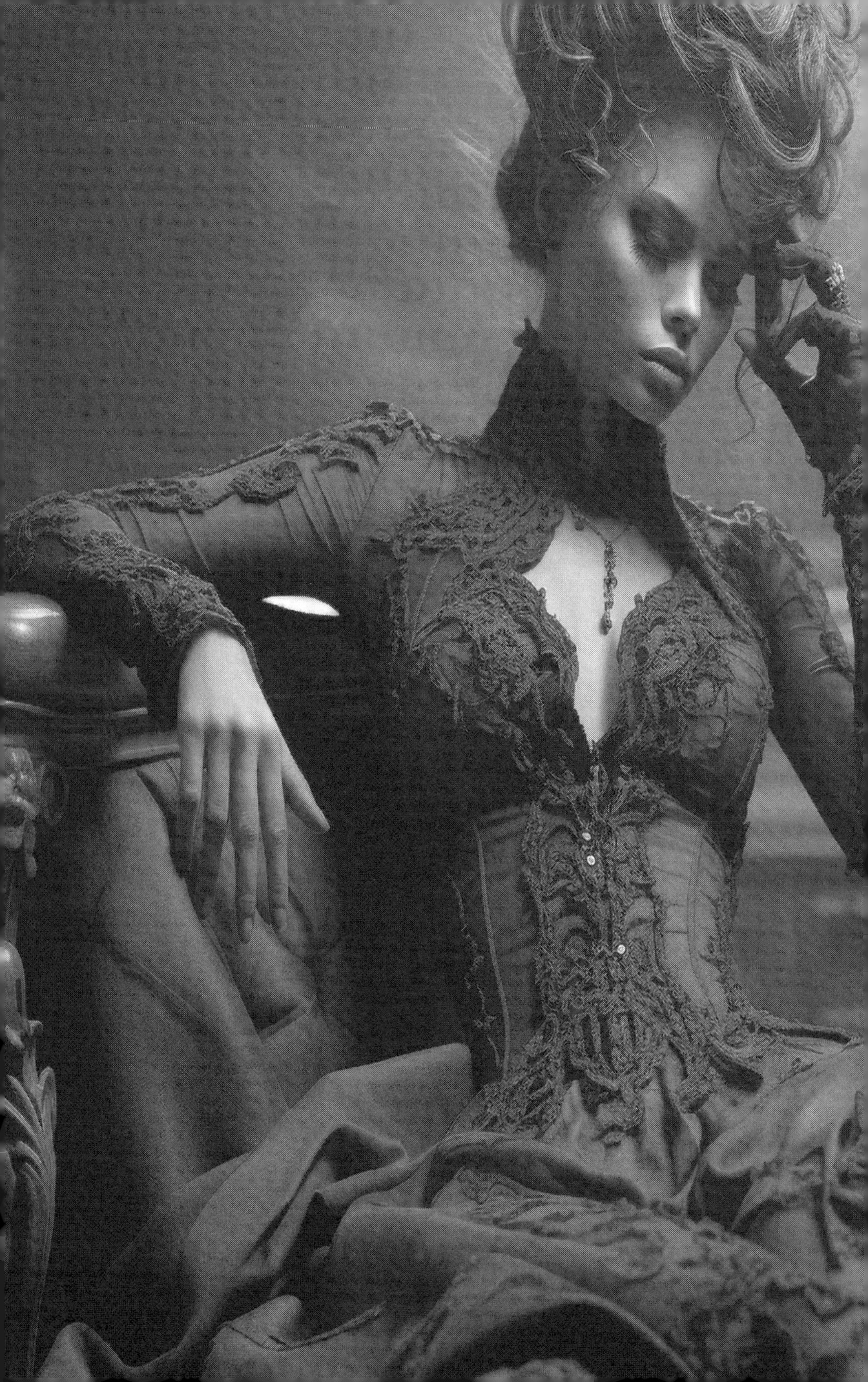

Chapter Sixteen
Octavia

I popped popcorn and browned ground meat for my two boys, setting a bowl in front of pig and wolf respectfully. Each took about three or four mouthfuls before sniffing each other's bowls and making the joint decision to switch. Wolf went to popcorn, porklet to Hamburger Helper. Leaning one hip against the marble kitchen counter, I folded my arms across my middle to watch them munch. The butler had offered to make the snacks for my boys, still I opted to do it myself. Granted, the grand manor wasn't like the bed bug infested, rent-by-the-hour motels we normally crashed at. But I wanted the feeling of taking care of my makeshift family any way I could.

Filling my lungs to capacity, I let myself exhale the stress for the first time in a long time. Chaos raged all around. We were damned near on the verge of war ... again. Somehow that tumultuous state had become my norm. So much so, that in the midst of it all I knew enough to claim this momentary calm reprieve.

Watching my boys blissfully munch, I laughed as they switched bowls two more times before Reid sat back on his haunches and happily licked his chops. Bacon took advantage of the opportunity to go from one bowl to the other, lapping and snorting up every extra morsel of food he could find.

Skirting around Bacon, safe out of scarfing distance, I squatted down beside Reid to scratch his ears. He responded by leaning into my touch and giving a moan of appreciation. "It's good to have you back, man. Though I do wish it was in a way that allowed for more effective communication."

Reid gave a huff of protest … or agreement. I had no idea which.

Letting my hand drop between my knees, I tilted my head and peered into his titanium stare. "I get what you're scared of. You shift back, and Nora's right back in your head. But you won't know if that's true unless you try."

Rising to his feet, Reid backed away, giving a growl not of threat but one of adamant refusal.

Staying in my squatted position, I raised both hands palms out to prove I was done pushing. "I'm not going to force anything. That said, it would be a lot easier to bring the gruesome twosome down if I knew what you experienced when you were there. Do you remember anything at all?"

Reid's wide wolf head dipped into a nod of confirmation.

Instantly, I perked. "You do? About Nora? Or Dotty?"

A shake of his head and a snort.

While a bit of the wind was taken from my sails, I tried not to let it show. "No? Was it about what you experienced?"

He hopped from one front foot to the other, excited I broke his code.

A lump of dread rose in my throat, choking me on thoughts of what all he could have endured. Nora made him brawl in her own personal fight club. There was no telling how far those fights went. My own reservations didn't matter. I would be there for him in any way he needed, as long as he needed.

Taking a seat on the floor, I curled my legs under me. "Do you remember much of what she made you do?"

Reid took a seat and shook his head with an iota less enthusiasm. His ears perked as if prompting me to dig deeper.

"If you don't remember what she made you do, what is it then?" My mind entertained a million possibilities. The primary one being what it would feel like to be locked in his own mind, a prisoner to a nightmare out of his control.

His mouth fell open and a wide smile curled the corners of his muzzle. Rising to his feet, he padded the distance between us. His cold nose nudged my cheek before he licked my face from chin to temple.

With a sigh, I pressed my forehead to his and scruffed his neck. "I'm choosing to take that as you don't remember the horrendous ways you suffered." He confirmed that hypothesis with another slurp to my chin. I pulled away enough to wipe away his slobber. "I'm happy to hear that. Though I'd feel much better about all of this if I could see your face."

His jaws snapped inches from my nose as he barked his canine rebuttal.

I calmed him with a scratch to his brow. "Not that your furry face isn't delightful, but I miss my incredibly handsome boyfriend. Yes, I said boyfriend. Don't look at me like that; I've said it before. This wasn't the first time. And I'll admit, I miss seeing you. Really seeing you. The sooner we can put a cork on Nora's powers, the better. And not just because mama has an itch she needs help scratching ... which I do. But that's a matter all its own." Leaning back, I raked my fingers through the fur of his neck. "The fact of the matter is that things are getting scary. Like, bolt the door and prop a chair against it, kind of bad. I don't know what's going to happen. For the first time in a long time... I'm truly terrified. Jinns, sirens, wraiths, vampires; they are all horrible in their own ways. What we're facing now? With so many obstacles coming at us all at once and Death literally breathing down my neck? I really don't know—"

"Times are tough and you're confiding in the family pet?" a voice fast becoming familiar interjected.

Pulling back, I found Reid frozen in front of me, still as stone and unblinking. Bacon was in the same state with his nose still buried in what had been Reid's food bowl. It was no mystery who was behind it. I felt his presence like an electric current. As much as I hated it, simply being near him caused fingers of sizzling energy to creep up my inner thighs. It heated my core with a desire I couldn't deny, no matter how hard I tried.

"Death." His name left my lips like a husky breath exchanged between lovers.

I turned and the world pivoted with me, blurring out of focus before centering on... him. Everything and everyone else faded away. The world was ours alone. My attraction to him was wrong in a plethora of ways. Not the least of which being the wolfman I was just nuzzling a second ago. I loved Reid. I truly did. In a way I hadn't thought was possible since Elba died. Yet in the presence of Death, everything changed.

Hands plunged casually in the pockets of his freshly-pressed slacks, he wore a sterling silver suit with a black shirt beneath. Every inch of him oozed charm and sex appeal. The cherry on top being the smirk tugging back one corner of his delectable lips. "A welcome like that would make any guy come back for more. Though I wager I would, regardless. There is something about you, Octavia Hollows, that I just can't seem to stay away from. Curiosity got the better of me and I had to peek in and see if you were heeding my warning or racing headlong into danger – which I fully believed you would be. An element that adds to your charm, by the way. Instead, I find you pouring your heart out to someone who can't even begin to understand the weighty responsibilities with which beings like us are saddled. A monumental mistake, if we're being honest. Really, what can the wolf possibly do? I mean no disrespect, but currently he's battling to be in control of his own mind. You put the weight of this kind of thing on him and he's likely to do something stupid that could have me coming for him far sooner than fate demands. So, yes. I intervened. For your well-being, as well as his."

My tongue flicked out to wet my suddenly arid lips. "And you… what? Swooped in here to be my knight in shining armor? You must have me confused for the kind of girl who needs to be rescued. Let me make one thing quite clear: I don't want a hero. If that's why you're here, by all means dissipate back into the void from whence you came. Because today is not the day, and I am not the one."

If he felt any sort of insult from my words, Death didn't let on. Instead, he closed the distance between us with easy strides. Reaching out, he let the knuckle of his index finger trace down the length of my arm, setting my entire existence on fire with his touch. "I would never presume to think you would require anything so archaic. No, what I have for you is an offer far more enticing. If you're up for it."

"An offer from Death. Nothing bad can come from that."

Dipping his head, he let his breath tickle over my cheek. "I would never intentionally hurt you, Octavia. In fact, I'm doing everything I can to avoid that. But I need you to meet me halfway."

In that moment, I would have met him any which way he wanted if he would just bridge those pesky few inches between us. Thankfully, for the sake of my slipping resolve, he held back and allowed me the clarity to ask, "What does that mean?"

To my great regret, he took a step back and injected an icy distance between us that I felt to my very core. My stare fixated on him as he paced a slow circle around me. "I've foretold the danger to come time and again. I even instructed that you get as far from here as possible. Yet here you are, in the trenches and ready to fight on the front line in whatever is to come."

My entire body ached to be near him. To feel the magic of our connection crackling through me. Yet I knew the deep need I felt for that wasn't something to celebrate or give in to ... if my willpower could hold out. Which I doubted it would if he kept giving me that let's have raw, animalistic sex look. I mean, a girl can only hold out so long before her panties spontaneously combust.

"What can I say?" I murmured, sounding far more sex-kitten than intended. "I like to be front and center for the action."

What was it about this guy's mojo that made everything seem like a dirty innuendo?

As if reading my thoughts, he planted himself in front of me and graced me with a saucy grin. "I need only meet you to know that. However, to what I'm sure will be your great regret, you wouldn't be leading us into battle in this particular scenario. No, you would allow me to be the one to lead the charge."

In terms of eliminating one's enemies, sending Death to level the playing field seemed a sure-fire kamikaze approach that would result in an astronomical body count. "You're

Death, and there are people I care about caught in the middle of this. Handing the reins over to you seems like a monumentally bad idea. No offense intended."

Taking a step closer, Death caught one strand of my hair and twirled it around his pointer finger. "You hesitate for good reason. But I give you my word... say the names of those you want spared, and I will honor your wishes."

Finding myself leaning towards his touch, I made myself take a step back... no matter how much it pained me. "Damned near half the town is caught under the fae's thrall! The fact that I haven't met them all and am terrible with names on my very best day shouldn't be why any of them are sentenced to death."

Turning my back to him, I narrowed my eyes and searched the darkness for some traces of Reid, Bacon, or the manor that had vanished around us. Nothing else existed in that void except us. Just me and a magnetic being of unsurpassed power, charisma, and charm. This situation was toxic with a capitol T.

Standing with his hands in his pockets, Death wet his lips in a way that was pure seduction. "Such literal terms are for mortals. What's between us borders on the cosmic. To save those people, you needn't speak any actual words, but give yourself over to it."

Grabbing fistfuls of my hair, I expelled a ragged breath. "What is it that you think this is? Tell me, please, because I honestly don't understand. I've been attracted to people before. This isn't that, and that's the part that scares the hell out of me."

A blink, and Death was before me. With one palm, he cradled my elbow and raised my hand to his. "Attraction is contrived in terms of magnets, whose molecular structure draws them together by an unseen force. As I said, what's between us is more cosmic. The energy within our cores grows stronger the closer we are to one another." The whispered caress of his skin on mine ignited emerald wisps that licked from my extended digits. Death added the spark of his influence, capping my tendrils with tinges of black. "We are forces of nature drawn together by a gravitational pull. Together, we could make the unfathomable... possible."

As if cued, an ear-piercing pop echoed all around. Our melding powers morphed into an ethereal white orb with swirls of shimmering shades of blue rippling over its surface.

Eyes bulging, my jaw fell open. "It's so... beautiful." Peering up at Death, I gasped at how enchanting he looked illuminated by the orb's glow. "What can it do?"

"I don't know yet." Releasing his hand, he closed it into a fist and the ball of light vanished as if it had never been at all. "We can find out... together. Let me handle this matter for you, Octavia. Allow me to swoop in as your hero and I will spend the rest of eternity cherishing you and guarding your heart as a rare and precious treasure to which I alone hold the key."

Staring into the depths of his sapphire stare, I saw specks of silver swirling there that made it seem the cosmos he spoke of lived within him. And maybe it did. That was one of many things I didn't truly know about him. That bit of doubt and trepidation proved to be the bucket of ice water I needed to extinguish the flames of longing raging between us.

"You ask for my heart when you've shown me nothing of yourself. Your face is borrowed from my celebrity crush. Your name is a noun, not an actual moniker. Everything you've presented to me is a façade. I love Reid. I do. He's a good man I will fight for. Maybe with the life and death thing you and I are the yin to each other's yang, but it's not real. It's chemistry. I refuse to give up something pretty damned great that Reid and I have built and fought for over a science experiment."

I turned on the heel of my boot, prepared to march through darkness until I found my way back or was lost forever in Purgatory, whichever came first. Over my shoulder, I shouted one final parting thought. "Oh, and you really need to learn to know your audience. I'm my own hero. I don't need anyone to fill that role for me."

I expected to see Death in a rage. Instead, he shook his head as sorrow shadowed his features. "I truly am sorry to hear that. The end is coming, Octavia. On swift wings. I hope you change your mind… before it's too late."

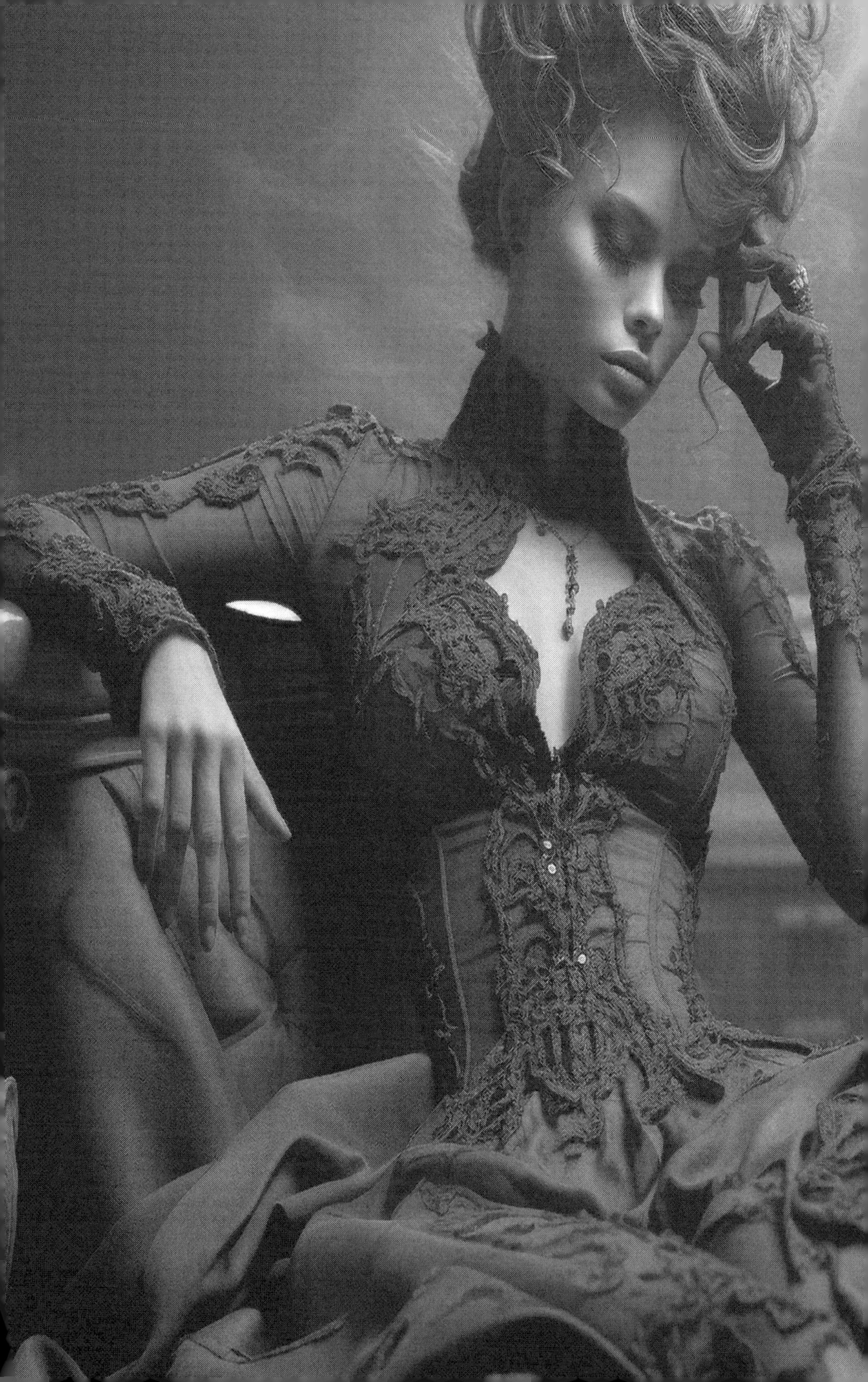

Chapter Seventeen
Connoll

I sat on the edge of the desk chair with my elbows on my knees and my head in my hands. My time wandering through Tormund's memories had accomplished nothing more than giving me a hell of a headache and second-hand PTSD. Knowing that for the sake of the entire town I needed to dive back in was why I was hunched in that position, reevaluating all my life's choices.

Yes, I was procrastinating.

But for a damned good reason.

Shit was brutal inside his head.

Straightening my spine, I slapped my hands onto my thighs with every intention of rising to my feet and getting back on task. The buzz of my phone from the front pocket of my shirt acted as a welcome distraction to delay the inevitable at least a little longer.

Glancing at the screen, a slow smile spread across my face. Ruby. The stunningly beautiful voodoo practitioner I fully intended to ask out as soon as I was confident in my control over my vampire side. I clicked on her message hoping for a little flirty fun, although what I got was anything but.

Ruby: Is Octavia with you?

I stared at the words for a minute with my brow furrowed. Was she implying that in the carnal sense? Fishing for information about my rather befuddling relationship with the pink-haired necromancer? Sure, Octavia was a smoke show. But death stalked that girl everywhere, my own demise being further proof of that. Not wanting to make things awkward by assuming a meaning she didn't intend, I went for a vague yet accurate response.

Me: She's with Reid.
Three dots popped up as she typed her response.
Ruby: Are they anywhere you can see them?
Okay, so this wasn't a relationship status thing. She meant in the geographical sense.
Me: They went into the kitchen to feed Bacon. Why? What's up?
Ruby: I did a reading. It has me worried about Octavia.
Me: How so?
Ruby: Death, Connoll. Death surrounds her from all sides in a way I have never seen before. I don't know what it means for someone with her abilities. Or those of us around her.
A chill prickled down my spine. My own thought of death stalking her blended with this new information in an oddly ominous way.
Me: What can we do?
Ruby: Watch her. Closely. Let me know if you notice anything odd. I'm going to research wards of protection to

cast around her. If all else fails, we may have to bind her powers.

I stared at those last words without blinking. A fist of terror tightened around my heart. If her powers were bound, she wouldn't be able to save me from myself if I lost control. I would be consumed by the monster within.

Offering her a dismissive "K" in response, I dropped my phone back in my pocket. After rising to my feet and stretching my back, I crossed the room on cautious steps. Easing open the bedroom door, I peeked out. Something in the manor felt ... off. Not evil, per se, but cold and isolating. The manor was utterly still and silent; not so much as a breeze rippled any of the fabric draperies. The stairs squeaked under my weight as I made my way down to the first floor, breaking the hush with the same jarring impact of a shotgun blast.

That should have alerted Octavia of my presence. After all, from where I stood at the bottom of the stairs, I could see her through the open kitchen door. Yet the heated conversation she was in prevented her from noticing me.

Hands on her hips, venom dripped from each syllable she uttered. "You ask for my heart when you've shown me none of yourself. Your face is borrowed from my celebrity crush. Your name is a noun, not an actual moniker. Everything you've presented to me is a façade. I love Reid. I do. He's a good man that I will fight for. Maybe with the life and death thing, you and I are the yin to each other's yang, but it's not real. It's chemistry. I refuse to give up something pretty damned great that Reid and I have built and fought for over a science experiment." Octavia started to turn away but glanced back with one final parting thought. "Oh, and you really need to learn to know your audience. I'm my own hero. I don't need anyone to fill that role for me."

It would have been a bold and brazen exhibit of female empowerment... if she wasn't alone. No one else was there, taking the brunt of her rage. Whatever was happening seemed to be all in her mind.

I couldn't betray Octavia by telling Ruby what I saw. Not yet, at least. I mean, who among us hasn't had a one-sided argument with someone who wasn't there, if only so we could say all the things we wished we had said? Even so, I intended to watch her more closely. Between this and the slipping control on her powers, the necromancer was definitely throwing up some red flags.

One thing I truly believed would help? Finally getting answers out of Tormund. That meant plugging my nose and cannonballing my way back into his psyche. Like it or not— and I definitely did not—I needed to get back to work.

For the first time since his father died and his mother abandoned him, the young vampire found true happiness. Not the hedonistic montage of sin he and Dotty indulged in, but genuine bliss. He drank from willing donors who trusted him and believed him to be a good man. Enjoyed dressing in fashion's latest trends, thanks to the vast resources of the hive. Best of all, he acquired balcony seats at the opera. A luxury that brightened his darkened soul.

He was returning to the hive after yet another captivating night of theater when his afterlife took a tragic turn once more. Sauntering in with his tailcoat folded over his arm, he was met by sounds of lighthearted laughter and clinking glasses. Neither of which gave him the slightest bit of pause. The heels of his shoes clicked over the marble floor as he made his way to the formal dining room. For this morning's fireside chat, he had a story prepared of how the male lead missed a cue yet somehow made the timing of the number even better. That anecdote and language in general fell out of his head when he stepped into the impromptu gathering. One glance and the world swam out of focus before him.

The smile died on Tormund's lips.

His vision tunneled on one person alone.

Dotty.

Clad in a silver slip dress with a feather boa draped across her shoulders, she held court at the head of the table. Locking eyes with her progeny, victory gleamed in the depths of her vindictive stare. "Oh, wonderful!" she beamed. Snapping her fingers beside her head, she waved to the butler. "Kindly pour the newcomer a glass before we toast. This donor is not to be missed."

The gray-haired butler scurried over to pour a glass of ruby-red blood and gingerly handed it to a visibly shaken Tormund.

Dotty tipped her wine glass his way before addressing the room with a winning smile. "As I was sayin', I appreciate you all takin' me in. I've been alone way too long since my mate left me." Pointed look in Tormund's direction. "But you welcomed me and made me feel like I didn't need to walk this life alone. For that, I am eternally grateful."

Murmurs of appreciation buzzed through the crowd along with polite nods and grins.

Dotty blew kisses to both sides of the table before continuing. "I don't have much to offer to show my thanks, but I do have this." She raised her flute a little higher. "Blood from a lovely donor I found in Greece who was sunning herself on the pristine shoreline while feastin' on mangoes and champagne. Please, enjoy."

Unease tiptoed down Tormund's spine. Fear tightening around his throat like a noose, he watched his hive raise their glasses to their lips. He might even have joined them, had he not watched Dotty lift her own glass... but not drink. Never had he known her to deny herself any sort of indulgence. That simple fact was enough to give him pause.

He thought to warn the others.

Yet what could he say that wouldn't reveal all the atrocities he had committed alongside his maker? Locking stares with her, he prayed her expression would give away some hint of what she had planned. It didn't. While the others sipped the heady brew and smacked their lips in contentment, Dotty raised her eyebrows in challenge. Was it possible he read this entire situation wrong and she truly was trying to make amends?

That question answered itself when the first member of the hive doubled over with a violent, hacking cough. The others quickly followed. Clutching their throats, crimson spittle bubbled from their lips. One by one, their eyes rolled back as they slumped to the floor, on the table, or dangling from their chairs. A mere blink later and they exploded into ash that filled the room in a thick, gray haze.

Tormund tossed his glass aside, shattering it to splinters against the fireplace mantel. "What have you done, you deranged twat?"

Her expression remained unperturbed and damned near indifferent. "And here I was, thinking you'd be thrilled to get a visit from an old friend."

Tormund's hands balled into fists at his sides and his fangs sprang from his gumline. "They took me in! They cared for me in a way you never could. They were my family, damn it!"

"I'm the only family you need!" Dotty snarled back, easily matching the heat of his tone. Her beautiful face morphed into a mask more beast than human. As quick as the transformation came on, all traces of it vanished. Her features iced over in a façade of indifference that was somehow even more chilling. Setting her tainted glass aside, she fluffed her curls. "You think these beings understood you? That they cared about you? They could never know you or love you the way that I do. Maybe what you need is proof?"

Tormund tensed, unsure of what would come but well aware it would be horrific. "What did you poison them with? At least tell me that."

Dotty clucked her tongue against the roof of her mouth and wagged one finger in the direction of her progeny. "Naughty boy, don't ruin your surprise. See, when I tracked ya down, I wanted to find just the right way to show ya how much I've missed you. I thought long and hard about the perfect gift to give ya. I didn't lie, you know. She really was in the Greek Isle, sunnin' herself and living off the tab of some rich old fella."

Dread seeped through Tormund's veins for reasons he couldn't yet comprehend. "Dotty, what did you poison my hive with?"

Her head snapped in his direction, each word spitting from her lips with pure venom. "Fine! If you're so insistent on spoilin' the surprise, have it your way! Dead man's blood, okay? The bottle I presented them with tonight came from a corpse. That happens to be very deadly to vampires, which you would know if you hadn't run away from me. Why, Tormund? Why did you leave me? Don't you realize no one will ever love you or understand you the way I do? We have an unbreakable bond, baby!"

The prickles at the back of his neck made Tormund fear there was still more to this story than Dotty was letting on. A dull ache ground deep into his long-stilled heart as he scanned the ash-covered room at the remnants of all those who had showed him nothing but kindness. And what did they get for their efforts? The eternal death served up by a callous and unforgiving hand.

Nostrils flaring, he glared daggers of hate at his maker. "Who is she, Dotty? Who did you find in the Greek Isle?"

Thick lips curling into a mischievous smile, she turned with a grand flourish to retrieve a hat box on the floor by her chair. "This is the best part, lover. I made sure I'm the only woman in your life you will ever want or need. I know how much it hurt you when she left, the unworthy cow. So, I tracked her down and made her pay." Plucking off the lid, she reached inside and placed her offering on the linen tablecloth beside her champagne flute. "Even better, I told her you sent me, and that every bit of pain I inflicted on her was in honor of you. She blubbered, doll face. Begged for her life. I showed her no mercy, because that's how much I love you."

Tormund blinked at the sight before him.

Once.

Twice.

And again.

At first, he couldn't see behind the horror of the decapitated head. Gray skin. Sludge matted hair. Stare fixed and glassy. It was studying the features that made black-tinged tears streak down his cheeks. Those eyes had once been blue. The complexion a warm peaches and cream hue. Wash that blood away and you would find the silvery-blonde hair… of his mother. She broke his heart when she walked out on him. Still, he prayed the day would come that they would somehow make amends and reconnect. Dotty robbed him of that, the latest in a growing list of turmoil she inflicted on him. Lips twitching into a snarl, he longed to rip her head from her shoulders and impale it on the fireplace poker leaning against the mantel. All that held him back was the knowledge that she was his maker, and therefore he could never overpower her. Vampire hierarchy saw to that. Still, he couldn't let her win. Not this time. Gaze drifting behind her, he noticed a sliver of light streaming in from behind the curtains.

The sun was rising.

His ticket to freedom had arrived.

This time he wouldn't fail.

Without offering a glance back at his mother's head or the remains of his hive, he draped his jacket over the back of the nearest chair. "You taught me a lot of lessons, Dotty. A handful of good, slathered with several lifetimes worth of agonizing. Even so, I refuse to become like you."

"Wh-what does that mean? You and me, we're the same whether you like it or not."

Offering no response, he turned on his heel and strode in the direction he'd come from. His hand was closing around the knob to the front door when she sprinted up behind him and grabbed hold of his arm. "Tormund, what are you doing? I did this for us! You have to see that!"

He glanced down at her hand clutching the sleeve of his shirt in a white-knuckled hold. "I would sooner meet the sun than spend one more second with you. Let go of me, Dotty. I mean it."

His maker reluctantly loosened her grip but didn't let go. "I did this for us, lover! Can't you see that? Everything I have done was for you!"

With a jerk of his shoulder, he shrugged off her touch. "Don't fucking touch me. I mean it." He wanted to unleash on her. To lash out and collide in a violent clash of fangs and fury. But that wouldn't hurt her; Dotty would easily overpower him. The only way to cause her any iota of agony was to destroy the one thing she cared for. Namely, him.

Tormund's gaze drifted back to the door and the painful oblivion that awaited on the other side. How he wished he could rewind time and not bring danger to the hive he loved. Not sought out a home. Simply remained a tumbleweed blowing from place to place, never forming attachments Dotty could use against him. He was lost in his reverie of what might have been when he noticed the first light of dawn seeping through from the crack under the door.

Sunrise.

After all that had happened, this was his only way out.

"Everything you did was for me," he parroted, his voice vacant of emotion. "And now, what I have to do is because of you."

Dotty pulled back with an abrupt laugh, offering up a confused smile. "Yes, as it should be. Everything we do is for each other from now on, building an eternity others can only dream of."

Tormund glanced over his shoulder at the bane of his very existence. "An eternity with you would be nothing short of a nightmare."

Leaving those words hanging between them, he wrenched open the door and strode towards the horizon with a determined gait. Let the sun scorch him. Let it blister his skin and reduce him to ash. The pain would be a momentary necessity to rid him of her, once and for all. Throwing his arms out wide, he smiled in relief as his skin began to steam and sizzle. It would be over soon. After Tormund endured one final trial.

To the stabbing anguish of his heart and soul, his maker proved she was stronger than him yet again by seizing hold of him with her own smoldering hand and wrenching him back inside. After slamming and locking the door behind him, she ripped the tablecloth off the table—sending his mother's severed head tumbling to the floor—and used the fabric to pat out the burning sections of his flesh.

"No-NO-NO! How could you do that? You can't leave me, Tormund. Ever."

Detached from his body, he merely blinked in the direction of his maker. "You stopped me this time, but I'll find a way. That is my vow from this moment forward. You taught me about dead man's blood. It would be easy enough to get my hands on some. Hell, there's a bottle left in the dining room. Daylight. Silver. I'll find a way. Of that, I promise you."

She gathered his hands in both of hers and peppered them with kisses. "Tell me what I can do. Whatever it takes, I'll make this better. I'll make you love me again. Name it, and it's yours. I just can't stand the thought of walking in a world without you in it."

The words left his lips in a haunting echo, the cadence of a man resigned to death. "You want me to live? Stay away from me. I will give you my word not to off myself the very first chance I get as long as I never have to look upon your face again. Because if I have to spend one more second in your presence, I won't just be praying for the end of time, I'll welcome it with open arms."

She jerked as if he slapped her, stupefied by the bold words tumbling from Tormund's lips. "You can't be serious."

"Let me go and see if I'm bluffing," he countered.

"I can't live without you!" Blonde curls bobbed against the apples of her cheeks as she shook her head. "I won't."

Lifting his head from the floor, he snarled up at her. "But you will. One way or another. Leave me alone or let me die. The choice is yours." Instead of waiting for her to answer, he pushed her aside and rolled to his side to rise from the floor. "There are coffins in a light-tight room in the basement. I'm going to rest. When the sun sets, if you're still here, I will make it my mission to be dead before sunrise. One way or another, my fevered determination will ensure I succeed. If you do as I ask and leave, stay gone. Time will not heal the rift between us. Nothing will. If I catch so much as a whiff of you, I'll light myself on fire to avoid so much as a conversation. I mean it, Dotty. You want me alive? Vanish."

And she did.

By the time the twilight hour fell and his coffin lid cracked open, his maker was gone. In her heart, the platinum vampress held onto the hope that one day he would change his mind and come back to her. Until then, she kept her distance and watched his afterlife unfold from afar. Her progeny never integrated into a hive again. The pain she caused prompted him to adopt a nomadic existence of remaining solo and hopping from hive to hive for brief periods of time. It suited him ... for a while.

Dotty knew there was trouble brewing the first time she saw the pink-haired girl Tormund seemed obsessed with. Instantly, she hated her. One night, she even scaled the side of the manor they were holed up in to find the two cuddled up in bed together. It was in that moment she made the decision to interfere in her mate's matters one final time. The girl had to die. But first, she would see to it that she suffered ...

My eyes snapped open, rapidly blinking in bewilderment that I had jumped from Tormund's thoughts to Dotty's. I bolted back from the bed when I glanced down to find Tormund staring up at me.

While his silver eyes were still glassy and unfocused, he turned his head in my direction. "It's all about the blood, young one."

It wasn't Tormund's voice that seeped from his lips, but Dotty's. How, the detective couldn't even begin to deduce. But Dotty answered his unspoken question anyway.

"Tormund was mine, and you are his. That ties us as family. Blood of my blood, take this as a warning. Give me back my boy, or I'll deliver the bodies of the people of this town to you one by one."

A shudder and then Dotty was gone, leaving Tormund empty and unconscious once more. Shoulders sinking, I stumbled to the desk and slumped down in its chair. Tormund didn't possess some magical weakness that could bring Dotty down. He was the weakness. Which left us two options... awaken a homicidal manic... or unleash one.

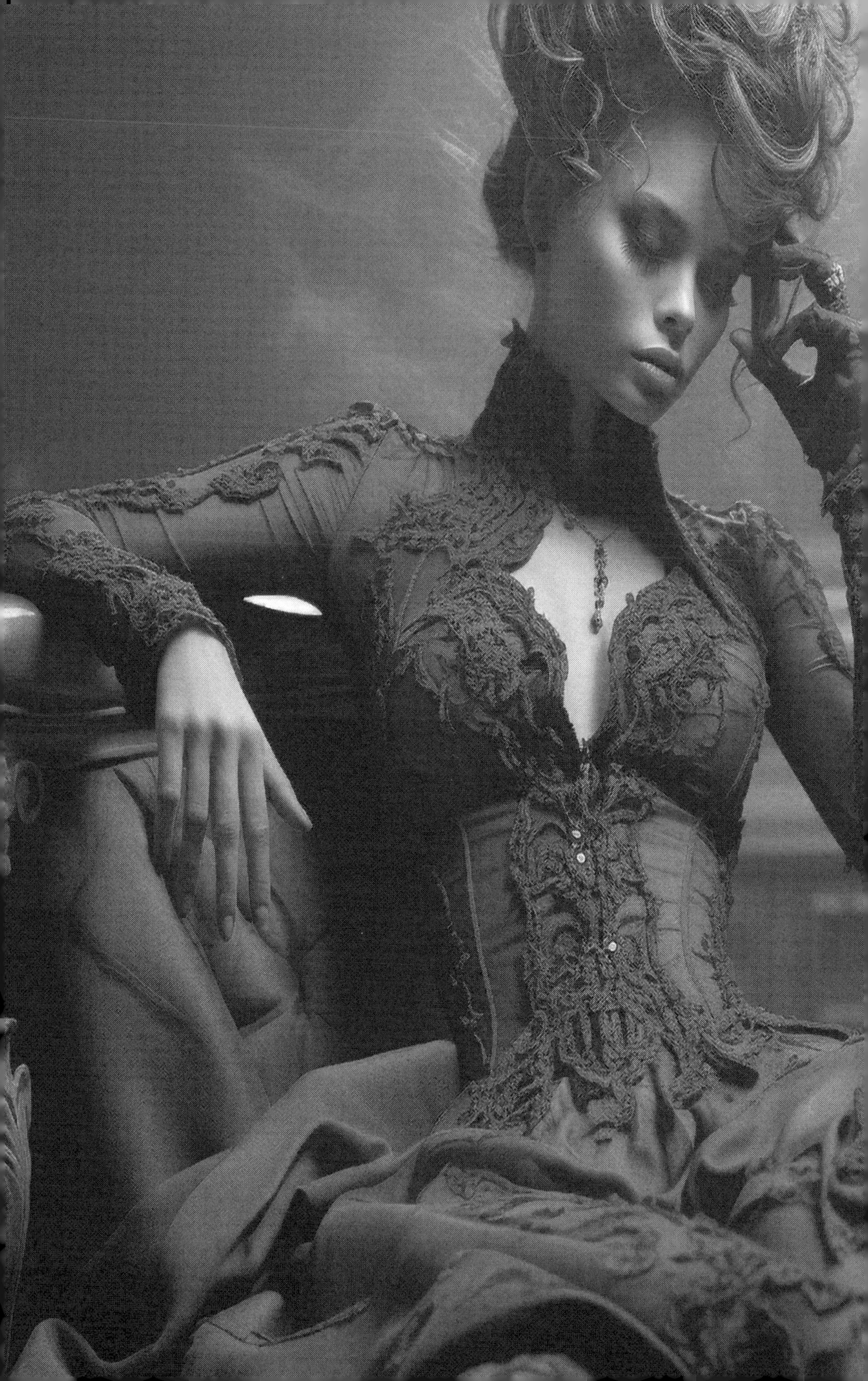

Chapter Eighteen
Octavia

Seated in front of me like the good boy he was, Reid-wolf tilted his head and pawed at my leg.

"Yes, something did happen. You're quite astute, even in canine form." I forced a tight smile, hoping his wolf side wouldn't pick up on the fact that it didn't reach my eyes. "But I promise you I'm okay."

Nudging me with his snout, he gave a soft whimper.

Yeah, no luck that anything would escape his notice.

"I'm okay, really." Folding my arms across my chest, I ran my hands up and down my arms to fight off a chill that radiated out from my core. I'd felt that ominous iciness since denying Death's offer, and prayed it wasn't a sign I had made a horrific mistake. Not that I would let Reid in on the burden of any of this. "Some shit went down, but it's nothing I can't handle."

Reid shifted on his rump, a whimper/bark escaping him.

Lips twisting to the side, I hitched one eyebrow. "You know if you want to have a heart-to-heart, it would be a lot easier if you at least attempted to shift back to human."

The wolf made a noise that could only be described as an argumentative merp, accompanied by him glancing from me to Bacon and back again.

Clucking my tongue against the roof of my mouth, I rolled my eyes. "Don't compare my communication with him to this. He's a pig. Always has been, always will be. You are a dude, whom I have slept with recently and often. Trying to have a meaningful conversation with you like this is justifiably weird."

His counterpoint came in the form of a plaintive howl.

Throwing my hands in the air, I let them fall to my sides with a slap. "I can't talk to you if you're going to purposely be unreasonable."

Further conversation was halted when the ground began to buck beneath our feet. The manor shook with enough force to throw open the kitchen cupboards and spill their contents across the floor. The outer wall cracked wide enough for daylight to spill in from the fissure.

Reid planted all four feet, riding out the waves of tremors with lupine grace. Bacon skidded across the floor on his butt, causing me to throw myself onto my side to catch him. Peering up at me, he squealed in panicked confusion.

I cradled him tight to my chest as I slid across the kitchen floor and caught a table leg to the spine. "Ow! I don't know, buddy. Last time I felt something like this, a demigod of carnage was unleashing his fury on the bayou."

"Ar-ro-ro-roo!" My wolf barked at the window, his silver gaze flicking my way as if in search of further explanation.

"Chances are slim that's happening again!" I covered my head and Bacon's as plates and glasses rained down from above. "Of course I can't know for sure, but it seems unlikely!"

As fast as the quake came on, the earth stilled. The silence that followed was broken by the slow claps of a human-shaped being comprised of flame materializing from the crack in the wall. "That was quite a performance in disaster preparation, but I'm afraid it won't be enough."

Easing Bacon to the floor behind me, I rose to my feet to position myself between my pork tenderloin and the flaming tart. "Earth moved, now we have fire. All that's missing is wind and we could have a funny little ditty about the twenty-first night in September."

Fire-crotch cocked their head in confusion.

"Earth, Wind, and Fire? Singing group from the seventies." Even as I spoke, I straightened the legs of my jeans and tried to appear unperturbed. "But that's enough musical education for today, wouldn't you say? Let's get to the point of your little visit. I'm guessing the King of the Winter Court sends you with his regards."

Fingers of licking flame rolled, casting dancing shadows up the walls. "This is about far more than pleasantries. The King's patience has run out. Before the sun sets on this day, you will deliver his daughter to him or he will see to it that all you care for will perish. Sunset, necromancer. The clock is ticking."

Black smoke belched through the room, and the messenger was gone.

I locked eyes with Reid, seeing more human understanding peering back at me than animal. "We've stalled for time as long as we can. Let's go see if Connoll found anything out from our sleepy psycho that could prevent a war."

--insert pig graphic here—

"My father was never good at honoring appointments and schedules," Connoll grumbled, combing his fingers through platinum hair that darted from his scalp in a messy disarray. "One of his many less than admirable traits. Right along with abusing his children and subjects and being an all-around deplorable person."

Standing just inside the doorway whilst making a conscious effort not to look at Tormund, I held Bacon tightly to my chest while Reid hovered protectively by my side. "We can compare notes on our traumatic childhoods later. Right now, I'm waiting for you to dazzle me with the plethora of useful information you've plucked from the head of that sycophant."

"Would you settle for jazz hands and some real bummer news?" Even as he asked the question, the detective raised his hands beside his head with spirit fingers that would make any cheerleader proud.

Jaw tensed tightly, I curled my fingers into fists and pretended not to notice the veins of darkness tracking up my arms. "I don't need to remind you that all our hopes were weighing on this. The two of them spent decades together. How could there not be anything we could use against her?"

Walking across the room, each step seemingly weighed by exhaustion, Connoll collapsed in the desk chair. "I learned a lot and saw a lot of horrific shit I can't unsee. Unfortunately, none of it was the magic bullet that would bring her down. There were…" he hesitated, choosing his next words carefully, "other things that came to light. Things about Tormund that may change how you view this entire situation."

Folding my arms across my chest, I leaned against the door frame. "What could possibly change how I view that monster? Did he rescue orphans from a burning building?

Pretty sure he would eat them afterwards. Rescue puppies and kitties from fighting rings? Not to sound like a broken record, but I bet he fucking ate them afterwards. He's a nightmare on legs, no matter what tragic backstory came before."

Elbows on his knees, Connoll steepled his fingers between his legs. "You might feel differently if you saw what I did."

Bacon's nose began twitching at something he caught a whiff of, causing him to wriggle for all he was worth until I lowered him to the ground. "Yeah, well, thanks to the ward you had me read off your skin whilst watching you die, that's not a possibility. So, I guess you're going to have to describe it in intricate detail."

Connoll dragged his tongue over the tip of one fang that lengthened from his gumline. "There is another way. If I were to consume even the tiniest bit of your blood, we would be one. Then, I could show you firsthand what I saw. It wouldn't take much. You must have noticed that I've gained control of my hunger and abilities. Think about it: I haven't even asked you to use your touch since my time with Tormund began. Why do you think that is?"

I let one shoulder rise and fall. "I figured you were feeding off him. Truthfully, I wasn't against the idea, hence not saying anything or trying to prevent it in any way."

Reid gave a sharp bark and nod as if seconding that notion.

Connoll's face folded with confusion. "What? No! I haven't been feeding off anyone. Don't diminish my accomplishments!"

Reid and I exchanged matching looks of resignation.

"If you say so," I relented. "Still, not loving the idea of you biting me."

"It would only take a drop or two of your blood."

"Is that the vampire version of just the tip?" My eyes narrowed. "I haven't fallen for that trick since I was sixteen."

A bark from Reid-wolf.

"Okay, fine. Nineteen."

Two more sharp barks.

Lips twisting to the side, I attempted to shrivel him with a glare. "Fine. Twenty-two. I'm never confessing anything to you again."

Taking a seat on his haunches, Reid's tongue lolled out of his mouth in a victorious grin.

Connoll raised one finger between us. "First, I absolutely need to be included in the next story time. Secondly, no. This is not the vampire version of a cheap frat guy trick. Prick your own finger if you want. Squeeze a drop or two onto my tongue, then I'll show you everything. You have my word."

Pushing off the door frame, I closed the distance between us. "I'm going to trust you, Detective. I have no reason not to. You and I have been through too much shit together for me to doubt you. Fang, please." He curled his lips back from his teeth, allowing me to grind the tip of one finger into his tooth until a ruby bead bloomed from my skin. Sucking back the sting, I squeezed my finger to draw more blood out. "Plus, if you do anything at all to hurt me, my wolf will most definitely tear you to pieces."

As if cued, Reid jumped to his feet and growled in ominous warning.

"Fair enough," Connoll agreed with a nod and stuck out his tongue in anticipation of my offering.

"Don't make me regret this," I muttered more to myself than him as I squeezed my blood into his mouth.

Connoll's eyes closed the instant he tasted me. An appreciative moan rumbled from his chest that made this whole situation insanely awkward. Chest swelling with desire, his eyes snapped open. Pupils dilating with ravenous hunger, his tongue flicked over one menacing incisor.

I stumbled back one step, then another. "Connoll? Detective Tiresias? I need you to get control, my man."

Reid's hackles raised and his muzzle curled into a snarl.

Eyes black with desire, Connoll's stare locked on my throat as he stalked straight for me with feline fluidity.

Heart hammering against my chest, I backpedaled until my shoulder blades smacked into the wall behind me. "This is what I get for trusting a vampire. Damn it, Detective, snap out of it! You don't want to do this!"

His palms slammed against the wall on either side of me, pinning me where I stood. Leaning in, he whispered against my ear. "You're right. I don't. I told you I had control." Pushing away, he inserted the distance needed for me to remember how to breathe. "Geez, where's the trust?"

Seeing the crisis averted, Reid expressed his emotions for the tomfoolery at hand in the only way he could. Meaning a long string of pissed off barks.

"Sorry, Cujo." Connoll laughed and pushed his shirt sleeves further up his tattooed arms. "Had to be done."

Bending in half with my hands on my knees, I tried to remember how a normal breathing pattern worked. "I should let him bite you, out of spite."

"You could," Connoll agreed, head bobbing in a nonchalant nod. "Or you could let me show you what I saw." He offered me his hand, his brows raised in impatient expectation.

"I highly doubt it will change anything, but let's get this over with." I sighed and closed my fingers around his.

The visions invaded my mind, fast and furious.

A poor little rich boy forced into poverty.

Abandoned.

Alone.

A second chance… that led only to death.

Chaos.

Carnage.

The exact kind of shit I expected of Tormund.

Then … Dotty began her little con games.

I wanted to believe the vampire who held me captive was the worst of the worst. However, his maker was on a whole other level. Tormund trusted her and was punished for it in vile ways that made my stomach churn.

He tried to leave.

Fought to better himself and escape.

She tracked him down and delivered death to his door.

Tormund wanted out.

Yearned for death if it meant freedom.

When he was granted it, he never joined another hive out of fear others would suffer the same morbid fate as those he lost. He sought family, yet endured solitude to protect anyone else from the cloud of darkness and sorrow that followed him.

Dropping Connoll's hand, I blinked my way back to the here and now. I should have taken Death up on his offer. Now, it was too late. There was only one way this story was going to end, and I had no choice but to embrace it.

Lifting my chin, I strode to the side of the bed and stared down at the sleeping Tormund. I would never forget what he had done to me, but for the sake of my own peace of mind, I would forgive. He hurt me as he had been hurt. That wasn't an excuse. It was a fact that I hoped would offer him some solace in whatever awaited in the beyond.

I didn't need to utter the reversal incantation. Not anymore. Emerald energy birthed from my fingers as I laid a hand on the former vampire's shoulder. Life was drawn out of him, shriveling him to a mummified corpse mere seconds before he crumbled to a pile of dust.

Stumbling back, I retracted my magic. Hearing Bacon clicking around my ankles, I scooped my boy up and dropped him into the detective's arms. Connoll's mouth opened, yet before he could utter a word, I silenced him with one raised finger. "Stay here. Lock the door behind me. Do not come out until you get the signal that it's safe."

Connoll's fangs sprang free with alarm. "Octavia, we need to talk about this. What are you going to do?"

I hesitated at the door with one hand on its door frame. "I'm going to end this."

Any fear I had that he was going to protest further was put at ease when I heard the door lock click into place behind me. Whatever happened from this moment on began and ended… with me.

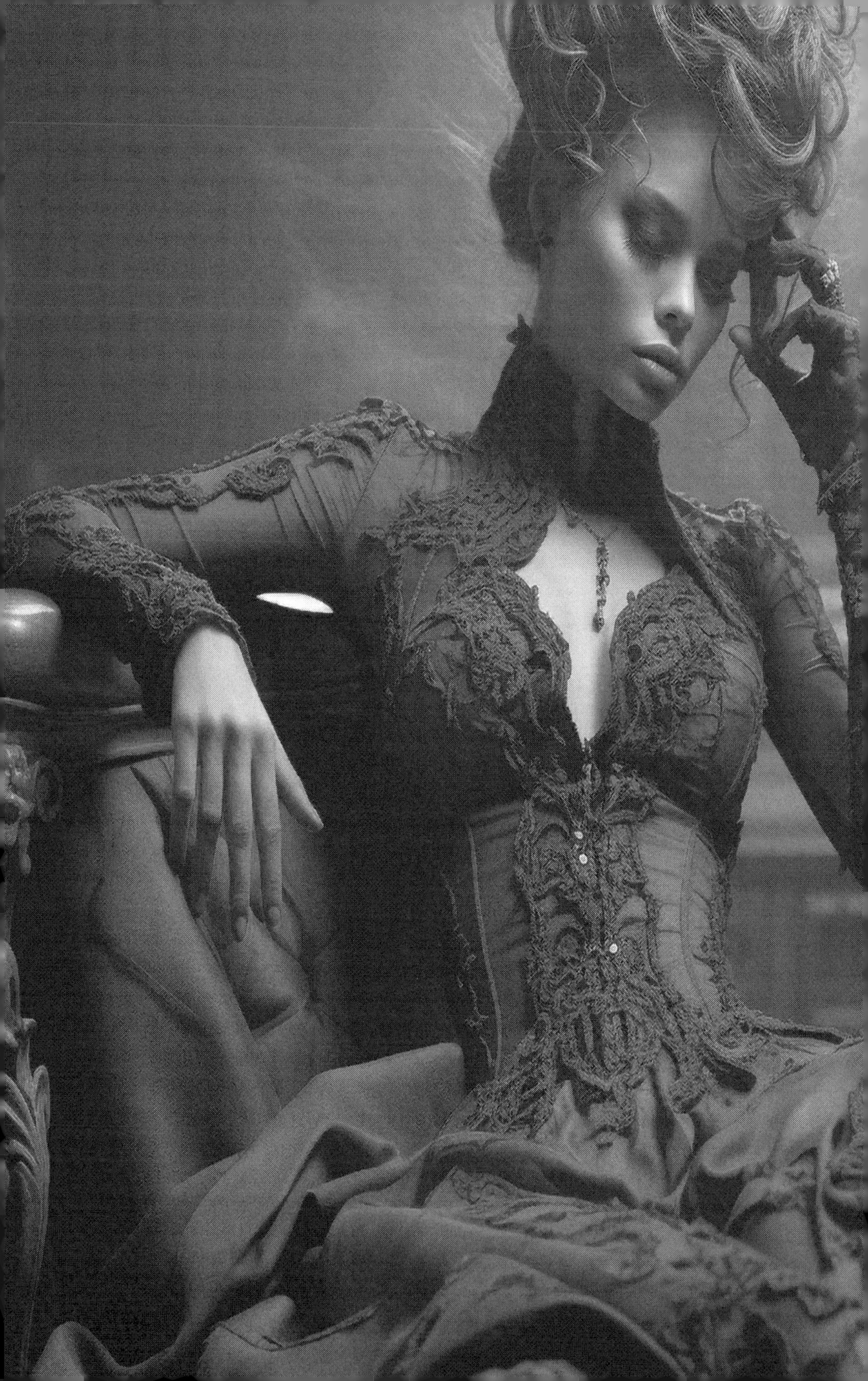

Chapter Nineteen
Octavia

You never know when you're going to need an army of the dead. Which is why you never throw one out if you happen to have it laying around. Pulling the book that would open the sliding shelves, I stared into the darkness beckoning within.

Filling my lungs, I drew energy from my core. Every fear. Every doubt. Every ounce of confidence. Every life that depended on me. I centered it all, drew my hands close to my chest, and cast it out in an emerald blast that illuminated the stone cavern with an ethereal glow.

Inhuman moans resonated from the depths. Scuffing and shuffling ambled up the winding stairs to heed my call. Dropping my hands to my sides, I waited. Rotting faces emerged from the blanket of black, dragging themselves onward with their stiff, jerky gait. Corpse after corpse answered my call to war.

Not giving myself time to doubt or reconsider, I snapped my fingers at my side to awaken a green flame meant to guide them. Turning on my heel, I led my decrepit troops into battle.

A necromancer flanked by her corpse minions. I had embraced the fate Sister Dina feared for me from the very start. There was a time when I was confident I would never fall into that fate. In my mind, ending up there meant spiraling into darkness, turning evil like characters in movies that were malicious for pure glee. Never once did I entertain the notion that the journey to this point would be out of love, duty, and self-sacrifice.

I'd received countless warnings. From Sister Dina. From Death himself. From my coven. From Reid. What would happen to me after this, I truthfully didn't know. But for my people—my makeshift family of misfits—I would be what was required of me. To hell with the consequences.

Down the stairs.

Across the grand foyer.

Out the front door.

Marching across the grounds.

My army grew as we moved. Every dead thing that fell under my umbrella of magic was dragged from death and animated just enough to join the ranks of my mindless minions. Bodies cast aside by the hive who resided in the manor before me. Woodland creatures who met their end in the surrounding forest. Gators who slunk into the murky waters behind the property as their final resting place. Without a thought in their empty skulls, they were drafted to my cause. They would fight for me without question. Kill at my whim. And be gone forever with a roll of my fingers.

We marched through the woods, only to be halted by tree branches coming alive around us to form a blockade. "In the name of the King of the Winter Court, we command you to stop!"

Beatific fairies melded from the scenery, seemingly appearing from nowhere. A pile of leaves took the form of a strapping, shirtless fae. The bark of a tree revealed a stunning chestnut-haired beauty who planted her hands on her hips and inserted herself as a commanding force.

I'd been in the South long enough to shrink her with a potent "bless your heart" look. So focused was she on looking in charge and intimidating that she seemed to miss the growing gaggle of death behind me. Her fae brethren, on the other hand, were shrinking back into the hiding spots they'd emerged from whilst trying not to piss themselves in fear.

Wise little fairies.

The guy who emerged from the pile of leaves raised a hand in the brazen speaker's direction. "Kerian, stop." Those were the only words he formed before disappearing into the landscape for the sake of self-preservation.

With wicked delight, I watched her take in the sight of the swelling army of decay behind me. "Carrion? Is that your name? What a funny coincidence. I could see you fitting right in with my friends here ... if you were so inclined."

All color draining from her features, Kerian stumbled back, her own blockade of branches retracting in her frantic backpedal. "I am merely doing the bidding of the King!"

Eyebrows raised, I jabbed a thumb over my shoulder. "I can let them know that. But I must admit they aren't the best listeners. I think that's because some of their ears have fallen off. That happens, you know."

Chin quivering, the trembling fae tried again to assert herself. "You have heard the King's demands!"

Holding one hand beside my face, I rolled my fingers in one direction and then the other, allowing the green flames to travel from one digit to the next. "Oh, he made himself perfectly clear. Deliver his daughter before sundown or all hell breaks loose. Some may say it already has."

A chorus of beastly groans rose up from the peanut gallery behind me, seconding that sentiment.

"I was... uh... tasked with ensuring you didn't attempt an escape." Kerian's gaze fixed on one of my Zombie-gators, her eyes bulging from their sockets. Not that I blamed her. He was cute in an ashy, missing an eyeball kind of way. I may have considered a full resurrection and keeping him, if I wasn't worried he would turn Bacon into pork rinds.

Eyes narrowing, I tilted my head. "Is this what a stealthy getaway looks like to you? That's not sarcasm. I'm genuinely asking because we might have a human-to-fae miscommunication happening here."

Kerian risked a glance at my face before turning her focus back to my horde. "I ... don't know what this is."

Finally, she was getting it. "This is me giving your boss what he wants. I'm going to go fetch your little fairy princess. You can join the fight or get the hell out of the way. What you don't want to do is get in my way, for obvious reasons." A flick of my wrist and my army surged forward in a false start meant to drive my point, and threat, home.

Gusts of winds rippled tree branches and Kerian blew away in a tumble of leaves. My message was received and the path before us was cleared.

There's nothing in the way now, Dotty. I'm coming for you.

With that as my driving thought, I resumed my march. Through the woods, down the street, striding towards the empty town with our numbers constantly growing. Not a person could be found in the houses, businesses, or milling anywhere around in Lavender Lotus. Nora must have been busy. Every citizen of the little burg now seemed to be wrapped up in this mess one way or another. Boots stomping over the concrete, that realization did give me a moment of pause. I had lost control of my horde before. They almost ate my pig. Hence the reason why I left my boy behind. I thought I had taken precautions, but now countless innocent lives could be caught in the crossfire.

My powers were growing in ways that weren't tested or trusted. All the more reason not to let myself waver or doubt. Hesitation could get everyone killed. Granted ... I could bring them all back, but with my powers spread that thin, chances were good they weren't going to come back right. A few would go through life like someone had twisted the top off their Oreo, figuratively speaking. So lost was I in my own thoughts and the chorus of haunting groans trailing me, that I nearly missed the dark silhouette leaning against a parking meter outside of the laundry mat.

Beautiful.

Hypnotic.

Alluring.

Death.

If it was possible, he was becoming even more attractive.

Then again, that could have been the daggers of danger flashing in the depths of his stare. Dressed in a stark black three-piece suit, he stuffed his hands into the pockets of his trousers and lifted his brows my way in open question. I hadn't heeded his warnings. My actions would have consequences, of that I had no doubt.

But not yet.

I couldn't let him stop me.

A raise of my hand tightened the ranks around me. Hobbling corpses moved closer, blocking Death's view of me entirely... and mine of him. They acted as my shield, for now. Though I was well aware they would never be enough to stop a being as powerful as him. My hope was a simple one. I just needed enough time to do what needed to be done.

He could rob me of my powers.

Deprive me of the ability to ever make a corpse so much as twitch again.

I would welcome it… if I could just overcome this last hurdle first.

One last ghoulish hoorah. Then I would willingly put it all behind me.

To my— albeit momentary—relief, Death didn't pursue me. He didn't have to. True disaster was waiting just around the bend. He likely knew that. As soon as the bowling alley came into view, my steps faltered for good reason. All the residents newly recruited by Nora surrounded the building with any weapons they could find. Chainsaws. Axes. Baseball bats. Tire irons. Each was held at the ready, the expressions of those wielding them frighteningly vacant.

The drums of war had sounded. No matter what happened from this moment forward … there would be blood.

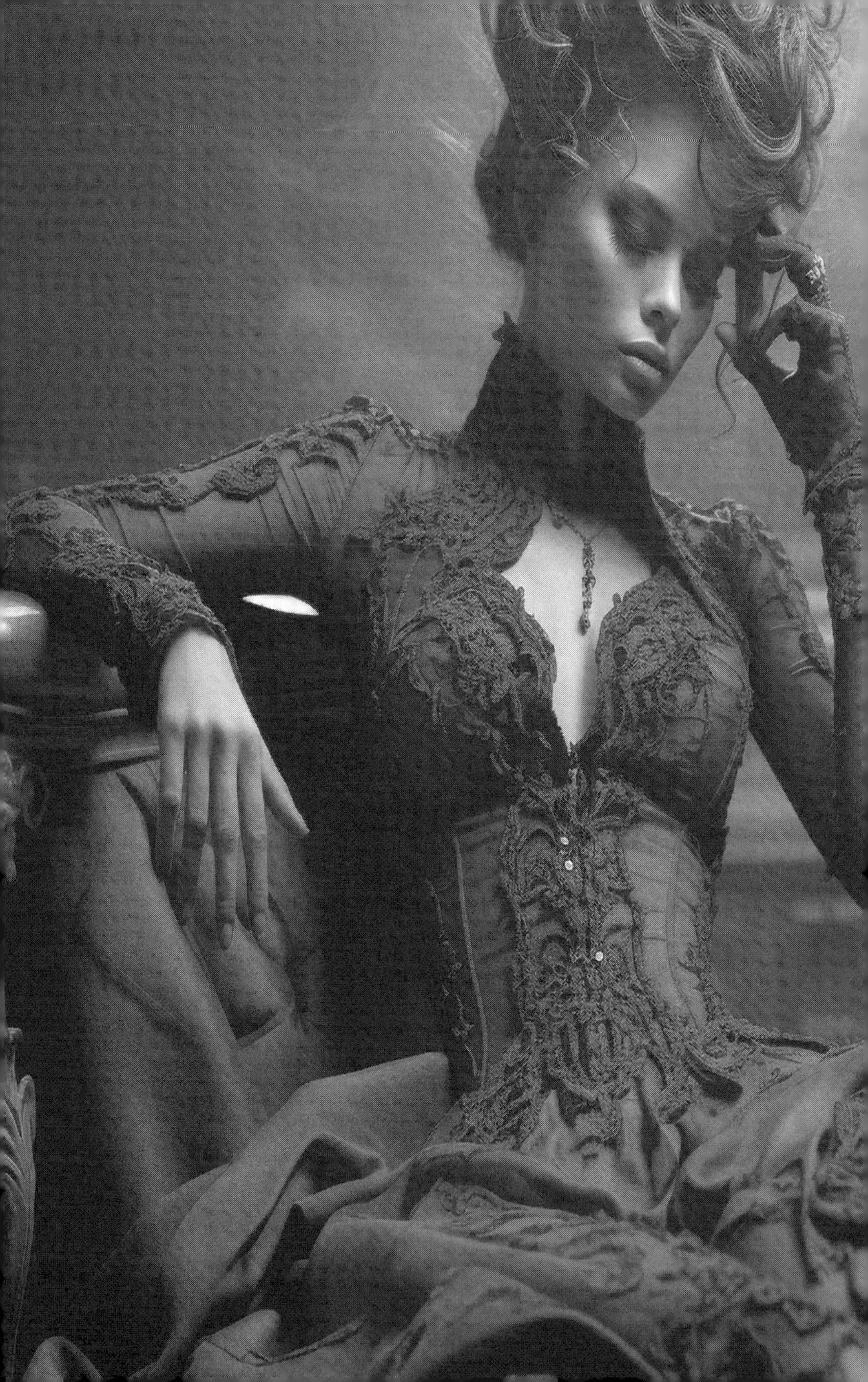

Chapter Twenty
Octavia

Fingers of dread raked up and down my spine, awakening bats of unease that flapped and churned in my gut. Whispering I'd lose control. Warning I couldn't trust myself. I forced those thoughts aside to the best of my ability—which was a laughably small margin. Squeezing my eyes shut, I let the pulsating power from my hands lick up my arms and engulf my shoulders in crackling emerald flames. When my eyes snapped open, tinges of black crept into the corners of my vision. Probably not a bad omen... right?

Chin to my chest, I whispered the words, knowing I could have conveyed them to each corpse behind me with a simple thought. "Bring me the vampire. Harm no one else."

A chorus of groans rose up in a lazy battle cry, and my horde shuffled forward at a speed that turtles would have found infuriatingly slow.

Lips parting with a pop, I called out to the bamboozled townsfolk protecting the smoke-filled bowling alley. "Now would be a good time to get out of the way. Not that you have to rush. I mean, you could probably take a nap first, run a brush through your hair, call an Uber, and still have plenty of time to mosey out of the way. But, ya know, when the threat arrives, it's still real. So, you know ... move."

None heeded my cautionary tale. Not that I expected them to. They were no more in control of their own minds than my army was. An ironic turn of events I planned to dissect in a moment of self-revelation once this was all over.

The two sides of the war met—finally—in a one-sided, violent collision. The people of Lavender Lotus came out swinging. Cracking skulls. Knocking eyeballs from sockets. Sending gray matter flying. It was a gruesome display, somehow made more horrific by the fact that my army didn't fight back or falter. They took each blow in stride because their nerve endings were as dead as they were, and kept ambling in the direction of the door.

I feared losing sight of my minions, because I didn't know the range of my control. (Were we talking like, drone or remote-control distance? Those were two very different units of measurement.) Playing it safe, I followed my masses, allowing some of the bigger cadavers to act as my own private security and protect me from flying tire irons and wide-swung bats. The waylay continued inside the bowling alley where I found people I knew and loved forced into the action.

Sister Dina whipped a bowling ball at a zombie's head and knocked it clear off his shoulders.

Paisley kicked the decapitated skull at the Dearly Departed Gator slithering her way.

The gator caught it in its jaws and chomped down with enough force to make bone bits spray.

And that was just what I caught out of the corner of my eye.

"Is this how you thought you'd win?" a nasally voice crackled through the bowling alley sound system.

I swiveled in search of who was speaking and spotted Dotty in a DJ sound booth behind all the lanes, holding the mic in her hand. I held my hands up alongside my face and let my flames stretch toward the ceiling. "It was plan A. Come on out and let me show you options B, C, and D. Sidenote: the D stands for death, not dickhead. Meaning it wasn't named after you."

"I see your lips moving and realize I must've given the false impression that I care what you have to say. I really don't. Not one bit. All I want is Tormund." Through the twelve-by-twelve, nicotine-stained window I watched Dotty grip her microphone in a two-handed hold. "Bring him to me and the rest of these meat sacks are yours."

Knowing she couldn't hear me, I shook my head.

"No?" she tsked through the crackling sound system. "You think you have control here because you brought the walking dead along? Girl, I have had the upper hand in this from the very start. I thought you knew that. But I guess you need more proof."

My corpse army beat at the door of the sound booth, cracking the wood into shrapnel that hadn't broken free... yet.

The fact that Dotty kept her gaze fixed on me without faltering should have been a warning, but I was trumped up on undead horde bravado. That shifted with five words that sent shivers of trepidation rushing through me.

"Nora, change of plans, doll."

Where Nora was, I couldn't say. Unfortunately, I didn't have to see her to feel her influence. The people of Lavender Lotus stopped fighting... but didn't drop their weapons. They came together in neat rows that stretched down the lanes, across the lobby, and out the front door. Off-putting, to be sure. But the next step was far worse. Each took whatever weapon they had and held it at the ready... to turn on themselves.

My breath caught in a fist of fear I hadn't anticipated. So many lives on the precipice of self-destruction. Yet a few recognizable faces in the crowd made this a much more poignant maneuver. Sister Dina pressed the claw of a crowbar to her own throat. Misty held a rumbling chainsaw at her side. Paisley dimpled the skin of her wrist with the blade of a knife. Every member of the quaint little burg was transfixed on self-destruction while I was powerless to prevent it.

What was I going to do? Order my horde to wrestle the weapons from their hands? That would end in the type of bloodshed Dotty was counting on. Out of options, I played the only card I had.

"Stand down!" My scream echoed off the walls and halted every corpse where they stood.

"Good girl," Dotty purred through the sound system before clicking it off. The door to the booth creaked open and out she stepped, looking like what you would get if you ordered a 1940s Hollywood starlet from Wish. "It's too bad it came to this. We gals could've been great friends. My fairy controlling human minds. You rallying the dead. Imagine all the things you could accomplish for me!" She gave a flirty giggle that made me want to rip one of the bolted-down chairs out of the floor and whip it at her.

That said, she had given something away without intending to. When she mentioned the fae princess, her gaze flicked to the bar in the back, complete with a tattered pool table and a dart board held together by duct tape.

Seeing this as my one and only opportunity to avoid a complete massacre, I raised my voice for the cheap seats (which could have been literally any chair in the nicotine-stained bowling hall.) "It doesn't have to be this way. Whatever you think is about to play out here, it doesn't have to."

With the palm of one hand, Dotty fluffed her platinum curls. "That's adorable, doll. But unless you have Tormund in your back pocket, I'm afraid it does."

"I wasn't talking to you." I kept my words clipped and measured. "And Tormund's dead, by the way. And not the up-and-walking-around version of about half the population here. I mean the dust to dust, ashes to ashes, blowing away on a breeze kind."

In a blink, Dotty's playful expression morphed to demonic rage. "What? No! You bitch. I'll have every measly human you care for skinned alive, and that boyfriend of yours turned into a fur coat!"

She started for me, and I flicked my wrist in her direction. That simple gesture was all it took for my rotting carcass allies to shuffle shoulder to shoulder in a blockade between us.

Taking advantage of the wall of bodies between us and well aware she could bulldoze through them with ease, I turned my full attention in the direction of the bar. "I know this isn't what you wanted, Nora. Connoll told me all about how your father exploited your gifts to build his own empire and that you ran away to escape that fate. Sure, making an orgy cult wasn't the best use of your time, but we all go a little nuts when we're out on our own for the first time. I get it. I drank no liquid other than Slurpees for three months straight. Girl, when I say I was pissing rainbows, I'm not even remotely kidding."

Composure a thing of the past, Dotty tried to climb or claw her way through the sea of corpses any way she could. Luckily for me, pain was an issue with which my soldiers no longer had to contend. "I will rip your eyes from their sockets and wear them like earrings!" the vampress fumed.

I jabbed one up-turned hand in Dotty's direction. "Think about it! She's controlling and manipulating you just like your father did. Is that really what you want?"

"She's worse," Nora rasped as she rose from behind the bar. Dried blood was crusted beneath her right nostril, and I counted at least three sets of bite marks on her throat. Dotty had not been kind to her. Chin quivering, the fairy princess broke down in sobs. "Please, I just... want to go... home."

"You are home! You belong to me!" Fangs exposed, the tendons of Dotty's neck bulged as she screamed. "If this bitch truly failed to deliver Tormund, we will feast on her as your first meal after I turn you. Then, we'll start a new family together. You need me!"

Sucking air through my teeth, I cringed. "Eek. You know who screams things like you need me? Someone you absolutely do not need. She's one vampire, Nora. Yes, she's old and powerful, but—"

Dotty was indignant. "Who are you calling old, you pink-haired trollop?"

"See? That's an old-ass thing to say." I pointed one finger Dotty's way while keeping my focus locked on the trembling fae. "Look at our numbers, Nora. Yours and mine together. We band together, and we can walk out of here without anyone else getting hurt." I jerked my head in Dotty's direction. "Unless we want them to be."

"No!" Dotty shoved one zombie aside, then another. To her annoyance, more of them easily filled the vacated space. "You can't do this! All I want is Tormund. Give him to me, or I won't stop until I kill them all! Every last mortal in this town!"

Something that resembled hope built behind Nora's eyes, yet it was edged by hesitant fear. "How do I know I can trust you and you won't turn your zombies on me?"

"Zombie is such an ugly word. I prefer mortally challenged," I quipped. An alliance was needed to prevent a bloodbath. For that to happen, Nora required proof we were on the same side. And I knew the perfect way. "The vampire bent you to her will. From the looks of you, by violent means. It seems only right you get the opportunity to return the favor." Fingers splayed, I called on the green wisps to churn and roil up my arms. Chin dropped to my chest, I stretched my essence to each rotting being in my brigade. "Hold her."

The oh-so-patient dead who had to this point allowed Dotty to hit, kick, and claw at them, snapped to attention. At my command, they closed in. I couldn't say for certain how many of them it would take to subdue the pissed-off vampress, but I knew how many they used. A swarm of no less than twenty swarmed Dotty, seizing any parts of her they could. Wrists. Arms. Torso. Shoulders. Back. Legs. Neck. Hair. They held tight as she flailed, preventing her from breaking free even as a few of their own body parts fell off.

I approached once she was secured, leading with one upturned hand that crackled with a show of my power. "I believe we played this game once before and you weren't a fan."

Dotty's eyes bulged and she threw her body back in a frantic attempt to get away. "No! Stay away from me! Don't touch me with your filthy magic!"

I slapped my hand to her clavicle, reveling in how her heart lurched to life beneath my touch. Mouth falling open, her shrieks echoed through the otherwise quiet alley in a deafening soundtrack.

Job done, I turned to Nora. "She'll be mortal for little more than an hour. Meaning she can be hurt, harmed, or even killed. Does that earn me your trust enough to join our resources and get these people the fuck out of here?"

Nora took a tentative step forward. "She's... mortal?"

I dipped my head in a nod of confirmation. "Blood pumping and all. So how about you have these people drop their weapons and we'll let them go home?"

Inching past Paisley, Nora plucked the blade from her hand. I thought that was a step in the right direction... for about fifteen seconds. That's how long it took for an expression that could only be described as fixated madness to steal over her features. She ran at Dotty and with a bold swipe of her knife, opened an angry gash across the vampire's breast bone. Blood bloomed from the wound, streaking the draped neckline of Dotty's silk dress in red splatter.

A fresh scream ripped from Dotty's lungs, earning a maniacal smile that lifted the fae's heart-shaped lips.

Feeling the control I had slipping, knots of unease twisted in my gut. "Okay, so you can see for yourself I'm a necromancer of my word. Dotty has no choice but to let us walk out of here. Or we can kill her. Your choice. That said, I think first and foremost we should take advantage of this opportunity and let these innocent people walk out of here."

Nora tucked a lock of her unwashed, knotted hair behind her ear. Her head tilted as she considered me. "We will. I want to put this whole nightmare behind me more than anyone."

"I wouldn't say anyone," I muttered under my breath, my stare drifting to the faces of the people I cared for who were still trapped by Nora's will.

"We've all suffered," Nora agreed, seemingly plucking that very thought from my head. "And that is why she must pay."

Eyebrows darting to my hairline, I pressed my lips together in a thin line. "I get wanting retribution, believe me. But we need to make these people our priority."

"Don't you see?" Nora's stare pleaded for me to understand. "She'll never stop chasing us. As long as she walks this earth, we'll never be free."

Dotty's head snapped in one direction then the other in search of some way to escape the shit storm of her own creation. "No, no! I won't! All I want is Tormund. This was all about him. Give him back to me and you'll never see or hear from either of us again!"

Nora took a bold step forward, seized a handful of Dotty's platinum hair, and wrenched her head back just as I had watched the vampire do to her. "Didn't you hear? Your boy-toy is dead. But don't worry. You'll be reunited with him soon enough." Taking one wide step back, Nora turned the blade in her hand and passed it to Paisley, who approached by a will not her own. There was nothing behind her eyes; her body moved as part of a game she wasn't playing.

"Nora, what are you doing? We need to go." I thought about commanding my minions to free Dotty and give her a chance to run, but there were too many innocent people there for me to take that kind of risk.

"And we will." Nora swatted my words away with a flick of her wrist. "Right after Dotty feels a fraction of what she's put me through."

"W-what are you going to do?" Dotty's voice betrayed her by quaking.

In place of an answer, Paisley caught Dotty's wrist and delivered one swift cut to her forearm.

Dotty's mouth fell open, but before a sound left her throat, Nora locked eyes with her. "Silence! That's right. You're human. I can control your mind now, too. And that means it's time for a little payback. Every person you hurt in here is going to make one small slice into your flesh. Paying back blood for blood. If you die by a thousand small cuts, so be it. But it's going to be slow … and agonizing … the same merciless treatment you showed us."

Tears tracked down Dotty's cheeks, yet her mouth remained firmly clamped shut.

Brow furrowed, I tried to inject myself into the spiraling situation. "Nora, I get why you're…" My right knee buckled. I clamped a hand on the nearest zombie to steady myself. Darkness crept into the edges of my vision, my head swimming. For reasons I couldn't understand, everything went black and the floor rose to meet me.

My eyes opened to a hand extended to help me up. I closed my fingers around it without question and was heaved to my feet like I weighed nothing more than a feather. The world that had been spinning around me in a dizzying array regained focus on the handsome face of Death. As soon as my feet were under me, I dropped his hand as if it scorched me. Like every other encounter we'd had, everything vanished around us. Considering the debacle I'd found myself in, it was the worst possible moment.

"No, damn it!" I pushed away from him in hopes it would propel me back to reality. "Not now. You can't do this! I can't be here!"

The sleeves of his button-down shirt were rolled up his forearms, his hands plunged into the pockets of his navy slacks. "Don't be coy, Octavia. You know exactly what this is. You were warned."

Desperation raising my voice to a shrill shriek, I closed my hands into fists to fight the urge to grab the creature of death. Thankfully, I held back. I'd done some dumb shit in my life, but even I knew not to manhandle Death. "I knew the consequences and tried not to let things come to this. Believe me, I did. Unfortunately, I didn't have a choice. I know I have no right to ask for anything. Still, I am begging you to let me see this through before you do whatever it is you're going to do. Please." I clamped my hands together in prayer, hoping he had even one ounce of compassion I could play to.

Death closed the distance between us, immediately mesmerizing me with the intensity of his magnetic gaze. "My beautiful queen, how I longed for you to reach out for me, that I may spare you even an ounce of agony. Yet you are so fiercely independent you feel you must take the weight of the world onto your delicate shoulders."

My face tipped up to his, battling the urge to eliminate those pesky few inches between us. The nearer my proximity to him, the more common sense fluttered right out of my head. "You can take my powers. I'm okay with that. I'll never raise another corpse again. It'll be a welcome relief. But please, let me finish what I started here. Let me save the lives of these people. Then, I'll return my horde to oblivion and happily take my place within the mediocrity of everyday life."

Death sucked air through his teeth and grimaced. "Oh, my darling. If only it were that easy. I'm afraid I never said anything about taking your powers."

My forehead creased. "What? You said…"

"I said you would lose the ability to give life." The instant the words left his delectable lips his hand shot out, his fingers digging into my abdomen. "From this moment on, only death resides in your womb. Now, the children to whom you were to pass your talents on will never be. Who they were to save and the good they would have done has all been… erased. I am so very sorry, Octavia. I sincerely didn't want it to come to this."

I stumbled back, folded in half by a dull ache that throbbed through my core. Gutted by emptiness. Filleted by a future that would never come. I could feel it as it was ripped away from me.

Truth be told, I never gave much thought to having a family of my own until the hollowness of what I'd lost resonated through me. "H-how could you?"

"Seek me out, my queen." Something between regret and promise swirled in the depths of his stare. "Hold only me responsible for this, and… come for me."

With that acting as his parting sentiment, Death faded before my eyes and forced me back into the scene of chaos and destruction.

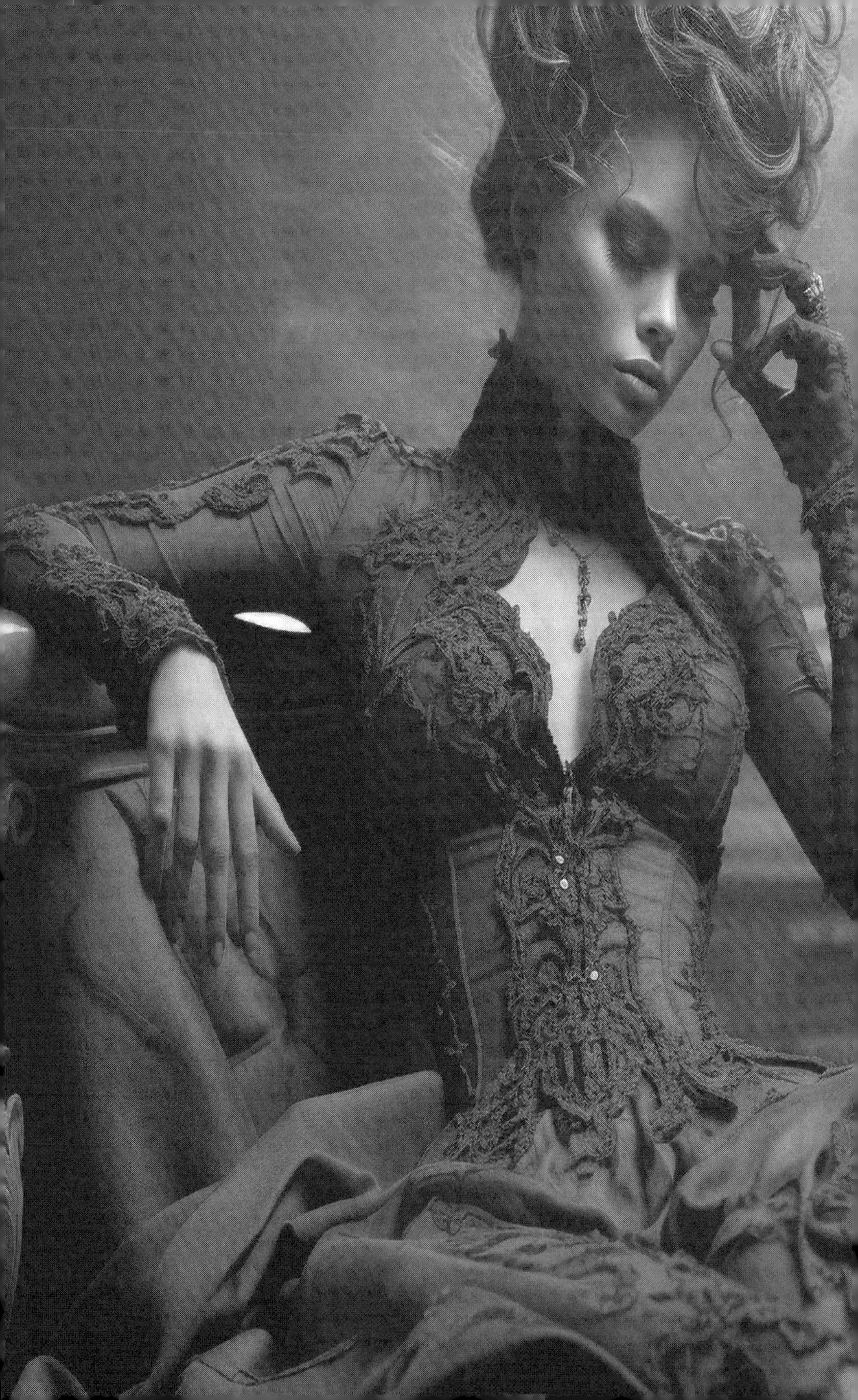

Chapter Twenty-One
Octavia

It felt as though I'd only been gone seconds, a journey into another time and space that lasted merely a blink. But however long I had actually checked out was enough time for Dotty to be sliced and diced into ribbons. Her slumped form lay in a pool of blood on the floor, covered in hundreds of cuts encompassing every inch of her exposed flesh. Torso sliced open. Arteries cut in two. Flesh torn to bone. Face down, her platinum hair floated in a pool of her own blood.

Still on the floor where I fell, I planted one hand to steady myself and rose on shaky legs.

As I turned out, my absence was felt in a way I couldn't have fathomed. Rushing to my side, Nora hooked her arm through mine and hoisted me the rest of the way to standing. "Octavia! I don't know what just happened, but we need you."

The rapid movement caused my head to spin and my stomach to lurch. "What? Did someone chip the knife when they were helping you turn Dotty into hamburger? Because it seems you more than handled this particular situation."

"Things got out of hand there, I admit that." The fairy princess cringed in the direction of the pile of Dotty parts. "She'll turn to dust when your touch wears off, right? You know what? That doesn't matter right now. We can dispose of the body later, if need be."

"As sentiments to wake up go, that one is not the best."

Nora rushed on in a long-winded ramble like I hadn't spoken at all. "You want to be allies? Now is the time. You help me, and you have my word I will let all these people go. Right now, I need your army to help me get the hell out of here."

My hand instinctively went to my stomach, where needles of pain stabbed deep into my core. "Catch me up; what did I miss? From where I'm standing, it seems you could walk right out the door." I felt as if I'd woken in the middle of a play and didn't know my next lines.

"Your horde went slack when you did, and we need them back. More accurately, I need them back. Stat." Nora glanced to the door, anxiously chewing on her lower lip. "My father and his army are outside. He'll kill everyone in here if I don't go with him."

Was it on the tip of my tongue to declare that to be her problem and not mine? Absolutely. But I had enough sense to know that wouldn't be productive in any way. Tongue feeling swollen and thick in my mouth, I battled my way back to some semblance of coherency. "What... is it you want me to do?"

Nora grabbed both my hands in hers, which were trembling in fear. "We can combine our forces and fight our way out of here. My father's warriors have surrounded the bowling alley. But if we create a diversion, I can escape into the night. You and this town will never see me again. I'll even forget that sexy-ass wolf-man of yours exists. You have my word."

Normally, I considered myself a rather quick-witted person, always ready with a sharp retort. This was not one of those moments. A lot had happened in a short enough span of time to leave me reeling.

Was what Death said true?

If so, how did I feel about it?

Those were questions I needed time to mull over and process. Unfortunately, a quiet moment of reflection wasn't on deck. "Wait ... what now?"

The doors to the bowling alley burst open and a flood of fae soldiers spilled inside.

"There's no time for this!" Nora didn't bother trying to explain again. Shoving away from me, she dipped her chin to her chest and let her voice boom off the walls. "My family! Protect me! Become a human shield around me!"

The people of Lavender Lotus moved at her command, positioning themselves between Nora and the Winter Court warriors surrounding us.

"No..." I uttered the word as if I could somehow deny what was playing out before me. Then, a second time with fiery conviction. "No! Nora, you can't do this. If you sacrifice these people to save yourself, you'll be no better than Dotty, using and abusing them just as she did to you."

Hair swept across the middle of Nora's back as she whipped her head in my direction. "I can't go with them and become my father's pawn again. I refuse to go back to sacrificing my own life and happiness while he and his kingdom enjoy the spoils of my efforts. I'd sooner die!"

"There's no need for that," the King himself interjected as he followed another wave of soldiers in. Nose crinkling at the sight of my horde, he scoffed in open disgust. "I knew following the necromancer would prove worthwhile, yet I'm afraid I miscalculated the stench that would accompany her."

I snorted. "Bold of you to blame me for the smell, and not the rotting corpses. But whatever, dick."

"Octavia! He's royalty!" Nora gasped, one hand fluttering to her throat.

"My apologies." I dipped in a melodramatic curtsey. "Your royal dickness."

"I will not lower myself by speaking directly to a being of such unnatural magicks." Folding his arms over his middle, the King peered down his pointed nose at me.

"There is nothing unnatural about what I do," I countered, only to have the sentiment punctuated by the bottom jaw falling off the animated corpse nearest to me. "Touche', gravity."

My awkwardly morbid interlude was glossed right over for their family drama… into which Nora fully intended to drag as many people as she deemed necessary. A furrow of her brow, and the citizens of Lavender Lotus arced back with weapons in hand.

"I won't go with you, Father. I refuse. I'll make these humans fight until the bitter end before I become a tool for you to wield again!"

Head leaned her way, I whispered out of the corner of my mouth, "You see the irony in that statement, right?"

The king's soldiers drew spears from the sheaths on their backs. But before the threat of violence could erupt, the King of the Winter Court raised one hand to halt them. "That won't be necessary, Nora. For, you see, my final frost is imminent."

Nora gasped.

The fae warriors swooned.

The jawless zombie beside me groaned in question.

I was with him, having no clue what was happening. "Is he becoming a snowbird? Spending the winter months in tropical climates playing pickle ball? What am I missing?"

Ignoring me entirely, Nora inched towards her father on tentative steps. "You can't possibly know that!"

His head hung in sorrow. "I do. The royal oracles have confirmed it."

Chin quivering, tears welled in Nora's eyes. "Wh-what does this mean? What are you saying?"

The hint of a smile warmed the king's features. "Well, if you're going to be dense and need it spelled out to you, the throne is in need of a successor. Your brother is a tainted bloodsucker. That means the only other option to be crowned... is you."

Nora blinked his way, processing so slowly I could practically see a loading symbol over her head. "You don't mean...?"

Both palms raised, the king bowed to his daughter. "The throne is yours, Nora, Queen of the Winter Court, if you want it."

Her gaze flicked to her army of unwilling minions, considering them as if seeing them for the first time. "I... would be queen?"

"If you so desire." The king lifted one hand in warning to his soldiers. "In the name of the elements, put your weapons away. I will not have you threatening your future queen."

Nora covered her mouth with both hands, her eyes bulging in shock and awe. "Future queen?" She tried the title on. Sampling it. Tasting it.

"If you'll accept it and all the responsibilities that accompany it, my child." This time, a beaming smile spread across his features.

Nora sucked in her cheeks, then let her lips part with a pop. "And that means all of these soldiers," with a roll of her wrist, she gestured to the same fae who had been pointing spears at her mere seconds ago, "they would answer to..." She trailed off, looking to her father with her eyebrows raised expectantly.

The king folded his hands in front of him. "Why you, of course."

"Innnnnn-teresting." She drew the word out as if genuinely deliberating what her father laid out before her, which fooled exactly no one. Chances were likely even my zombie horde saw the writing on the walls. Sure enough, the fairy princess's agenda flipped like a switch. Swiveling my way, she grabbed my hand in both of hers. "Thank you so much, Octavia. You can have your people back. Give that sexy wolf of yours my love. He's not a snack, but a whole damned meal. I might even have considered taking him as a consort if his lupine blood wasn't considered tainted among my kind. Queens can't be associated with that kind of thing. You know how it is."

"I absolutely do not, but thank you for allowing me to keep my boyfriend." Sarcasm dripped from my tone, to which she seemed completely oblivious.

Personality wise, it turned out fairies were just the fucking worst.

"Oh, of course!" she gushed. "Please know, you will always be considered an ally to the Winter Court." Nora practically skipped to her father's side—you remember, the same guy she was ready to go to war with a few blinks ago. Linking her arm with his, she hugged it tightly to her chest. "Can we talk about my crown, Daddy? I would love to have something specially designed. I'm envisioning a gorgeous spectacle comprised completely of jewels."

Patting his daughter's hand on his arm indulgently, the king steered them both in the direction of the door with their legion of soldiers falling into step behind them. "Remember, child, the throne—and crown—don't become yours until I die."

Nora let one shoulder rise and fall. "Still, it doesn't hurt to plan ahead."

"Quite right," the king chuckled.

Lips pursed, I nodded to myself and muttered under my breath. "Turns out, I hate fairies." Clearing my throat, I called out. "Uh... princess?"

The soldiers spun on me with their spears pointed my way, incensed that I would dare speak to their soon-to-be-queen. All of which Nora found delightful.

Laughter bubbling from her lips, she swatted at the air with one hand. "Oh, for the elements! Didn't you all hear me? She's an ally! There's no need to kill her just to please me."

Yep, I definitely hated fairies.

"What is it you need, my necromancer friend?" Despite still looking like a war criminal due to Dotty's cruelty, Nora assumed the role of a royal and held her head high and haughty.

Wetting my lips, I silently gestured to the humans still trapped under her thrall.

Brow furrowed, she glanced around, blinking her confusion until the realization set in. "Oh! Of course!"

I was breathing a sigh of relief when I realized one crucial detail I'd missed. "Wait! One second!" I shot a quick glance at the Zombie Gator. "Scarecrow, I'll miss you most of all." With a sigh, I filled my lungs to capacity and let a blast of black-tinted energy pulse out. My corpse army crumbled to dust that coated the floors, bowling balls, and plastic furniture. When the last of them fell, I gave Nora the nod. "Go ahead. Now we don't need to worry about my army eating yours."

Another giggle, then Nora dipped her head and concentrated. The people of Lavender Lotus blinked their way back to clarity. Some openly wept their relief. Others embraced. A few crumbled to the ground in exhaustion. Of course, my attention went to my people.

Misty immediately checked in with every member of her pack to make sure they were okay.

Sister Dina and Paisley hugged and inspected each other for injuries.

No real surprise that once she was secure in the fact that her love was okay, the High Priestess noticed the thick layer of dust covering the alley and cast a side glance my way. "Do I even want to know what this mess is all about or why I have a sinking feeling it has something to do with you?"

"I'll leave you to deal with this. Tah!" Giving me a finger wave over her shoulder, Nora sauntered out with her father. "So, about my coronation…"

"I'll be dead for it," her father stated matter-of-factly.

"That means I can orchestrate it however I like!" she chirped. "I envision a sea of flowers and a lavender gown to complement my fair complexion." She was still hashing out the details as the fae filed out and disappeared into the night.

"Octavia?" Sister Dina pressed. "We have you to thank for our freedom, do we not?"

Scratching my nose ring with my pinkie nail, I gave a one-shoulder shrug. "It's what I do."

"Do I need to know how you accomplished this?" Fingers laced with that of her love, Dina raised Paisley's hand to dot a kiss between her knuckles. The pre-Lavender Lotus Dina would have demanded every detail of what transpired, or else enacted some sort of incantation to allow her to see it for herself. Yet the ebony beauty before me, who only had eyes for Paisley, seemed to be making her inquiries out of habit and not actual concern.

I couldn't help but feel a twinge of guilt knowing I had seemingly earned and betrayed her trust in the same night. Skirting around the issue, I offered a tight-lipped grin. "There will be plenty of time to talk about that after you've all had a chance to rest and recover. For tonight, let's focus on getting everyone home."

With a nod of agreement, Dina unlaced her fingers from that of her love and walked to me with resolute strides. Cradling my face between her palms, she pressed a kiss to my forehead. "I am so very blessed to consider you family. Will you be coming back to the house with us, or are you headed back to that opulent manor of yours?"

"I'll go back to the manor to make sure Reid is free from Nora's fuckery. But I'll stop by in the morning to check up on you both." I spoke around the lump that had formed in my throat.

"Language, Miss." Dina booped my nose, then backed towards Paisley and the exit. "Come over early. I'll make us all a well-deserved breakfast buffet."

All I could do was nod. For years, the wayward band of misfits I'd bonded with had become the only family I needed. So why did my heart ache that the possibility of anything more had been stolen from me?

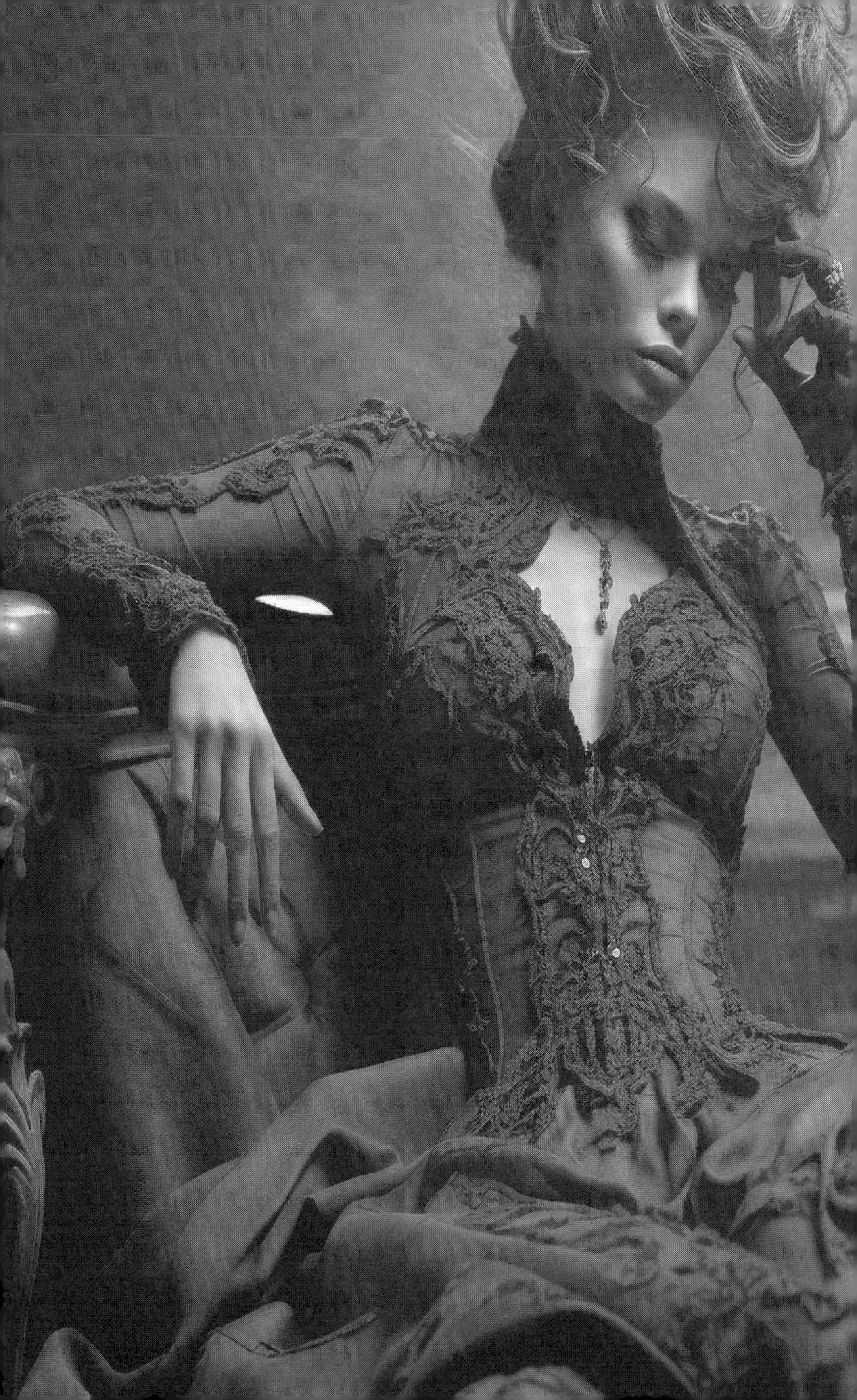

Chapter Twenty-Two
Octavia

Misty had been shopping at the Piggly Wiggly for ingredients to make fresh pico de gallo when Nora sashayed through the sliding doors and recruited her, against her will, to her pain and pleasure cult. Sure, nothing but a hot damned mess followed. However... that did mean that her truck was within walking distance from the bowling alley. In light of everything, I chose to celebrate the small victories. Even if it followed a zombies versus fairies showdown—which thankfully resulted in moderate bloodshed and minimal loss of limbs. Except for the bitch who masterminded the whole ordeal and the corpses whose parts fell off—the latter being a preexisting condition, in my opinion.

Regardless, it meant I didn't have to make the long walk back to the manor on foot. Granted, I rode on the back of my Zombie Gator for a good portion of the trip into town, but it was still quite a trek. And that made the drive back to the manor in an actual vehicle a delightful change of pace. The extra blessing was that Misty and I matched each other's energy ... and rode in silence. After everything that had happened, we both had our windows down and were enjoying the night breeze. The Alpha had her elbow propped on the window ledge with her free hand gripping the steering wheel. I leaned my head out the open window and let the crisp night air lash at my face. So many thoughts swirled through my mind, exhaustion making it impossible to focus on just one.

That was until the tires crunched over the gravel of the manor driveway and my thoughts turned to only one thing: Reid. As the headlights bobbed up the drive, they illuminated his god-like frame. Lifting my chin off the car door, I squinted into the glow of the lights. My breath caught when I saw him break into a sprint. The way he moved. How he pumped his arms. His muscular thighs straining against the fabric of his jeans. I didn't need anything more than his silhouette to recognize him.

Reid.

My Reid.

Back to me and one hundred percent himself.

Misty barely had time to ease the truck to a stop before I wrenched open the door and leapt out. I skidded to find my footing, raw determination keeping me upright.

"I'm going to go ahead and go. You seem to have things under control here." Misty chuckled as I slammed the truck door shut behind me. The Alpha threw it into reverse and backed down the driveway as I broke into a sprint straight towards my wolf-man.

Reid's shoulders hunched forward as he ran, his posture hinting at the lupine within. The long waves of his hair rode the wind behind him with each of his wide strides. He was sex on two legs. A freight train of desire racing for me.

We collided with each other midway across the yard. Our lips met with urgent need, a surge of desire threatening to consume us both. His hands seized my waist and lifted me up like I weighed nothing at all. I wrapped my legs around his hips, drawing him closer still.

A low growl of appreciation rumbled from his chest as I playfully bit his lower lip. Both hands cupping my ass, he carried me back into the manor. I couldn't tell you one thing about the route we took. My attention was stolen by the white-hot need pulsing through my core as I ran my hands across the broad terrain of his back. Life had served me such a heaping platter of shit as of late that I hadn't been able to contemplate just how much I missed him… until now.

Every cell of my body fired with electric longing. All I wanted was a space—any would do—where I could stake claim to every impressive inch of him. The tips of his fingers were venturing towards the heat between my legs when we burst through the front door. At the base of the stairs, I curled my fingers under the bottom hem of his black t-shirt and tugged it over his head. Halfway up, our breaths coming in unsteady pants, he eased me down on the stairs and pressed himself against me in an enticing tease. Hand venturing further down my leg, he raised my thigh to grind himself against me.

We likely would have shed the last of our inhibitions and done it right there on the stairs, had we not been interrupted by a high-pitched squeal coming from the second floor. Bacon's hooves tippy-tapped over for an ill-timed interruption to our reunion. In an incredibly confusing sensory moment, I had a sexy wolfman panting his hot breath against my neck while Bacon's cold little snout nudged my cheek.

Head falling forward, the scruff of Reid's cheek brushed mine as he chuckled against my ear. "Any chance you're suddenly okay with swine voyeurism?"

Inching my way out from under him, I eased myself to sitting. "I just don't think I could look him in the eye again after that."

Reid filled his lungs to capacity, his exhale sounding like more of a growl. "Okay, then on to plan B. Out of the way, Porky." With a gentle hand, he eased Bacon aside and scooped me up in his embrace.

Wrapping myself around him, I glanced over Reid's muscular shoulder to my little pork tenderloin. "Bacon, stay. Give me twenty minutes and I'll make you popcorn."

Reid pulled back, chin to his chest. "Really? Only twenty?"

Lips pursed, I tried again. "Thirty? Forty? Fuck it. Bacon, take a nap, buddy. I'll order you a pizza. I promise."

They say pigs are smart. I think my boy had this all planned out. With a contented little snort, he trotted downstairs with his curly-tail bobbing behind him.

Snaking my arms around Reid's neck, I teased his lips with mine. "We're on the clock, cowboy. I'd move, if I were you."

To my absolute delight, he needed no further invitation.

insert piggy picture

Sweaty and satisfied, I rested my head on Reid's broad chest with one bare leg draped over his. My index finger traced his nipple, which perked at my touch. "I guess I don't need to say I missed you. I feel I made that known with that second position."

Reid dipped his head to dot a kiss into my tussled hair. "Your flexibility was as impressive as it was a delightful little treat. But... and hear me out before you get mad... I didn't miss you. Because I was never without you."

A coy smile twined over my lips. "Is this where you say I was always with you in spirit? Look at you, being all sappy."

Reid curled one knuckle under my chin and tipped my face to meet his. "No, I mean literally. I have been with you this whole time."

Eyes narrowing, I played along. "Are we talking in a creepy watching-you-sleep way? Because, and I mean this in the most respectful way possible, your attributes can wake this girl up any time."

Reid leaned in for a kiss, awakening fresh fingers of hot longing that crept up my thighs. "Look at you, angling for round two while I'm trying to be sincere."

With the heat of his breath on my passion-raw lips, I fought past the cloud of desire fogging my brain. Kind of. Even as I spoke, I reached under the covers to make my intentions known. "I'm listening, I promise."

Head falling back against the pillow, Reid threw one arm over his head and closed his eyes in appreciation. "I hate to bring up painful topics, but it has to do with while I was under Nora's control."

My hand hesitated. "Tell me about it."

Chest swelling with a deep inhale, he began. "I don't remember much at the beginning. But when Dotty began her reign of cruelty, the fairy had mercy... on me, at least. I can't speak for the others."

I pressed a kiss to his stomach and inched lower. "Go on."

A low chuckle reverberated through him. "I'm trying, but you're making it hard."

I glanced at the tented blanket. "I can see that."

"Wily minx." Hooking his arms under mine, Reid flipped me over and pinned me beneath his massive physique. "As much as I would love for you to keep that up, I want you to hear this. While my body was being used to further the vampire's agenda, Nora built a failsafe in my mind where I could escape. It was a perfect existence I could sink into and find happiness."

Peering up at his sweat dampened face, I fought to keep my hands to myself... for now. "What did it look like?"

Reid dropped down onto one elbow and nestled in alongside me. "It was our future. Yours and mine. We had built a life together and it was all I could ever want. It wasn't the typical suburban, white picket fence existence. That's not us. Instead, we were still traveling the country, battling all sorts of ghouls and goblins—"

"Goblins are surprisingly docile," I injected, hiding a yawn of exhaustion behind my hand. "I have no desire to ever battle one. It would be like kicking an, albeit ugly, puppy."

"Noted." Reid gave a lock of my hair a playful tug. "In this other world, Bacon was there, of course. But he wasn't the only one."

I glanced towards the hallway at the mention of my boy, knowing full well it wouldn't be long before he was pawing at the door. "I can't handle more pigs. He's a high maintenance swine."

"That he is, but that's not what I meant. We had a family of our own." Reid studied the lines of my face, watching my reaction.

My mouth fell open. Fate couldn't possibly be that cruel, could it? "Family? Is that something you ... want?"

A sheepish smile added boyish charm to his rugged features. "I hadn't thought about it much before, but now?

Yeah, I do. We had two boys and a girl. Octavia, I didn't just see them; I knew them. Their personalities. Their laughs. How it felt when their little hands closed around my fingers. They were real to me. So much so, that I miss them with my whole heart even now. I completely believe that's the future waiting for us. When we're both ready, of course."

I had to believe he tagged on that last part after misconstruing the anguish carved on my features as doubt. Swallowing hard, I croaked my question around the lump of emotion lodged in my throat. "That's a future you need?"

Inching down my frame, he nestled in with his head on my chest and his silky hair tickling my side. "Only with you. Being stuck in wolf form these last few days, there was so much I wanted to say and couldn't. The biggest being that I love you, Octavia Hollows."

Grateful he was no longer looking at my face, I freely let the tears slip down my cheeks unchecked. "I love you, too." I sniffed, unsure what that meant anymore. What he wanted was the one thing I couldn't offer, not anymore. "So much. But... I have to ask... what if that's a future I can't give you?"

Silence.

"Really? It's that important?"

Muscles falling slack, his only response came in the form of a chorus of soft snores.

My head fell back against the pillow, soft sobs shaking my shoulders. I turned my cheek to the side to wipe my face with the back of my hand when I caught sight of something beckoning to me in the night sky.

The eyes of Death stared back at me from amongst the stars. Taunting. Daring. Summoning me with the last words he spoke to me. "Seek me out, my queen. Hold only me responsible for this, and... come for me."

He did this.

He could undo it.

Jaw clenched tight, my grief was chased away by raw determination.

Death had made an enemy out of me.

And now… I was coming for him.

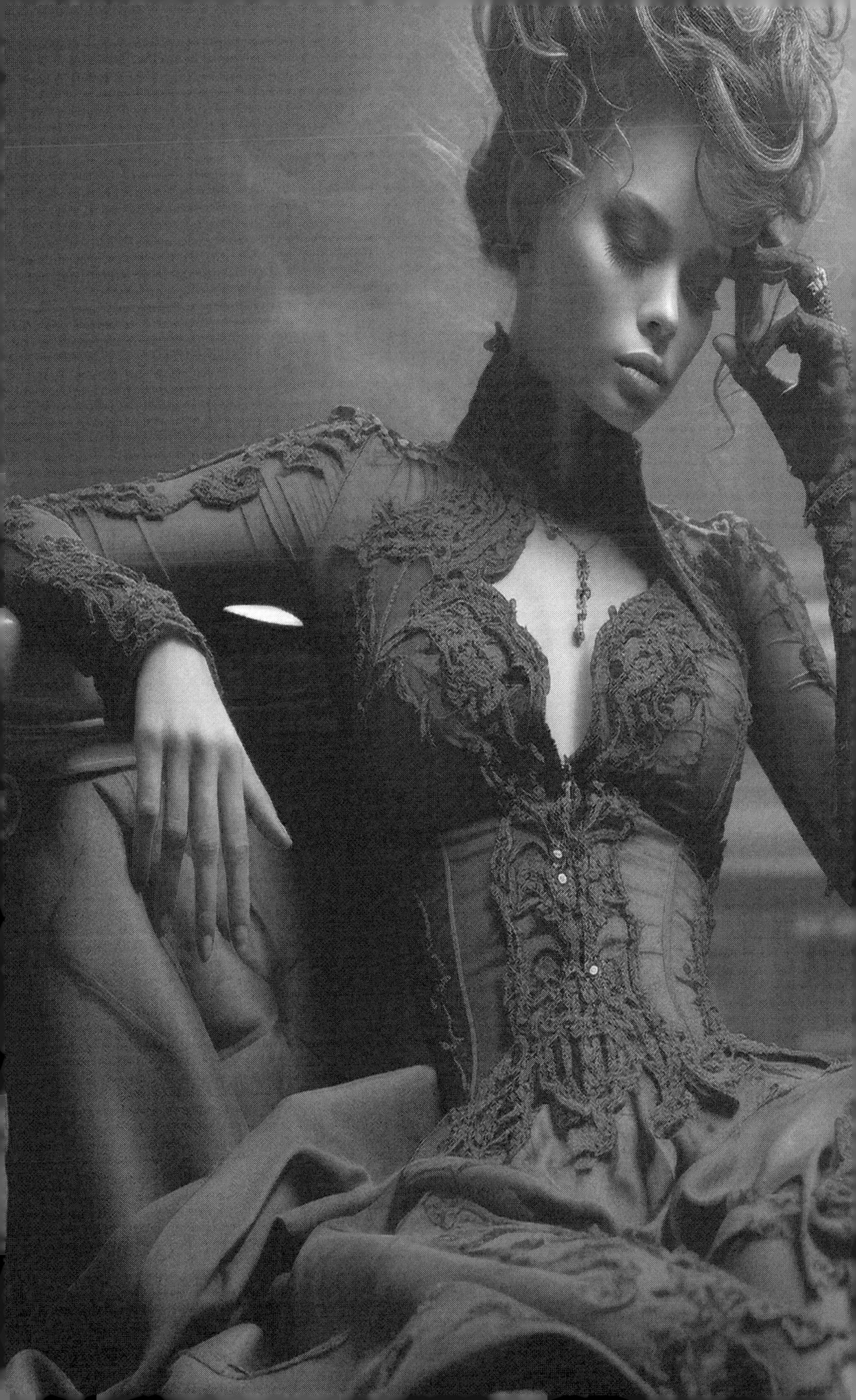

Chapter Twenty-Three
Reid

I woke with a contented moan. Rolling onto my side, I kept my eyes shut and patted at the mattress beside me in search of Octavia. A bit of snuggling. A dash of pre-coffee kink. I was up for whatever she was—literally. But all I found was an empty side of the bed and cold sheets.

I pried one eye open, then the other. "Octavia?"

Nothing.

Pushing myself up onto one elbow, I scanned the room. The bathroom light was off and the door leading into the hall was open. For a beat, I thought she had ventured downstairs for coffee. That idea dissipated when I noticed her helmet and motorcycle boots were gone.

Still, I wasn't concerned. Octavia had a wild nature and went wherever the urge took her. If that meant an early morning donut run, that's where her spirit would take her.

After sliding on my jeans and tugging a t-shirt over my head, I ventured downstairs to wait for her whilst secretly hoping she got jelly-filled ones. I padded to the foyer on bare feet, pulling up short when I saw Connoll sitting outside on the front stoop with his head hung in his hands.

I opened the door. "You alright, man?" I asked, bumping his shoulder with my knee.

"She took Bacon and left," the detective rasped and held a piece of paper up to me over his head.

Brow furrowed, I took it and scanned the words that made my blood run cold.

"Death started a fight. I intend to finish it."

I heard the rip of my shirt before I realized I was shifting. Hair sprouting. Teeth elongating. The bones of my face cracking and morphing into a snout. A sniff at the air and I caught her sent. That was all I needed. If she was chasing down a death wish, I was ready to gallop straight through the gates of hell alongside her.

"Where are you going?" Connoll rocketed to his feet, shouting after me as I sprinted across the yard.

"To get my girl back," I growled, falling onto all fours.

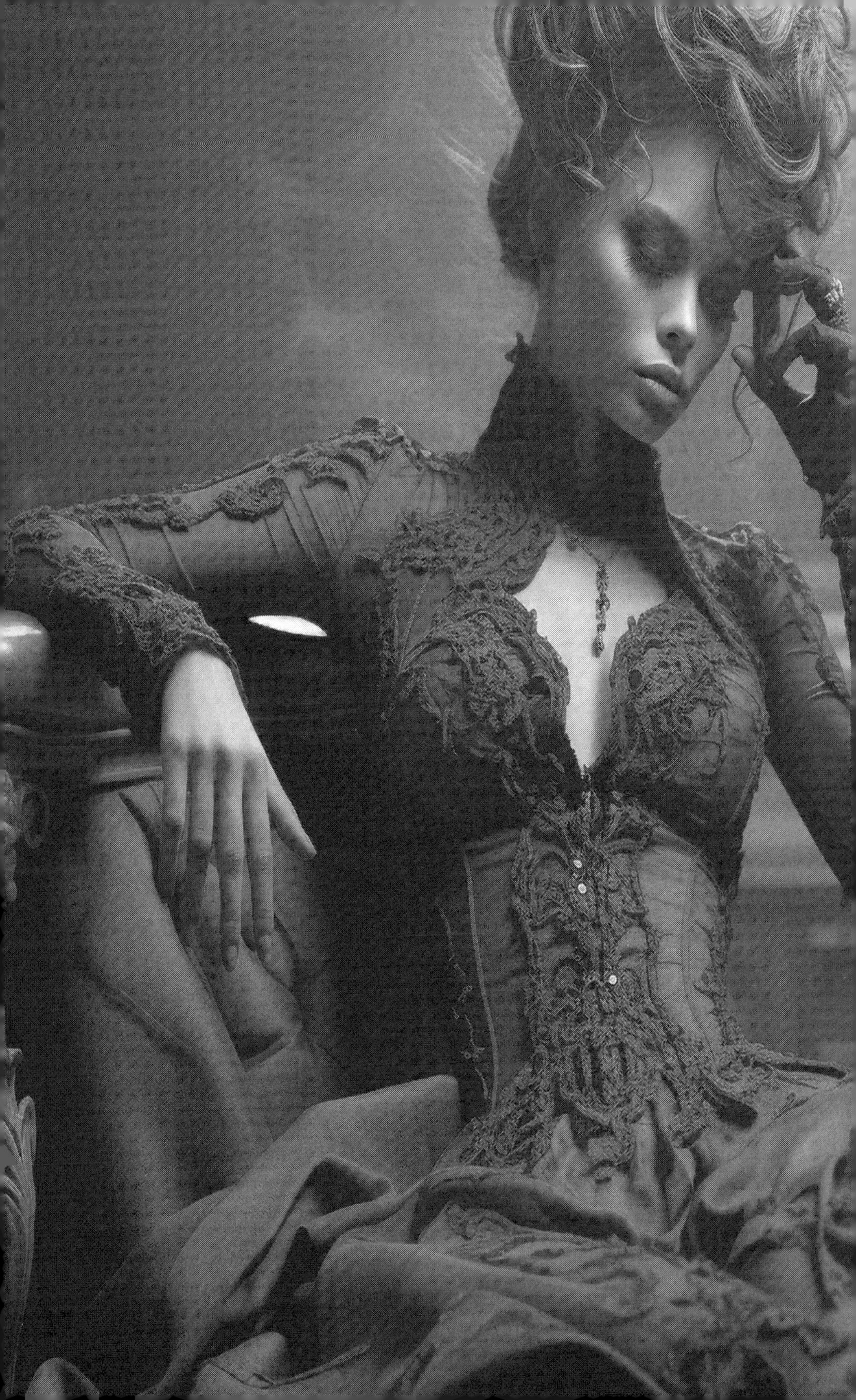

The Journals of Octavia Hollows continues
with Dance with Death

About the Author

Stacey Rourke is the award-winning author of works that span genres but possess the same flare for fast-paced action and snarky humor. She lives in Florida with her two beautiful daughters, two spoiled rotten dogs, and one chaos goblin/kitten. Stacey loves to travel, is obsessed with all things Disney, and considers herself blessed to make a career out of talking to the imaginary people that live in her head.

PennedCon Award Winner Author of the Year 2020
PennedCon Award Winner Best Book Blurb 2020
TopShelf Award Winner Best Science Fiction 2019
Utopia Award Winner Author of the Year 2018
Utopia Award Winner for Best Villain 2018 for Ursela in Rise of the Sea Witch
Readers' Favorite YA Fantasy Bronze Medal Winner 2017
Readers' Favorite Fantasy Silver Medal Winner for 2015
Turning Pages Magazine Winner for Best YA book of 2013 & Best Teen Book of 2013
RONE Award Winner for Best YA Paranormal Work of 2012
Young Adult and Teen Reader voted Author of the Year 2012

Connect with her at:

www.staceyrourke.com
Facebook at www.facebook.com/staceyrourkeauthor
Amazon Author Page: http://amzn.to/2l8FlbH
Instagram & TikTok @rourkewrites

Other titles by Stacey Rourke:

The Gryphon Series
The Conduit
Embrace
Sacrifice
Ascension

The Legends Saga
Crane
Raven
Steam

Reel Romance
Adapted for Film
Turn Tables

TS901 Chronicles
Co-written with Tish Thawer
TS901: Anomaly
TS901: Dominion

Veiled Series
Veiled
Vlad
Vendetta

The Journals of Octavia Hollows
Volume One
Volume Two: Fate Worse than Death
Volume Three: Jaws of Death
Volume Four: Death's Door
Volume Five: Dead Wrong
Volume Six: Dance with Death

The Unfortunate Soul Chronicles
Rise of the Sea Witch
Entombed in Glass
Pursuing Madness

The Archive of the Five
The Apocalypse Five
Coming Soon: Rogue Five
Coming Soon: Freedom Five

Fear the Reaper
Reaper vs. Ripper
Reaping a Pain in the Axe
Reaping Rasputin
The Devil You Reap

Death Diggers Handbook Chapter One:
Corpse Queen
Rotting Reign
Divine Decay

Death Diggers Handbook Chapter Two:
Monsters & Mayhem
Chaos & Carnage
Hauntings & Havoc

Made in the USA
Columbia, SC
08 July 2024

43c30d39-802a-4eb2-a43f-e07c8bc94e67R02